Praise for Gwenda Bond

"Offbeat and imaginative, *Blackwood* mingles past and present, dark forces with a hint of pulp SF, along with many kinds of drama—from Shakespearean revenge to an amphitheater show where the island's legend is just an entertainment for passing tourists. Whether viewed as young adult, genre mix, or a first novel, it belongs with the year's best."

—*Locus Magazine*

"It's definitely a wistful sort of novel about being different and dealing with scary stuff like losing your family and falling in love, as much as it is about ancient evils and terrible curses and supernatural menaces. It's nice to see a gentler, more personal sort of coming-of-age-and-battling-evil novel."

—Charlie Jane Anders, *io9.com*, on *Blackwood*

"Unique, fast-paced, and rife with tension, *The Woken Gods* brilliantly pits loyalty against survival, trust against inevitability, and love against fear."

—Carrie Ryan, *New York Times*
bestselling author of *The Forest of Hands and Teeth*

"The concept had me hooked from the start—I love mythology, and the idea of the gods 'waking up' and returning to the world makes for a great premise. If you like mythology and fast-moving YA novels with decisive and strong female protagonists, *The Woken Gods* might just be for you."

—*Tor.com*

girl on a wire

girl on a wire

GWENDA BOND

SKYSCAPE

SKYSCAPE

Published by Skyscape, New York

www.apub.com

Amazon, the Amazon logo, and Skyscape are trademarks of Amazon. com, Inc., or its affiliates.

ISBN-13: 9781477847824 (hardcover)
ISBN-10: 1477847820 (hardcover)
ISBN-13: 9781477847916 (paperback)
ISBN-10: 147784791X (paperback)

Library of Congress Control Number: 2013922670

Book design by Neil Swaab

Printed in the United States of America

For Jenn, ringmaster of my career and friend,
and for everyone who dares to dream big.

prologue

I planted my feet on the wire that ran parallel to the rafters. My new act involved a series of ballet-inspired moves, building to a trio of slow but tricky pirouettes, and the barn was the best place to practice. If I mastered these moves today, I'd be showing them off at the next show our traveling family circus offered—Fridays and Saturdays, entry for twelve bucks.

Before taking my first step, I peered thirty feet down at Sam, who was only just getting around to the stall-mucking. As far as I was concerned, it was the most important of his duties as caretaker of my mom's coterie of enormous white horses.

"Sam, hurry up," I called down, wrinkling my nose at the strong, musky smell of manure, hay, and horse sweat in the barn. "Please. It reeks in here."

"You're supposed to be rehearsing," he said, and brushed overgrown sandy hair out of his eyes with his forearm. "But if it's that bad, take a break and come back later."

Sam had come to live with us the year before. I'd gotten so used to having him around that he felt like my brother instead of my cousin. I'd even gotten used to his annoying habit of being right all the time.

Late-afternoon sunlight streamed through the open back doors, a sadly natural spotlight to go with the unwelcome odor.

"I bet the Cirque American doesn't smell like this," I said.

"We'll never know," Sam said. "But I promise you that horse manure smells the same everywhere."

To that, I said nothing.

The Cirque American. Pronounced *Americ-ah-n*, even its pronunciation was glamorous, with the *ah* sound promising a classy continental vibe. Its financial backing also had a pedigree, since the owner, Thurston Meyer, was an actual billionaire. The Cirque was a brand-new touring production aimed at adults, not kids—no sad elephants or angry big cats, just old-style glamour and logic-defying feats under a big top tent. Lots of the most famous family names in the business had joined up already. Despite the fact that my father happened to be the best wire walker in the world, we'd never gotten an offer to work on any show this size. Until now.

And Dad had turned the unbelievably great offer down flat.

Our tiny circus was already in serious danger of dying. Even the presence of the Amazing Emil, as my father was known onstage, wasn't enough anymore. Traveling a circuit takes money, and these days it was obvious we weren't making enough. Mom had wanted to join the Cirque, but didn't challenge Dad when he refused to budge. My grandmother Nan, whose brilliant career as a trapeze flyer and expert tarot reader had become a quiet retirement of tutoring Sam and me, took his side. Sam hadn't bothered to vote.

Our family had finally been given a chance. And nobody but me was willing to fight for it.

After the family meeting at which my father had delivered his decree, Nan insisted on consulting her tarot deck. She'd immediately started in on some mumbo jumbo about "bad blood" and "old threats."

"There's no need to discuss it further," my father had said, putting a reassuring hand on her shoulder. "We Amazing Maronis will never accept any job that includes working alongside the Flying Garcias."

I stared at both of them, mystified. I didn't even know the reason this crazy old rivalry existed. The Flying Garcias were a Latino family of trapeze artists, as legendarily gifted as us, but far more successful. Our paths hadn't crossed in decades, and as far as I knew Nan had never performed anywhere near them. But every so often the Garcia name would come up, and I'd be reminded anew that we were all supposed to cling to this ancient feud, no questions asked.

Well, that made zero sense with the way things stood. Soon enough, we'd be stuck in the middle of Indiana year-round, out of cash and off the circuit, with no way to remake the Maroni name. Dad would probably end up working a factory job, and Mom would land behind some desk, answering phones instead of being the Amazing Vonia and controlling her magnificent white horses with only her voice and a few hand gestures—while wearing a costume that made her look like an equestrienne superhero. I had no idea what would happen to me.

Just thinking about it made me feel queasy, never good this high up in the air.

I'd been mulling how to change the course of things. With the start of the Cirque's inaugural season and the expiration of Meyer's offer coming up fast, I couldn't wait any longer. I whirled on the wire and traipsed easily over to the ladder nailed to the wall. There was no net to dive into. Dad never took a bad step. I didn't either if I wanted to live.

Descending the rungs, I called over to Sam. "Mom and Dad went to buy feed, right? And Nan went with them to shop?"

Sam didn't pause in his busy mucking away at the other end of the barn. "Yep."

That was a two-hour errand, minimum. Perfect.

I'd stashed a pair of jeans and a few other things in a navy hard-shell overnight case that used to be Nan's. I pulled the pants on over my practice tights, swapped out my walking slippers for my favorite pair of red sequin ones, and shut the case with a satisfying click.

"See you later," I said, picking it up. I gulped in the fresh, clean air as I slipped out the open barn doors into the brisk early evening. This was it.

I had to hike past our neighbors' cornfields to get to the highway. The road met my two requirements: a decent amount of traffic and enough trees to hide behind while I waited for a ride that looked safe. I wasn't going to hop into the first semi or pickup that blew past. Being bold and being stupid aren't the same. They're as different as falling and flying.

Tucked behind a wide tree trunk, I watched traffic fly past and prayed that my overnight case wouldn't be needed. Living in an RV during peak season was a familiar way of life. Camping wasn't. Finally a blue hatchback hit the horizon going not a mile per hour over the speed limit. There was enough light left to make out the shape of a woman's bouffant hair on the driver's side.

I grabbed the overnight bag, left my hiding spot, and leapt over the ditch to the roadside. Then I raised my free hand and dropped an invisible racing flag.

The brake lights flashed as the car stopped.

I zipped over to open the passenger door. "Thank you, thank you," I said, checking out the woman to confirm that she wasn't a serial killer. Early thirties, with masses of curled hair around a kind, tired face I expected to see more makeup on. She looked as harmless as a friendly crowd. Tossing my bag in the back seat, I climbed in.

"Your hair is extraordinary," I told her.

The woman couldn't keep from smiling, but her eyebrows lifted. "How old are you?"

Sixteen. "Do you really want to know?"

She said nothing.

"Eighteen." What she wanted to hear. "My name is Jules."

She ticked her finger on the steering wheel, frowning like she'd decided that picking up a hitchhiker—even a blonde one in shiny red slippers like me—hadn't been the best idea. "I don't see a car anywhere. Did you have trouble?"

"Not really. I just need a ride." I had to get to the truck stop before my parents noticed I was gone or my plan wouldn't work. "We should probably get going."

She put the car in drive. "Where can I drop you?"

"The Flying J off Exit 85?" I suggested. It was a good forty minutes' drive.

A long moment of consideration. "That's out of my way, but all right."

I high-beamed my brightest smile. She cringed. Okay, maybe an audience needed that smile and one person didn't. I adjusted it to normal wattage.

"What are you doing out here anyway?" she asked.

No reason to lie. "Running away to join the circus."

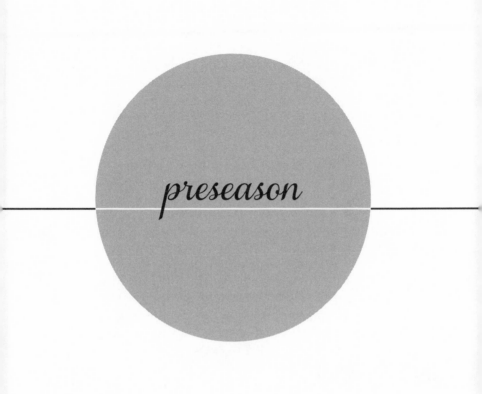

preseason

one

Only a few days after I'd hitched that ride solo, I sat in the passenger seat of our aging, oversized RV with the rest of the family as we lumbered into the Cirque American's grassy lot in Florida. Our pace slowed to a crawl while Dad navigated through the tightly packed caravans and trailers of the other performers. I could hardly believe that we were really, truly here.

Nan alternated between giving me meaningful stares and the cold shoulder. She was angry that I'd forced my father's hand with the runaway stunt. And I had—that was the whole point. When I'd called him from the Flying J truck stop and explained that we had to take this chance or the family would split apart, to my eternal surprise Dad hadn't put up much of a fight. He must have understood that we were doomed to extinction if we didn't make a move. So my wish had been granted. Within twenty-four hours, we'd made the arrangements to drive to Sarasota, home of the Cirque's winter quarters, where everyone gathered to train and assemble the show in the preseason.

We were late, showing up just a few days before the show rolled out for three months of touring, from mid-May through the second week of August. My mom's horses were due to arrive the following day. But so what if we'd barely made it in time? We had. The truth was, whatever "bad blood" we might find here would be a small price to pay.

Dad parked, and I stepped out of the RV. The sultry, humid air—nothing like the harsh, dusty heat of Indiana—embraced me as I took in the field that hosted our new neighbors. Many people assume all big circuses travel by train, but only the Greatest Show on Earth rides the rails these days. They were our chief competition, and driving meant we could hit mostly different cities from them. These mobile homes were the ones we'd travel in all summer.

My father climbed down the stairs and stopped beside me, slight but straight as a blade. He moved with the grace of his gift.

"We belong here," I said. "You must feel it too."

His expression was tight when he responded. "Julieta, you brought us here, but you need to be careful. Between the Garcias and your grandmother . . . there are old hurts. Gossip. Do not mention to her how happy all this is making you. It will only upset her more."

"I promise." I held my arms out and spun around. "I'll double-promise if I can have a few minutes right now to go look around."

"Your mother—" he started.

"Is still mad at me, but she'll get over it." She'd given me a good chewing out in Russian after they'd picked me up from the truck stop, but I suspected she was happy about the outcome. "You'll see, Dad, and so will Nan. This is right."

"I hope the past stays past, for your sake." He didn't sound convinced it would.

"Forget the past," I told him over my shoulder, the slightly overgrown grass tickling my ankles as I set off, "and bring on the future."

After a few minutes of exploring the grounds, I reached a cluster of newly constructed practice spaces. They included a generously sized stable and ring for horses, several hulking barns and warehouses, and a handful of one-story buildings designed to mimic the look of old-style traveling circus tents. On the side of each building was the show's logo: the words *Cirque American* in a toss of red, white, and blue stars, outlined in a gold that gave it a touch of glamour and steered clear of tacky.

I desperately wanted to see the inside of one of the fancy practice buildings. Checking first to make sure no one was around to stop me, I ducked into the next large warehouse that I came to. Carefully, slowly, I shut the door behind me and crept forward into the deep shadows around the entrance. My slippers wouldn't make a sound on the mat floor unless I wanted them to.

And, obviously, I didn't. Not once I understood where I was.

Floods lit the other half of the building. From my vantage point, I could see everything in perfect detail. The solid black bars of the rigging hung from the ceiling, and a giant net tilted to the side far beneath it. I'd never seen a trapeze act in person. But I'd watched videos with Nan, and listened closely as she described each element of the performance. She knew her stuff, since she'd been a gifted practitioner herself.

The trapeze began to swing. I took several steps forward without meaning to, lured by the prospect of witnessing a flyer for the first time live and in the flesh.

It was a boy—dark-haired, muscular, and close to my age—gripping the bar with steady hands, his strong legs kicking out to send his body soaring through the air. He was like a shark cutting through water, a knife slicing through air, a body breaking through reality into a dream. Whoever he was, he was good.

In fact, he was so good, I suspected there was only one *whoever* he could be: a Garcia.

I took a few more steps forward, though I was barely conscious of moving. I'd stumbled into a chance to spy on someone Nan would likely brand as our enemy, and I wanted a better look.

Back and forth he went, building speed with each powerful kick of his legs. I wondered how he handled all that controlled energy when he wasn't flying. No ambient noise disturbed the quiet, even the air-conditioning silent as a held breath, so I could hear the whistle of air around his limbs as he gathered speed. His last pass brought him high on the left, and when he started to swing out, he released the bar and began to spin, knees tucked to his chest.

He went around once—

Twice—

A third time and—

A fourth.

He spun in a fourth revolution, extending his hands at the last moment, as if reaching out to meet the catcher's grip, if one had been there. Except he was a fraction too low. I knew enough to conjure a catcher into place and understand that this boy would have just done the hardest trick in the history of the trapeze, *if* he'd extended his hands ever so slightly sooner. He'd missed it by the tiniest portion of a second. That was incredibly close to achieving a move that was rarely attempted, let alone *successfully* attempted, by even the best trapeze artists. The fabled quadruple somersault.

He bounced down into the net, and I still didn't move. I had the impulse to say something to him, though I hesitated, trying to decide whether to go with a simple hello or maybe ask if he'd ever made the quad. But then he brought his arms up and down, punching the net in frustration.

And that was my cue to leave. I turned and slipped out as quietly as I'd entered.

I couldn't believe I'd considered speaking. My face heated as I imagined what might have unfolded if he'd spotted me watching him uninvited. One thing was for sure: if he *was* a Garcia, feuding with him was definitely *not* my first instinct. I wanted to know more about him. I wanted to get closer, and I wasn't sure why. Maybe it was his ambition. Attempting the quad was bold.

Clearly I wasn't the only one at the Cirque who had big dreams. The two of us really might turn out to be rivals.

Somehow, the idea of a competition between us did little to help my flushed cheeks. But a worthy distraction came a moment later, when I caught sight of the big top and gasped. I thought I'd been impressed by the practice buildings. This was far beyond them.

A striped circus tent the size of a small stadium crowned the top of a rise. Its three spires created a dramatic silhouette against the darkening sky. The closest thing to it I'd ever seen was in old photographs. Later, that tent would be the backdrop for our welcome party, which the Cirque's famous owner, Thurston Meyer, had insisted on hosting. The grandest big top in existence, and our family would enter it as the guests of honor.

Adrenaline surged through me as I flashed on what we could achieve here, of the successful future within our reach. If that boy was a Garcia, and he was attempting the quad, then I'd need to come up with a dream act of my own. I stared at the soaring circus tent, and thought of my heroine, Bird Millman, the best wire walker in history, in my not-so-humble opinion. During her heyday in the early 1900s, she'd pulled off stunts like strutting above city skylines on simple wires strung between buildings. Being here, gazing up at the spires of such a grand big top, made me seriously consider that maybe *I* could try something that jaw-dropping. That dangerous.

I walked forty feet up without a net all the time, and I'd trained plenty on outdoor wires. But could I envision myself out of the circus tent, hundreds of feet higher, above the real world? Even if the answer was yes, my dream act would probably be forced to remain a little closer to earth for the time being. Nervous parents, nervous owner, nervous audiences. First we had to prove that we belonged here.

But if I was certain of anything, it was that we did.

I shook my head to clear it. The idea of imitating Bird might be madness for now, but I still walked back home to change for the party grinning so hard that my cheeks ached.

two

Thurston led the way to the big top. He wore his ringmaster tux and tails, bow tie undone, face animated below a waxy crown of brown hair. The whole trip across the grounds, he had done nothing but fawn over my parents. Nan wasn't with us, of course. She'd refused to come out.

As we approached the massive tent, electronica beat out a crazy song in welcome. Elaborate masks covered a table set up outside the entrance. Painted and sequined, beaded and glittered, they proved that leather and papier-mâché could be transformed into marvels. Butterfly wings splashed with a sparkle of colors, twisting vines that gleamed green, fox ears that curved above golden cheeks. Some were scary, colored deep red or black and sprouting horns and spikes.

"It's a masquerade," Thurston explained. "I had the costumers making them all night. Please, take your pick."

Selecting one turned out to be easy. I tried the fox, but set it down for the butterfly. Wings would be a handy thing for a wire walker to have, after all, and I liked how the holes were positioned so my eyes became part of the wings' intricate design. The soft leather of the mask hugged my cheeks, stretching up and out on either side.

My mother had found a horse, the material manipulated to mimic a long nose. She grinned at me, high blonde ponytail swishing behind her. I assumed that meant I was officially forgiven.

Thurston directed a slight frown at my father. "Emil, nothing to your taste?"

My father's gaze roved over the table, but he made no move to choose.

Sam had managed to find the plainest black mask available, and he still looked uncomfortable wearing it. "Don't laugh," he said.

Which, of course, made me laugh. "It suits you. You're like Batman. If only I could find you a cape." I glanced around, pretending to look for one.

"'Some men just want to watch the world burn,'" he said, in a goofy deep voice, no doubt quoting one of the action movies he loved and I'd never seen. "Without a cape."

"Alas."

Dad finally responded to a still-frowning Thurston. "I choose to show my face."

"Okay," Thurston said. He must have sensed the tension and the possibility for our deal to fall apart, because he swept a patch of the table clear and removed a set of papers from the inside pocket of his jacket. I knew what the contract said: it was a two-year commitment with Dad as headliner, Mom as primary equestrienne, and me as a bonus. "Let's just get the signing over with and then have a party," he said, and presented Dad with a pen.

Dad hesitated at taking it. I held my breath, suddenly afraid he'd change his mind.

Mom said, "I want to dance, Emil."

What she was really saying: *I want to be here. Sign the papers.*

And so he did. Scribble, scribble. Done. He handed off the pen to Mom, and frowned toward Sam and me. I was already backing discreetly away, toward the party. Dad said, "You still have a curfew."

"Yes, Dad." I tugged Sam with me toward the tent flap. "Who's the best cousin in the world?" I asked him.

"Batman?"

"Me." I shoved him inside and stopped short.

The center ring roughly contained the party's chaos. Everything but the tracks of the rings had been removed. There were no stands erected where an imaginary crowd would watch the show, no other spotlights left on to lift the shadows. Within the moodily lit, swarming circle, about a hundred people pressed close together dancing, and some couples whirled in fancy turns. A light bird of a woman flipped into the air off a man's shoulders and he caught her, in time to the music.

I instantly wanted to dance, but I didn't have a partner. Sam, like all boys my age, wouldn't. But it was crowded, and I was disguised as a butterfly, and I'd danced alone before.

Doing it mixed into a crowd would be easier. Next to me, Sam was scanning for the booze table, but I headed toward the ring.

And tried not to notice the frowns that followed us, or the way people shied away as we passed. The chilly reception got harder to ignore with each step. Why?

I slowed and glanced over my shoulder. Thurston was escorting my parents into the tent, and I watched as the people gathered there reacted to their entrance, stepping aside or averting their gazes coldly. Instead of going to the dance floor, I stopped near a cluster of older men who were drinking. One of them spat into the dirt. Near me.

I nudged Sam in the ribs. "Did you see that?" My attention landed briefly on a pack of boys nearby, our age but acting older and fake tough with stolen beers in hand. And not dancing. Though they did get points for wearing masks, at least.

Sam scowled at the ground. "I'm going to pretend I didn't."

Within a few seconds, the boys had moved close enough that they were practically standing on top of us. They blocked my view of anything beyond. At least, until some of them split off, one striding into the crush and press of the dancers, and another two off toward the exit.

At the exact moment the music stopped, I blurted, "I don't know what everyone's problem is." I might as well have shouted it. The music restarted a moment later, with a slower tempo.

"And on that note, I'm going for a beer before I have to pick a fight," Sam said, and walked away. I hoped he was joking about the fighting. It was one of the reasons he'd been sent to live with us. When his parents retired from touring life, regular school hadn't gone well for him.

A strong hand landed gently on my arm. The boy it belonged to said, "Let's dance." He wore a grinning devil's mask, and the brown eyes behind it pinned my mouth shut.

But only for a moment. "I suppose," I said, my best attempt at blasé. But I was already trying to judge by his height and the close-cropped dark hair whether this was the boy from earlier.

I wanted it to be him.

My heart picked up its rhythm at the same time the music did, as one of his arms went around my waist. His other hand clasped mine, and he tangoed us into the crowd with steps that weren't a tango. I'd been dancing with my parents for years, and knew the difference. But I followed his lead anyway.

He had on dark jeans and a soft black T-shirt. It had short sleeves, and my hand gripped his bare arm. His warm, muscled bare arm. His hand tightened a fraction on mine, and I swallowed.

Blasé, I reminded myself.

"That was a very First of May thing to say," he said. "Not surprising, since you are one."

I knew my temper flared in my eyes. It was a trait that Nan always likened to a dragon, or Bette Davis. I attempted to soften, but with little success.

"*You* must be one," I said, "since I've never heard anyone actually use that phrase."

It was a reference to the starting date that old circuses used to observe, and what new green hires were called when they went out on the road for the first time.

"You know what it means?" he asked. "A novice, someone who doesn't know the score."

"Oh, I know the score." Being annoyed would have been easier if I wasn't also enjoying the dance at the same time. This devil wasn't half bad. What I wanted to know was if this devil was a Garcia.

"Clearly," and he dipped me, "you don't."

I gasped, and he lifted me back up. When I straightened, we were closer. Our faces were inches apart. "I haven't been a First of May since I was seven years old."

Dark eyes considered me. "If you weren't, then you'd know what everyone's problem is. It's that you're here."

I bristled. "What are you talking about?"

Another boy in a suit approached us, apparently not picking up the tension, because he gave a shy smile and asked, "May I cut in?"

From the voice, I realized the person in the suit wasn't a boy, but a girl with a pixie cut and a striking, angular face accentuated by a Phantom-style half mask. She was definitely wearing a man's suit—black and vintage, with wide lapels—but pale pink lipstick too.

"Not now, Dita," the boy said.

I decided I was glad for the distraction. "You certainly *may* cut in."

Smoothly I removed my hand from his and offered it to the girl named Dita. She shot the boy a surprised look. He blinked like I'd shone a spotlight into his face.

I asked her quietly, "You do know how to lead?"

A grin slanted across her face. "With brothers like that? Yes."

The boy was this girl's brother. I didn't understand why that was a relief. He'd called me a First of May, which was insulting enough, and I was almost certain both of them were going to have the dreaded last name Garcia.

Dita danced us away from him.

"You're a talented dancer," I said. I believe in giving compliments, but only when truthful. People know what they're good at. And what they aren't.

"Thanks. Most new people, I make them nervous," she said. "They think I'm, well, the girls assume since I dress . . ." She looked away, though she didn't miss a step.

"People think too much. It's one of their main problems. The suit is gorgeous. And you saved me from your brother. He's good with an insult."

"Really? Usually my other brother's the problem there." She changed her grip as the music shifted again, to a faster beat. A salsa?

We picked up our pace to match it. I scanned the crowd for her brother, who was easy to spot in his devil mask. He sat in a chair, leaning forward with his elbows on his knees. I waved, and sent him a falsely bright smile.

"Why'd you just get here? Are you one of the iron-jaw cousins?" Dita asked.

Now was the time to find out my answer. "Late arrival. What's your act?"

"We're the flyers."

So she and her brother were definitely part of the Garcia clan. "Wow," I said. "My grandmother was a flyer."

Dita seesawed us between couples. "What's her name?"

I took a breath. Then, "Nancy Maroni. Have you heard of her?"

Dita stumbled forward, stomping my left foot. I grimaced at the pain. Apparently not everything Nan had said was mumbo jumbo.

"S-sorry," she stammered, but she sounded like she wanted to run away.

The boy materialized again. "Everything all right here?"

Dita nodded, but there was strain on her face. "Did you know who she was?"

The boy shrugged. "Of course. That's why I was dancing with her."

Releasing the light grip she still had on one of my arms, Dita pasted on the worst fake smile I'd ever seen. She wouldn't be getting any compliments on that. "This is awkward," she said.

"No kidding. I'm Jules," I said, slowly. "Jules Maroni. And you must be . . ."

"Remy Garcia," the boy said. "You should know you're only here because Thurston's an outsider. He doesn't understand that nobody wants to work with the Maronis."

On the wire, the best walkers have an invisible line that extends the spine up into the sky and down into the earth.

Their posture is beyond straight, almost a miracle. Suspended between earth and sky, they always seem like they should float away, but instead they become steadier and more controlled. I wasn't as good as my father yet, but I tried to find that line. I drew myself up, too subtly for them to see, but not too subtly for them to notice.

Behind the mask, Remy's eyes narrowed. Dita elbowed him, and pointed. "Rem," she said. "Trouble."

"What?" His lips had curled into a smile that made him sinister with the devil mask's black leather hugging the curves of his cheeks. If I hadn't seen him attempt the quadruple somersault with my own eyes, I'd never have pegged him as a flyer. He was all muscle, and didn't have the right quality about him. Most flyers—including Dita and Nan—moved in a way that was effortlessly weightless, even when their feet were on the ground.

I turned to see what Dita was pointing at. Across the ring, I spotted my parents sitting on a raised platform, chatting away with Thurston. Mom was glowing, but Dad was scanning the crowd. He rose to his feet.

"Novio," Remy said.

His sister responded, "Master of the obvious."

Remy rushed past me, Dita following, and I chased after them. The crowd parted for us. My eyes flicked to the dais, and I saw that my father was off it and into the crush. Only a few people continued to dance. Everyone else had grown quiet. Mom was on her feet and frowning, but stayed where she was. Thurston leaned back in his seat.

A moment later, I reached the edge of an instant clearing, the kind that always forms for a fight. A lean, compact older boy in a black leather jacket was circling Sam. I'd never seen such a fierce look on Sam's face before.

"Say one more thing. I dare you," Sam said, his hands balled into fists.

Oh no.

The boy—it had to be the famous Novio—wore no mask, and the hard set of his features made me question whether he'd ever had a happy day in his life. I kicked myself for wondering whether he and his brother looked anything alike.

"What's going on here?" Remy asked, approaching the two of them.

His hands were upturned and flat, but I didn't buy him as peacemaker. I stepped in. "Yes, I'd love to know too. Because it seems like you're ruining our party."

If there was any talking still going on in the crowd, it stopped then. *Yes, I said it. Our party.* The music had vanished.

Novio approached me, and I hoped that would give Sam time to calm down. "I can see why my brother was dancing with you, even if you are a Maroni."

My father wasn't far, because I heard him shout, "Let me through, imbecile!"

I could defuse this before he got involved. I could. This wasn't how I wanted our first night at the Cirque to go. I hadn't wanted any of Nan's feud nonsense to be real, and here it was already causing problems. I refused to let ancient history ruin things.

"I'm a good dancer, I know," I said, laying on the charm.

Novio came in closer to me. I held my invisible line, refused to flinch from him. He said, "You're pretty for a thieving dog."

Odd choice of comparison, but, "Woof," I said.

Novio almost smiled. His cheek jerked, and a hand landed on his shoulder. I expected it to be Remy, pulling his brother away, and felt a wave of gratitude. Thurston wouldn't like the fighting, and it was better for everyone when owners were happy. I said, loudly, "Sam, let's go. This party's dead."

But, of course, the hand belonged to Sam. His fist landed dead center on Novio's square jaw.

I stood, more or less in shock, as Sam and Novio laid into each other, locked in a close scuffle like some sort of perverse hug. Until a devil mask appeared in front of me, blocking my view.

Remy placed his hands on my shoulders, forcing me to walk backward away from the fight. I peered over his shoulder. "Let me go. Sam!"

The crowd sealed off behind us, separating us from the mayhem. "They'll break it up in a minute," Remy said. "You'll be safe back here."

He stopped, and we stood there, glaring at each other through our masks.

"You should have stayed out of it, butterfly. Look at the carnage, already happening."

And then the tent began to go dark. The lights died in a progressive swoop of spots going out, section by section. When the black descended, I couldn't see Remy or his devil mask anymore. He lifted his hands from my shoulders and said, "Stay put." I tried not to feel unmoored without the anchoring touch as the crowd jostled and shouts of confusion rose around me. In the crush, someone got close enough that I felt the heat of breath. I sensed that it wasn't Remy, and stepped back.

"Stay away from my daughter," my father called, from nearby.

"Turn them back on!" A voice boomed out. Thurston's.

The lights popped on again, brighter than before. Thurston stalked through the mass of performers to the middle of the ring. "What a lovely welcome for our newest members," he said, soaked with sarcasm.

Behind him, my father clutched Sam's bicep. My cousin's face had a long gash across the right cheek that oozed a thick line of deep red. One of his eyes was pinched shut. He wore a cocky smile that must have been painful.

Remy was several feet away, pressing his shoulder into Novio's chest. Staying between him and Thurston. And, more importantly, between him and Sam. Novio's face was also going Technicolor with bruises.

"I see the rumors about how well the Maroni and Garcia clans get along are true," Thurston said. "And since we have members of both right here, I may as well say this. As it currently stands, the finale belongs to the Garcias. But now I have Emil Maroni to fit into the order." I resisted checking Dad's reaction. "And it's hard for me to imagine where else to put him. There's the matter of Jules to decide too."

Our wire act was rare in that it wasn't a large-scale family affair, but just the two of us, and typically each walking solo at different spots in the show. Thurston hadn't mentioned Mom because horse acts never got the grand finale.

Novio said, "You can't be serious. You wouldn't end the show with a rope walker."

We did *not* walk on ropes.

Thurston ignored his outburst. "The day after tomorrow, our wire walkers and our trapeze artists will perform before the final dress rehearsal. Whoever impresses me most will get the finale, the runner-up will get the plum placement right beforehand, and last place closes the first act. Everyone wins, so no more fighting. Figure out how to get along."

My father nodded, regally. "Maronis have never minded proving ourselves."

Novio shrugged off Remy. Thurston took their silence as agreement, smiling as he headed back to the dais. I was about to start toward Dad when I glanced down and spotted it.

There, at my feet, lay a red rose, with a stem clipped to the length of a finger.

I bent and picked it up. The thorns were covered by some kind of rough gray string or cord wound around the stem. Odd. An even odder feeling passed through me when I touched it . . . like a shiver, but on the inside. I straightened and looked around for a secret admirer—or any kind of admirer—but all I found was Remy shaking his head at me.

"Julieta," my father called, "let's go home."

I kept the mystery rose with me as we left the big top, but it hardly made me feel better about the disastrous evening.

Neither did my final look back, where Remy was still watching me. He raised his hand in a wave good-bye, and I couldn't read his expression. All I could tell was that it lingered on the flower.

I was sure it wasn't from him.

three

Sam and I followed a couple steps behind my mom and dad on the journey from the big top back to the RV. We passed the long trailers that housed the men and women of the work crew, and the shouts of laughter ringing from doors open to admit cool air made me even more aware of our outsider status. Would we ever be at home here? I wasn't so sure anymore. After the fight and blackout, the night felt unfamiliar and alive with threats.

"What did he say to you?" I asked Sam.

Sam said, "That we shouldn't be here. And that we'd better not be here to try and steal his family's spotlight, since that's what the Maroni voodoo is all about. I hope we do take the finale. Jackass."

"What Maroni voodoo? They're crazy," I said.

"You wanted to come here," my dad said, startling me. I hadn't realized he'd been listening so closely to me and Sam. "And now we're here."

He was right. But things were turning out so much different than I'd expected. Before, I hadn't cared about details from the distant past. Now I needed to know how the old hurts and bad feelings had come about. I had to, before I could fix things, and make this work the way it was supposed to.

"What happened back then? Why do the Garcias"—I hesitated, not wanting to say it and make it real, but there was no other word that fit—"hate us like this? Why does everyone else here seem to feel the same way?"

Dad didn't answer, and Mom put a worried hand on his arm. "Emil?" she prompted. "What should we know?"

My stomach clenched as our little foursome came to a halt. If something was being kept secret from Mom too, it made me worry even more.

"We'll talk when we're in private," Dad said, shooting a stern look at me and Sam. Then he zeroed in on the rose I held. "Where did that come from?"

Probably best not to tell him a mysterious someone had left it at my feet during the blackout. There was enough uncertainty swirling around us already. Besides, I planned to find out. I wanted to know the identity of my admirer way more than he did.

"I found it," I answered, with a shrug.

He grunted acknowledgment, and we were walking again. When we reached our RV a few minutes later, the windows were dark. That and the front door being open didn't strike me as strange right away. Nan would be inside, watching an old movie if I knew her. And I thought I did.

But Dad's shoulders pinched together as he stood in front of the door. He put out his arm to block us from going around him and inside. "Wait," he said. "Something's wrong."

I ducked under his arm, and up the stairs. He was right behind me.

There was no light inside except from the TV. *Bringing Up Baby* was playing on mute, turning Hepburn and Grant's banter into a soundless, sinister flicker. My slipper crunched on something that shouldn't have been there.

Dad hit the light switch, and the wreck came into sharp relief. I'd stepped on a broken glass, which had been knocked off the kitchen counter and crushed into a glimmering spiderweb. The curtains were torn down, the seat cushions tossed around. The cabinet doors hung open. The drawers had been yanked out and were spilling their contents.

"Nan?" I asked, half turning to Dad.

"Mama," he called.

"I'll check the back," I said, too afraid to stand and do nothing. Nan was invincible. I thought of her as a glamorous tarot-reading force of nature, not fragile enough to be hurt. But in truth, she was increasingly frail with each passing year.

I picked my way through the debris and into the back. A glance into the first small sleeping berth—Nan's—confirmed it had also been tossed. There was no sign of her there. In Mom and Dad's larger space at the back, the mattress was ripped, the midnight-blue sheet torn to reveal a white seam of stuffing guts. Sam's bunk was tiny and undisturbed. I left my own small room for last.

My things were strewn everywhere. The closet had been emptied, clothes heaped on the bed. I dropped the weird rose onto my dresser.

Above the mess, the framed photograph of my heroine, Bird, hung slanted on the wall. Beautiful Bird, smiling while she held a parasol and walked a wire between buildings in Chicago, making it look as easy as walking down a street. She was stylish in a cream sweater and knee-length skirt, the outfit topped off with a beautiful hat. Whoever had broken in had managed the impossible. They'd made Bird lose her balance. And also me.

"Nan's not here!" I called, loud enough to be heard up front.

But it was Nan who answered. "I am, sweetie! I'm back!"

I hurried toward the kitchen, where she'd obviously just entered from outside. I was comforted by the sight of her, tall and stately and commanding enough that we never questioned her ban on being called granny or even nana, because only Nan, short for her full name, would do. She was dressed for going out in a white blouse, flowing pants, and heels, a black scarf knotted at her neck. She wore Monroe-red lipstick, like always.

There was no surprise on her face at the mess. "You wouldn't listen until you saw proof you could recognize," she said, directing her statement to me. "But now, now you will."

The night officially had too many mysteries for me to disagree. I nodded, and let her take my hand. Hers was cold.

In the kitchen, my dad sank into a chair at the table as Mom moved to clear the mess from it—crumpled napkins dumped from their holder, the calendar that usually hung on the wall above, Nan's latest tabloid. I closed the front door and replaced a couple of couch cushions, so Nan and injured Sam would have a place to sit for the emergency family meeting.

Mom rummaged in the freezer and made an ice pack for Sam, then extended the lumpy cloth to him. "On for fifteen minutes, then off," she said, and before he could protest, "I don't care if it hurts. Now, let's everyone tell me why my house is a disaster area."

Nan crossed her hands one over the other, manicure perfect and red. "First, what happened to Sammy?"

"I fell into a doorknob," Sam said.

Mom clucked her tongue, annoyed, and motioned for Sam to put the cold pack to his eye. Which he did, wincing.

"A doorknob that looked exactly like Novio Garcia's fist," I said.

"Oh," Nan said, but, again, without surprise. "Only to be expected. That's one of the children?"

"Yes," Dad said. "Where were you?"

"I went to see Maria Garcia," Nan said, "to pay my respects for Roman's passing last year and try to smooth the waters, now that we're here. He was her father, after all. It was the least I could do. I wasn't gone half an hour. Maria's husband was with us. So if that's what you're thinking, Emil, the answer is no, they didn't do this. And it sounds like their kids were otherwise occupied."

I was afraid to breathe, afraid to miss something. Nan had paid a visit to Remy's parents while we were at the party meeting the rest of the Garcias. That much was clear. Why she'd felt compelled to pay respects to Roman, I had no idea.

Sure, he'd been a famous flyer in her day, but I'd never heard his name pass her lips before.

Nan focused on me again. "You see now, don't you? The bad blood I tried to warn you about."

"But why," I said. "I don't understand. What's the problem?"

"There were . . . accidents. Tragedies, long ago, when I was still a flyer," Nan said. "Roman told everyone I was responsible, and there was no way to defend myself."

"You were on a show with the Garcias?" I asked, shocked as much by that revelation as the one about Roman. Though, now that it was confirmed, things made slightly more sense. Slightly.

"Yes. The Greatest. Touring all over the country," she said. "It was the biggest show I was ever on, and the worst summer of my life. When Roman told people I was behind the accidents, there was no way to make anyone believe different, because everyone knew I could do magic. Like my mother before me. You know my cards originally belonged to her."

My eyes gravitated to Sam, but I couldn't tell if what she'd said had registered with him. This side of his face was too swollen to reveal much.

"Magic?" I said, not trying to hide my skepticism. "I know you're good with the cards, but . . ."

"I'm better than good. Think about every reading I've ever given you, Jules. You never believed them, but they were all true, weren't they? Just last week, you asked me for that reading about what direction you should take your career, and I," she smiled a brittle smile, "like a fool, didn't look far or hard enough to see what you were up to."

My head ticked down. Of course I remembered the reading. I'd taken what she'd told me as another sign it was time to take action—it had helped spark the idea of running away to make my point. I didn't believe in the cards literally, though. I never had.

"That's right, you should hang your head. I never imagined you might use my reading as an excuse to press the issue and prod us here." Her eyes got a distant look as she went back over the details. "Remember? I told you that you were about to go on a journey, and that there would be danger. But there's always danger on the wire. I wasn't looking hard enough at the cards you received, so I didn't see all the implications. You know how accurate my readings are, but you can't know how powerful my warnings are. And I was right. You are in danger. We all are. We should not be here."

Magic? So this was my explanation. Everyone hated us because they thought Nan did magic. I wished Sam was less out of it so he could appreciate the bizarre reality we'd just stepped into.

"But we *are* here," I said. "And we can't leave now. Dad, tell her."

"She's right. The papers are signed," he said.

Nan didn't speak for a long moment, and then, "It will not get any easier. The Garcias remember too well. They've spread the stories too far. Everyone will be looking for bad luck to fall now that we're here."

Silence descended on us, here at the circus that should have been nothing but a golden ticket, with our home in shambles. I refused to accept it.

I cleared my throat. "Well, nobody at Cirque is going to find proof of any voodoo magic or bad luck curse. Because, I'm sorry, Nan, I trust you on most things, I really do, but this is crazy talk. They'll see how good we are, and these rumors will fade away."

"That might be true if they were only rumors," Nan said. "But you have to listen. There are specks of truth that give them weight. It makes them impossible to dispel."

"You want me to believe magic is real, and you can do it," I said, shaking my head at her, "at the same time you're telling me that ignoring lies is impossible?"

Nan gave me a cool stare. "Yes."

That Nan appeared to buy into her own bad press was a problem, but I'd make her see reason. The Cirque could get over it. We were here to stay. My mother took my hand, and I read it as an indication that Nan's claims troubled her too.

"That's enough for tonight," my father said. "Everything will be clearer in the morning. The children need their rest—especially you, Julieta. You'll be rehearsing tomorrow." From the look he and Mom exchanged, the two of them needed to have a long talk. She released my hand and went to lean against Dad in his chair, lending him support.

I wasn't ready to be sent to my trashed room, not just yet. "We should call Thurston about this. Have whoever did this made an example of. I bet his security team's the best."

Mom started, "That's a good idea—"

But Dad interrupted her. "We tell no one."

"What?" I didn't think I'd heard him right. "We have to tell someone."

"No," he said, "we don't. No one was around because of the party. No one will know."

"Whoever did this will know," I pointed out.

"They're not going to tell anyone about it," Sam said.

True enough. But Mom put her hand on her hip. "How can we afford to replace these things if we don't report it, Emil?"

They studied each other, but Dad had an answer. "I'll ask Thurston for our signing bonus. We'll take the RV into town tomorrow and replace what we need to replace. We cannot start this engagement from a place of weakness." His tone softened. "We have too many enemies, too many people with hard feelings toward us. This is not up for debate. You will all be careful. We will rely on each other. No one else."

Nan nodded to my father, approving.

I wondered exactly how many enemies we had and what it was they wanted from us. And I wondered if one of them had left me that odd flower.

four

After a long day of replacement shopping, I found our practice space easily that night. Not only was the building numbered—lucky thirteen, which someone must have thought was funny—but the entrance was marked with a sign that said The Amazing Maronis. I unlocked the heavy padlock with a key from Thurston, who'd sheepishly admitted to Dad that he'd been so certain we would eventually sign on that he'd had the space designed especially for us.

I fumbled my way in and threw on the lights. They illuminated an interior triple the size of the barn back home—and, I noted with gratification, a little bigger than the warehouse where I'd caught Remy practicing. Actual spotlights lit the wires far above. Yes, wires. There were two. One a little lower, one higher. Thurston had set it up so we each had our own wires. Not that Dad needed to rehearse. He'd show up tomorrow and nail it.

There were nets beneath the wires, which Dad would order removed, but otherwise it was perfect. Jogging across the mats, I was more determined to stay with the Cirque than ever. When I stopped, my eyes drifted up again. The nets made a pattern like a see-through honeycomb, and far above them the thick cables of our wires stretched taut and perfectly level, waiting for someone to claim them.

"Now that's magic," I murmured, and touched the rose from the night before. I'd pinned it onto my practice top, letting the short stem dangle. A makeshift corsage. The bloom was as fresh as the night before. The cord must have kept it from wilting.

If someone thought to scare me with it, I figured wearing it would show I wasn't bothered. And if it was flattery, then the admirer—possibly an unknown ally?—would see I'd kept it.

I coated my palms in gym chalk so they wouldn't slip on the rungs, and started up the ladder to the lower wire. Climbing, I was all nerves and determination, determination and nerves. It was the same emotional seesaw I'd been on all day long. One minute I felt sure I'd mastered my act, the next I felt 100 percent certain I was a hack who'd get booed as soon as I put my stupid feet on the wire. My mental state was worse because of our reception, but the up and down was normal enough. I would never trust anyone who didn't get at least a little nervous on the cusp of doing something important to them in front of other people.

I climbed onto the platform with my parasol and took a breath. Arranging my arms into the balletic carriage I'd been working on—difficult because it wasn't a traditional balancing strategy and I had to account for the gauzy umbrella—I traipsed onto the wire. I canted my upper body to the left and to the right, gracefully I hoped, and took another three steps until I was about a quarter of the way across.

A few more high steps brought me to the center of the wire.

The pirouettes were a little crazy. No one did this kind of thing anymore on wires this high, not without a safety wire or harness. They were my best chance to wow the audience, though, so I wanted to nail them. And I was still toying with the idea of trying to do something even more spectacular than this.

I started the series of three twirls that would take me to the end of the wire. *Spin*, I told myself. I did, and the wire felt as solid under the ball of my toe as ground would beneath my feet. I breathed easier when I completed the first and then second rotations without a wobble.

When I went into the third spin, I saw Bird as clear as if she were right in front of me. It was like she stood on the wire, and I was traveling toward her. Except it wasn't this wire. I saw her between those buildings, leaning forward, her skirt ruffled in the wind. Most of all, I saw her crooked. Off-kilter, unbalanced like her portrait on my wall.

Everything around me spun into motion, my third pirouette incomplete. Interrupted. Air raked across my face and through my hair. Confused, I dropped the parasol and my hands clawed the wind. My feet pawed in a desperate search for the wire.

I didn't stop trying to right myself until I bounced into the net. I hit hard, exhaling in a whoosh, the diamond-shaped pattern of rope biting into my skin.

I hadn't fallen since I was four years old. I hadn't had a net to save me since then either.

When I went outside, the grounds were deserted, which was a relief.

I was freaking out. *I fell I fell I fell.* At least no one had seen. I hugged my arms against a cool breeze and started my walk home. But it was only a few steps before I decided on a detour, past the Garcias' practice space.

Remy had acted like he knew everything, so maybe it was time to find out if the Garcias' side of the story matched up with Nan's. Maybe he'd be alone again and I could get some answers. After plummeting into the net, I wanted to feel like I was back on solid footing.

Luck was with me.

I opened the door to find the same tableau I had when we arrived. The lights were off in the entryway, but shone down on Remy as he practiced solo. Once again, I stood quietly and admired the way he moved through the air, strong and purposeful. I shivered as I remembered how I'd touched those warm, muscled arms the night before, the same arms that were now propelling him high overhead.

Last night while he was insulting your family, Jules. Get a grip.

To distract myself, I traced the fading diamond impression the net had left on my skin, touched the rose as if for more luck, and took a few steps forward just as he launched from the swing into the revolutions of a quad attempt. One, two, three, four—

Holding my breath didn't help him. His placement coming out of the spin was too fast and a little low. His body rocketed down and down into the net, where he punched it. Swore.

I squared my shoulders to come forward and announce my presence. But I waited a beat too long. He saw me first, and when I took an involuntary step back, he leapt out of the net, his feet scuffing the mats as he rushed toward me.

I backed up. "It's not what you think—" I started.

But he reached me and his strong arms surrounded me, forming a light circle that my back bumped into before I stopped.

"You're not spying? Or here to hex me, maybe?" Remy asked.

His body wasn't touching mine, only his arms, but heat radiated from him. I didn't move. I didn't even want to.

He dropped his arms.

"I'm here to talk." I was ready to apologize for sneaking in. I'd invaded his privacy.

He smirked. "If I'd known I had an audience, I would have tried harder."

He was the most infuriating boy of all time.

"I already saw you the other night," I said. "Just like tonight."

His rich brown eyes narrowed. Sweat beaded on his temples. "You saw me do what, exactly?"

"Try for the quad. What you did was amazing."

A corner of his mouth lifted. "So you do know how to spy successfully. But I had no idea you were so easily impressed."

The line of his shoulders was as straight and tight as a string about to snap. "Maybe you don't know any better, but I didn't actually *do* anything, amazing or otherwise. I didn't do it. I'm trying to do it. Two different things."

I should have known better than to offer praise. Performers are never more unpredictable than when they're full of adrenaline and failure. I didn't think it was possible for us to be standing any closer together, and I wanted to put distance between us so badly I imagined how to achieve it in seconds. In one second, I could move six inches back. In another second, six more. All I had to do was move two seconds' worth. Then I could get control of the situation.

But there was no way I was going to give in and move first.

"How many people have actually done the quad? Three?" I asked.

"Four," he said. "But only one in the last ten years."

I shrugged. "Yes, well then, you're a huge failure."

His posture relaxed. The tension left his shoulders and chest. He gave me a skeptical grin. "I wouldn't go so far as to say 'huge' failure. You wouldn't feel the need to spy if that was the case." The grin left. "Or maybe you would."

"You mean because I'm a Maroni?"

He nodded.

"Tell me why. What do people say about us? What do the Garcias say about us?"

He paused. "You really don't know?"

"I don't know enough."

He still hesitated. "And you want to?"

"I don't like being in the dark, and what I've heard sounds made-up." I put some challenge into the words.

He shrugged one sculpted shoulder. "Accidents happened when your grandmother was on the same circus as my family, years ago. She caused them, and she benefited. She could bestow her curse or her luck on whoever she chose, and no one wants to work with that kind of person. She was discovered. They ran her out on a rail."

"That's not true," I said. But it was almost exactly what Nan had said the night before. It explained why Dad had never booked big shows despite being the best in the business. Not that I thought for a second Nan had been at fault.

"What do you know about these so-called accidents? She would never hurt anyone."

"People did get hurt, though. Badly. People died." He went on, quietly. "You can see why I might be disturbed to find you in here."

I could, if he believed we were a family of saboteurs with no moral code when it came to hurting others. I tucked a stray hair behind my ear. "I was curious. That's all." But there was one thing I didn't understand. "Do you believe in magic?"

He studied me, and when his black eyebrows lifted, I noticed the slant of a tiny scar just above the right one. For a second, I thought he was going to make a joke of it. Of me and my question. But his face settled into a serious expression.

"No," he said. "But my grandparents did, and my mother does . . . and I do believe that something happened back then that's hard to explain in other terms. I don't know if it was magic or not, but it was bad. And your grandmother was to blame."

I nodded, though the words hit like a blow. He really believed she'd done terrible things. They all did. It was time for me to head for the door, so I turned.

"Leaving so soon?" Those words were said lightly, but not the ones that followed. "Don't go run and tell your boyfriend that I'm doing a quad, because it's not part of the act. I was just playing around."

My boyfriend? "You mean whoever gave me this?" I angled back toward him and touched the rose. When my fingers brushed the corded stem, I shivered inside again.

He frowned. "No, the blond guy."

"You mean Sam?" Even with the shock of falling, and of what he'd relayed about Nan, I couldn't help it. I laughed so hard that my eyes stung with tears. Dragging in a deep breath, I managed to pull myself together. Mostly.

As I left, I gave Remy one last look over my shoulder, and let it linger. "You should try it again. An attempt at something great . . . it's not nothing. And I'll be bringing my own personal best tomorrow. The Maronis have no need to put a hex on anyone."

five

When I came in, Nan was the only one still up, sitting in her shiny red dressing gown in front of TCM. It was the Barbara Stanwyck movie about the professor collecting slang. I knew all the old classics from our years of watching her favorite films together. She muted it as I came in and settled next to her on the couch. I wanted to try to smooth things over. But when she looked at me, she froze.

"Jules . . ." She pointed to the rose. "What's that?"

"A flower."

"Hold still," she said, and unpinned it from my top. As she held the stem, she went pale, as if instead of holding a rose she was communing with a ghost. "Where did it come from?"

I hesitated.

"Where did it come from?" she asked again, clearly intent on getting the truth.

Fine. "Somebody dropped it in front of me at the party last night."

"You didn't see who?" she asked.

I shook my head no. "It was during the blackout. Why?"

"I keep telling you there's danger, and you keep refusing to see." Nan tugged at the cord on the stem, and it began to come free. She unwound it, and once it was loose, I saw it wasn't a cord at all. The long gray shape Nan held up between us put me in mind of a rat's tail. Fronds of fuzz trailed off each side.

It was a long, dark, thick *hair* . . . of some kind.

"I wore that. Ew." I couldn't believe I'd touched it. "What is it?"

"It's an elephant hair," she said, squeezing the words out like they were sour.

I frowned. An elephant hair—from trunk or tail, so circus lore went—was supposed to bring good fortune. Getting one would be next to impossible, especially when there were no elephants in the show.

"Aren't they a good luck charm? But it couldn't have come from here. So maybe it's a gift? What if someone is helping us, someone who doesn't believe all the lies about you?"

She considered the hair, lowered it between us. Her green eyes were troubled.

"No one who gave you this is a friend. I've seen it before, long ago. Someone gave it to you thinking it would unsettle me. Or . . . Jules, has anything bad happened to you today?"

Thrown, I glanced over at Barbara Stanwyck for guidance. Nan reached for the clicker and turned off the movie. She set it down and tipped my chin back to her. "Jules," she prodded.

"Okay, yes. But it doesn't have anything to do with that weird hair," I said, confident that was the truth.

"So tell me."

I knew that expression. She wasn't going to take no for an answer.

"I fell." When her eyes widened in alarm, I clarified, "There was a net. It was no big deal."

"Right, not a big deal. You never fall, not since you were four. I still remember that day. My heart almost stopped. Thankfully you weren't so high, and Emil was there to catch you." She lifted the hair again. "This is what caused your fall."

"Are you joking?" As the words came out of my mouth, I knew the answer was no. I'd never seen her look older or more serious, all the color drained from her face.

"I wish I was, sweetheart," she said. "But don't worry. I'll get rid of it. You'll be safe from the bad luck it brings once I destroy it. Still, you have to be more careful. You understand that there are people here who want to hurt us now, don't you? This proves it."

Her grave expression kicked my worry into high gear—my worry that she really thought what she was saying was true. "Nan, you can't think that someone planted a magic elephant hair to make me fall. You see how it sounds when I say it?"

She stood, towering over me, and propped one hand on her hip. "Do you trust me?"

I rose too, and faced her. "I trust that you believe what you're saying, but . . . I don't believe it. I can't."

Because it's nonsense. We belong here. You can't do magic. No one can. Which means no one can use it to hurt us or vice versa.

Nan didn't back down. "Good luck, bad luck, superstition . . . Power is power, and magic is usually more complicated than good or bad. Things are what they are. Someone gave this to you. Then you fell. You can't deny that."

Lots of people in the circus are superstitious. My mom didn't follow any kind of religion, but she had a small crucifix sewn inside every costume she'd ever worn. What's more, Nan's crazy theories sounded less weird when I thought back over everything that had happened since we'd arrived: the rose at my feet after the blackout in the big top, the destruction of the RV, the deep shivers when I'd first touched that hair, my unprecedented fall into the net. Remy certainly believed that Nan had hurt people . . . and possibly with the inexplicable powers she claimed to possess. I didn't have a logical explanation for any of it. Now I understood just how easy it would be to believe mysterious forces were at work.

But even if I wasn't ready to buy into the whole idea of magic being to blame, I resented whoever was stirring up the past to frighten Nan, to try to frighten the rest of us.

"Go to bed," she said. "I'll take care of this."

I lay in bed staring at the ceiling, turning the situation over and over in my head. If Nan was right, someone who knew all about her bad history wanted to exact some kind of psychological revenge on our whole family. I needed to stop them. The first step was obviously to prove to everyone else that the Maronis weren't into black magic that caused harmful accidents. If I could do that, there'd be another benefit: proving to Nan that nothing bad was going to happen to any of us because we were here. So she could put her doom and gloom to rest.

When the *snick* of a lighter sounded, I slipped out of bed. Noticing that the framed picture of Bird was still off-kilter, I reached over and set it straight. I eased out into the hallway, against the shadowed wall.

Nan knelt in the center of the living room, facing the dark television like she planned to worship it. I stayed flat to the wall and watched her. The silk of her robe shone dully in the flickering light of a short, fat, white candle, which sat on the floor in front of her. She was murmuring, too low for me to make out the words.

She lifted the stringy gray elephant hair above the candle. As she lowered her hand to the flame, it flared and sparked. Her eyes were closed. In her fingers, the hair seemed to writhe in the flame. The movement had to be a trick of the light, because it shifted like it was alive. A moment later, she jerked the hair back up, at least the portion of it that hadn't been scorched away.

The flame flared again, and then Nan blew it out. She laid the remainder of the hair across her palm.

I wanted to hurry back to my room, but I went a few steps closer. "What are you doing?"

She unfolded at the knees, standing. Her hand closed around the hair. "I was making sure it causes no more harm. Getting rid of it."

"By burning it in a candle and chanting?"

She sighed like I'd never understand. "Yes. This shows someone is rooting against us, inviting our failure. We have to do something about it."

Finally, something I agreed with. "I'm going to," I said.

"No, Jules." Her voice was steel, her expression set. "Let it be. You don't need to do anything but be more cautious. Let me handle it."

I'd never been afraid of Nan before. But I was in that dark room with the lingering scent of burning candle. If not afraid of *her*, exactly, then of her acting this way. Maybe this fearsome quality explained why people still told stories about her, decades after she'd left the circus. Maybe it explained why someone would still have a vendetta against her, and give me a rose that would send a message.

I *would* find out what was going on. That was what I vowed when I went back to bed. I'd start by planning the next day. The attempt at greatness I'd promised Remy was definitely coming. The stunt I'd dismissed before came back into my mind, and suddenly it was perfect. This would be a walk so dangerous it would test Nan's theory that someone was out to get us.

six

From my vantage point below the wires, I looked up into the big top's main spire, and my heart beat faster. It was part nerves—I'd woken up with them—and part awe at the elegance of the setup. Above the center ring on either side were the familiar black bars of the rigging, tucked amid the lights. Our wires were staged to the left, with Dad's slightly higher than and five feet away from mine. The trapeze accoutrements were to the right.

The start of our season was tomorrow. The first show was two days away.

"Dad," I asked, nudging him with my elbow, "if I want to do something crazy once the season starts, will you go along with it?"

He wasn't listening, not even a little. I knew this wasn't the time to tell him about my intention to follow in Bird's footsteps. That now my sights were set on walking on air high above cities, like I was born on a cloud. I loved the idea so much I almost didn't care if he approved, so long as he gave his consent to Thurston. I was confident I could pull off the incredible—and I wanted this stunt to be so big and so daring it would prove once and for all that whatever bad magic my Nan thought was out to get us didn't exist any longer. Or never had.

I lowered my voice to a wheedle. "So you will?" A harsher tone was needed to prompt him to respond, so I used one. "*Dad?* You will?"

"Of course, sure."

He didn't even look at me. If he had, he'd have known I was up to something. Luckily, just then Thurston swooped into the center ring.

He removed his top hat and swept it in front of him, favoring the tough crowd of seasoned performers and work crew with a bow. "Ladies and gentlemen," he began, before pausing to let practiced chagrin steal across his face. "Never mind. I'll save the spiel for rehearsal."

The crowd laughed, and a few people cheered.

"As you know, we leave tomorrow for our first dates. Jacksonville doesn't know what's waiting for them—well, they know we're coming, but there's no way they know what to expect. We're going back to a time when things were done right. We're going to reintroduce this country to the glory and glamour of the true circus. In a world where everything is faked, staged for the cameras, we're going to show them something undeniably real." He paused to let it sink in. To make sure everyone was with him before he asked, "Right?"

Thurston was a born showman. Despite that, there were a few nervous smiles mixed with the applause that came in response. Hoping was dangerous. Hoping could hurt. We all wanted it to, and many needed it to, but the Cirque might not make a go of it. Thurston had never run a circus before, and for all we knew, this was a whim.

He carried on, "So . . . we need a final running order, don't we? And we need to decide who is going to close out each night's performance. I don't have to state the obvious: this comes down to our two new solo wire acts, from two generations of Maronis, and the Flying Garcias. Shall we begin?"

The performers shouted wholehearted approval to the competition. Thurston mused, "Who shall go first?"

Someone shouted, "The Garcias!" This touched off another round of clapping and a few shouts aimed at the beautiful blonde twins, who were the only nonrelatives in the act.

The three Garcias and the twin flyers straightened to absorb the attention like cats preening in the sun. Remy and Novio wore tight black bodysuits with a few red details, and the girls were in pink and red that showed plenty of skin. Dita's number was a scanty sequined thing with shiny pink and red flowers and a few strategically placed flesh-colored cutouts. I barely recognized her.

But even if the costume wasn't one I could picture her choosing, after seeing her in the suit, I had to admit that she—and the others—looked great. No tacky Eurotrash figure skating–style costumes in sight.

Remy caught my appraising look, and our gazes caught and held. We were challenging each other again. I smiled at him, and he looked away. First.

Ha. I win this round.

I turned back toward Thurston and his adoring audience of employees. If I was going to do this, I had to do it. Before he could give first dibs to the Flying Garcias, I stepped forward, and called, "I'd like to be first."

The applause died, but even if they wanted to, no one had the guts to boo. Not with Thurston standing right there.

He made me wait a long moment, then grinned. "Julieta Valentina Maroni, everyone." He slipped into the first row, in front of my mother.

"Julieta," my father said behind me, but it was too late for talk. "Not now," I said.

Thurston's taking his seat must have been a signal to whoever was operating the lights and controls, because a ladder began to lower slowly from the rigging beside the farthest left-hand wire. My wire. I found the line of my spine and timed my crossing of the center ring so I'd reach the ladder just as it finished the journey.

My costume was a prima ballerina's dream, or maybe more like a crazy dream about a prima ballerina. Instead of white or pink, I'd gone with rich red for the color—inspired by the rose that had turned out *not* to be a gift. The bodice was simple and fitted with clean lines, and at the waist frothed into a relaxed rather than stiff tutu.

Sensing that unnecessary flourishes would turn this particular crowd even more against me, I climbed the ladder without adding any showy smiles or significant pauses. I concentrated on grace and speed, and soon enough I was at the top. I stepped onto a small rectangular platform. The wire ran from it, continuing across a wide swathe of the tent.

A rehearsal is never quite the same as a performance. Every extra set of eyes on you brings extra intensity. People add a charge to the air, a spark. I was keenly aware of the crowd of experts watching, probably hoping I'd screw up.

Before I took my first step, I let the people below fade away, let go of my worries about my fall and Nan's weird actions and how people at the Cirque treated us, until it was just me and the wire and nothing else. I was an upside-down rose, a suspended drop of blood, a floating ballerina.

I was alone on the wire. I was whatever I felt like being.

Lost in the nothingness, I did my best, executing my aerial ballet like no one was watching and like everyone was. Soon enough I reached the platform on the other side. Done.

The performance had been flawless. That took the sting out of the subdued applause—polite, nothing more—from below. I heard a wolf whistle and recognized it as Sam's.

I had to bite down on an unprofessional grin as I took my bow. When I finished, I headed back down and into the stands, where I'd need to be for the next phase of my plan. Mom pulled me in beside her and Sam. Even Nan gave me a nod, signaling approval.

Too bad that won't last.

Dad went next, walking straight and sure, adjusting his speed when it suited the walk. Faster, slower. But no tricks. None were necessary. The way he moved was enough, so easy that everyone watching believed gravity had given up on trying to keep him tethered to earth. He simply walked on air.

Even this harsh audience couldn't help giving in to applause that was more than polite when he finished. Thurston was on his feet. From Dad's pleased expression, I could tell he was sure he'd secured the finale spot.

I experienced a moment's concern that he'd flip out when I put my plan into action. *If* I really had the guts to do it. But before I decided to raise the guillotine above my own neck, it was the Garcias' chance under the spotlights.

They didn't hold back on the pausing and smiling on the way up their ladders. And they got affectionate applause and shouts from the crowd in return. There were two sets of platforms, one higher and one lower, and two sets of trapeze swings. Novio and Remy were on opposite platforms, Remy on the higher one and Novio the lower. The girls were all on the platform below Remy, beaming.

Remy and Novio unhooked their trapezes and started things off by sending them sailing across to each other. Each of them grabbed the bar of the tossed swing at the exact same moment and their bodies launched into the empty space, crisscrossing because of the height difference. The brothers released their grips on the bars of the swings, and I expected them to plummet, to bounce off the net—I was sure it was a mistake—but Remy grabbed Novio's trapeze and swung his legs powerfully over the bar, letting his torso dangle below. Novio stood on Remy's swing, gripping the thick cords, sailing back to his platform. Remy swung his body back upright, and leapt onto his feet. He waited in the air for Novio to swing out and tap him forward with a cheeky kick that sent Remy close enough to jump off onto the platform that held the girls.

They caught him, playacting an adoring swoon as they wrapped their arms around him. *Please.*

Next, the twins flew off the platform and did some elaborate—and effective—interplay in the air. Novio caught them in turn, and then dangled one blonde from each arm. They speared down to the net at the same time. Dita was the last of the girls to go, and she did several pretty twists on the swing, before launching herself into a perfect triple somersault. Novio caught her, and she spun again on her way to the net, landing featherlight and bounding to her feet. It was an old-fashioned act. None of the gimmicky safety-wire-enhanced stuff so popular elsewhere.

Dita's dismount would have been a natural end, the cue for Novio and Remy to catapult to the net for bows.

When I saw Remy take the swing one last time, I realized I was clutching my mother's hand. She'd believe it was just nerves about the decision to come. But it wasn't. I wanted to know what he was going to do. And then it was clear.

He was going to try it.

He built up speed even more quickly than he had the night before. Novio bided his time, swinging back and forth, waiting for the catch.

Finally, Remy sallied forth. Until he started to spin, I wasn't sure he'd go through with it. After the third revolution, the audience lifted to its feet, shocked when they saw he was attempting a quadruple.

Remy made the fourth spin look easy, just as he had the night before. And, just as the night before, he missed his mark coming out of it. Barely. Novio's hands slipped past his, and Remy plummeted into the net.

But he didn't punch it. His hands were relaxed. If his shoulders were tight, he made a good show of making way for Novio's own flip down to join him, smiling as he grabbed his sister's hand and joined the troupe for a line of deep bows.

The crowd showered its favorites with adoration. Thurston was on his feet in front of me, gaping at Remy in surprise.

So Remy tried the quad, after all. I was . . . proud of him, which was ridiculous.

I released my mom's hand and stood up, knowing it was now my turn to be shocking. I was going to show whoever gave me that rose that they had another thing coming if they thought they could scare me off with a creepy hair. It was time to prove to Nan she had nothing to fear here.

I ignored my mom's frown, and stepped up next to Thurston. "Can we talk for a minute?" I asked him.

Now? his expression said.

"It can't wait."

He pitched his ear closer, listening, but not looking so happy about it.

"We're doing parades, right? Into the towns?"

He nodded.

"I'd like to remove myself from finale consideration." Not that there'd been much chance I'd land it over Dad or the Garcias. "I can go right before Mom, and she'll cap the first act."

"But why—"

I was confusing him, but there was no other way—this wasn't the easiest thing to propose. "How good are your permit lawyers and advance people?"

I had his full attention now. Mom started toward us, but I waved her away.

"The best in the business," he said. "Why?"

I couldn't show the nervousness of taking a deep breath, but oh, how I needed one. "Do you know who Bird Millman was?"

He nodded, eyes widening.

"And you know about her building walks?"

I didn't need to say anything more. He got it.

"You're sure you can do it?"

"Yes."

"Even so, your parents will never agree—" he started.

"Let me handle them. You handle the permits."

He paused, and when he nodded, the dip of his chin was brief. We had an agreement. "I have to do this now. We'll work out the details later."

"Make your announcement," I said, "but not about this, not just yet. Okay?"

I hoped he'd take my meaning. He did. "Of course."

I needed to tell my parents first. My dad came over and took my hand as we waited. When Thurston announced my placement, he was outraged on my behalf until Thurston and I both clarified that I'd asked to be before Mom. Mom was smiling, sure that was all the conversation she'd started to interrupt had been about.

The moment of truth. Thurston looked from our family to the Garcias, still glowing from their almost-triumph. Well, all except Remy's mother. Maria had left the crowd and stood at Remy's side, frowning. Guess she'd been surprised by Remy's quad attempt—and not in a good way.

"The quadruple somersault is one of the most impressive feats in the history of the circus," Thurston said. "And it's difficult to see how I could put it anywhere other than the finale."

Remy's eyes were on me. I couldn't look at Dad.

"But what we have is an *attempt* at the quadruple," Thurston continued. "While I'm sure the Garcias will make it happen at some point, we can't risk ending the show on an incomplete trick. No matter how impressive. Emil will close the show."

There was no booing. The logic was too sound. This wouldn't win over any of the other performers. If anything, Remy's almost-there attempt might create more gossip that Nan was somehow back to her old tricks and doling out bad luck.

My gaze caught Remy's again, and held. He smiled at me this time, but it was that skeptical grin from the night before. I imagined his expression when he heard about the stunts I was planning to pull, my wire walks high above the great outdoors. Then I imagined the expression of the mystery person who planted the rose, when they heard.

And I smiled too. The real fun was about to begin.

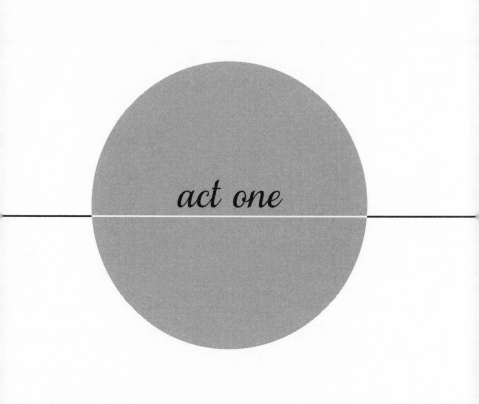

act one

seven

We arrived in Jacksonville the afternoon before the Cirque's opening night, taking over a giant parking lot and nearby grassy field across the bridge from downtown. The crew got busy setting up the tent right away. I was using the downtime to study at the kitchen table with Sam, with the idea that I should keep a low profile until it was time to hit the mess for dinner. Nan was on the couch, quiet thus far. Mom was grumbling under her breath while washing dishes.

My big announcement had led to some furious discussion, and Mom still wasn't completely sold. But Dad was out finalizing the remaining details for the next day's outdoor wire setup with Thurston. Even keeping my head down, I felt a little like I was on a ship, the waves rocky and the arrival at my destination uncertain.

The front door to the RV opened, and Dad came in. I decided to try to slip away to my bunk, but I wasn't fast enough.

Mom whirled from the kitchen sink to face him. "Emil, *how* could you agree to this?" She dried her hands, then smacked the dish towel against the counter. "And now you've committed her with the owner. I can't believe you helped her cook this up."

"She didn't need my help with that. You know our daughter," Dad said. "Julieta Valentina Maroni always seems to get her way."

They both turned toward me.

I stared down at the empty sheet of notebook paper in front of me. Sam coughed like he was swallowing a snort, and I looked up, but only far enough to scowl at him.

"Vonia," Dad said, his tone softer, "you know she's more than capable and ready for this. And I'm confident now that the crew who'll be taking care of the wire are the best in the business."

Speaking up on my own behalf would be like steering directly into the storm, but I had to, in order to make my way through it. "This is a calculated risk. All of it," I said. "Dad's right. I'm ready, Mom. This is what the circus is all about. I've been training my whole life, and you know that I'm as good as any Wallenda."

Thurston had been the first to make a reference to the famed family of wire walkers, especially well-known for the latest generation's stunt walks in places like the Grand Canyon and Niagara Falls. The promise of extra publicity from my doing something similar made this a win-win for the Cirque.

"Fine," Mom said. "I will not stand in the way of this opportunity, if it's what you want. I trust you, and Emil." With that, Mom extended her hand to Dad.

I'd won.

Or so I assumed.

Nan cleared her throat loudly enough to command our attention. "I cannot believe you would be so foolish as to attempt this walk, Jules, after everything I've told you." She glared at my parents. "And I cannot believe that you two are considering going along with this."

Ah, so that was why she'd held her tongue until now. She'd been waiting for my parents to forbid me from moving forward.

"That you would let your daughter risk her life, for what— a publicity stunt? To prove something to people who despise us? Emil, I've warned you about the danger here. You should know better. But maybe this will change your mind: Jules *fell* the other night during practice. Someone here is out to get revenge, and they will hurt us however they can."

I closed my eyes. I hadn't wanted to talk about my tumble into the net with my dad.

My parents' hands unclasped, and Dad crossed the few steps to the table. "Is it true? Did you fall?"

"I was just rattled from the night before. And seeing the net there was strange since I'm not used to having one."

"She's not telling you something," Nan said, looking from me to my parents. She took a deep breath. "I found an object, old and still very powerful, that was planted on the rose she was given. She was wearing the flower when it happened."

And the storm had blown back in, just like that. What if Dad reversed course now?

"Dad," I said, "that wasn't what caused it. I can do this. You know I can."

Sam peered at me over the edge of his silver laptop, but stayed quiet.

Dad gave a short nod, and turned toward Nan. To my surprise, his voice was raised when he spoke to her, pointing a finger. "It was *you* that made her fall, don't you see that? You started putting doubts in her head as soon as we arrived, telling us constantly about old grudges and danger. Now you're blaming some flower, some old object, and upsetting her even more." He dropped his hand. "No. We are here now, and we have to stick together and make our way. I know how you were mistreated back then. I know why we had to stay away, and I've gone along with it, all this time. But you will *not* fill my daughter's head with fears now. Fears are what cause falls."

Nan stood up from the couch, and raised pleading hands to my mother. "And you, Vonia, you agree with him?"

But whatever Mom thought about the magic talk, she wasn't easily cowed. "I would never support my child in something she wasn't capable of. Emil assures me that she is ready."

"How can you say these things?" Nan asked my father. "I raised you. It was always you and me. You must understand my powers, what I can do. You know there are forces at work in this world that are beyond what can be seen and easily understood. Do I have to remind you of what could happen to her if those forces come into play?"

My dad crossed and put a hand on Nan's arm, guiding her down to sit beside him on the couch. "I know what Grandmama thought she could do, and what she convinced you that you could do too. But we have to be real here."

There was a long, quiet moment, and Sam chose it to chime in. "Jules is the one who wouldn't let us pass up the chance to join the Cirque. She's already shown that she's willing to fight for this family. Now she has another big idea, and we should support her."

"Thank you, Sam," I said, and touched my eye where his was still ringed with a bruise. "Back at you."

Nan smoothed her hands across her lap, shaking her head, and I noticed something strange. Her fingernail polish was chipped. Not on every finger, but on her thumb and at least a couple of others. I had never known Nan to have one hair out of place, let alone to allow her manicure to lapse into such a state.

I decided to cut her a break. "Thank you all, actually, for supporting me. And you, Nan, for caring. I promise you, I will be careful. No fears." I nodded at my dad. "I'm going to go take a look at the tent."

Sam started to get up to come with me, but I pressed down on his shoulder when I walked past. I needed some time on my own.

Outside, I moved slowly toward where they were raising the big top, my slippers scuffing the gravel, thinking over the promise I'd just made to my dad. It was impossible to have no fears. But I would try my hardest. And when I did feel scared—which was inevitable—I'd remind myself of Bird. I knew her life backward and forward, and I'd let her story inspire me.

She was born into a circus family in 1890, but they must not have seen her destiny shining out of her tiny baby eyes, because they named her Jennadean—Jennadean Engleman. Jennadean may be many things, but it's not much of a star's name.

Her parents ran a small store in Colorado, and they traveled here and there playing mud shows. These small circuses—not so different from my family's before we joined the Cirque—couldn't afford big tops, but some probably had a cluster of small tents to house a decent freak show and some naked ladies, a horse act, and an acrobat or two. When Bird was six, her parents formed an act for the three of them, the Millman Trio. And half of Jennadean's real identity was born. She'd walked a wire in the backyard growing up, and she knew how to do some stunt riding on a pony, along with other tricks of the vaudeville trade.

When she was ten, her dad fell from the high wire.

Stopping in the grass and hugging my arms around myself, I had no trouble putting myself in her shoes. She'd have been there. She'd have seen him lying in the sawdust, his bones shattered like broken glass, his fragile body ruined by the impact. Though he lived, that's not something she'd have ever forgotten.

It would probably have scared many people off the wire, but it did the opposite for her. It was after that, that Bird was finally born. Whatever fear she felt after the accident, she hid it. She conquered the air. Within a few short years, she was one of the most famous women in America. A star in vaudeville, then embraced by the higher-profile circus. She danced and ran on a low wire, and walked the high wire with ease when she wanted to. Sometimes she used a parasol for balance, and sometimes she didn't. When she was a Ringling star in 1920, the side rings stayed vacant when she was on. No other act could compete.

And, to raise bonds for World War I, she did building walks above various cities. Her most notable outdoor walks took place in New York City, including one twenty-five stories above Broadway, and in Chicago—as captured in the photo on my wall. She made the cover of magazines, with delicately colored illustrations of a grinning Bird above a city.

She was charming, graceful, funny. She is usually called the best "woman wire walker" of all time, but I hate it when people add "woman" to make an achievement seem smaller than it is. She was one of the best wire walkers ever. Period.

Her story didn't end well, though. She met a rich man and retired from the circus and show biz for good. He died ten years into the marriage, felled by the stock market crash, and left her broke. She moved back home to Colorado and passed away of cancer before her fiftieth birthday. An inspirational tragedy was what she was for most people who bothered to remember her now. Her hometown wanted to build a golden statue of her, perched at the top of their downtown clock tower and about to begin a walk, so she could stay up there forever. Maybe it was even there by now.

For my part, I believed she'd *like* to be remembered in motion, far above it all, a bright light in the sky. And I believed she'd approve of another girl on the wire, proving herself. She'd approve of me.

Not to mention the beautiful big top I finally neared. She'd have fit right in here.

The tent, already up, rose from the gravel and concrete like a striped mirage. It was as if a different world had poked through into this one to improve it. Wrapping my head around the fact that the parade would happen in the morning wasn't easy. The entire troupe would march and dance and twirl into downtown, hoping to draw people to the opening-night performance.

But I'd be above them all, the real lure.

I could hardly believe my first outdoor walk was almost under way. Well, the first one in front of an audience. I would have pictured it on a wire strung between two buildings, like Bird. But in this case, I was going to be walking a bridge.

Thurston had called Dad and me to his trailer a few hours after our competition performances, and pulled up a picture of Jacksonville's skyline on his computer. His permit lawyers, after first telling him the whole idea was nuts and shouldn't be pursued, had been adamant that there was no way to get a permit for this kind of thing in two days, not with a minor involved, not even with parental consent. But these were lawyers who wanted to keep their jobs. One of them finally pointed out that the Cirque already had a half-day permit to close down the Main Street bridge for the parade route. And that the bridge had two towers, jutting high above its middle span. A little more Googling told us the towers were two hundred feet tall with a 365-foot span between them. We'd string the wire between them, and I'd be off.

It was ideal. Illegal, but ideal.

I made it to the tent and kept going, heading inside the entrance flap to the adjoining tent that had been raised behind it. This would serve as the backstage area, and was currently deserted, save for trunks and dressing tables set close together. Not fully unpacked yet.

A light breeze wafted over my bare arms, and I looked up to see Remy step inside and pull the flap closed behind him. He had on a pair of beat-up jeans and another T-shirt, this one dark blue, a uniform he wore so well he could have marketed it as the Remy Collection.

"Hi," I said, then kicked myself for not coming up with something pithy.

"Hi," he said back.

Okay, then. We were on equally awkward footing.

"Are you really going to do the walk tomorrow?" he asked.

Remy's dad was in charge of the rigging at the site Thurston, my dad, and I had agreed on. His dad and mine would be the ones who oversaw the crew responsible for setting up the outdoor wire.

"You must already know the answer is yes. Come to wish me failure?"

He took a couple of steps nearer. "Aren't you tempting fate?"

"First you bring up magic, now fate. I may need to stage an intervention. You're just jealous they can't get your trapeze set up that high. If this does go wrong, the Garcias will be thrilled, from what I can tell."

He nodded, though it didn't strike me as agreement. Then, "Seriously, though. You're going to do it?"

Either he was trying to psych me out in some way I'd never encountered before or he was . . . concerned . . . at least a little, on my behalf. Despite my best efforts, I was touched. Hoping I wasn't about to make a fool of myself, I offered him an explanation.

"We had an open air setup back home that I spent hours and hours on, growing up. Dad is a big fan of learning to deal with wind currents, because it's good training for walking in any conditions. And I . . . well, I've always idolized this famous old performer named Bird. My whole life, when I walked outside, I wanted to be like her."

I studied his face, but couldn't read his expression.

"Don't make fun, or I'll kill you, okay?" I cringed as I realized it was perhaps not the best choice of words, but he just raised his eyebrows, and I kept going. "For whatever reason, this is my dream."

"Birds can fly, people can't," he said. But then he added, "I'm not making fun. And I wouldn't be thrilled."

"Good." I swallowed. "Then you can live. Besides, don't think of it as tempting fate. Think of it as embracing my destiny."

"Cheesy." He gave an eye roll.

"What can I say? I was born with a theatrical instinct."

I punched his arm, and he let me.

I was reminded we were alone. No one else was here.

One hand—well, one finger, actually—would be sufficient to count the number of boys I'd been alone with that I wasn't related to. The two of us were making a habit of it.

So it was probably for the best that voices approached outside. The crew, coming to set up the dressing tables. Yes, definitely for the best, since it made us step apart. That was what I told myself.

"Break a leg tomorrow," Remy said.

And before I could say I didn't plan on it, he was gone.

eight

The process of getting ready conspired to make me late the next day. I finished adjusting my hot-off-the-sewing-machine outdoor walking costume in the full-length mirror in Mom and Dad's room.

The costumer had made it beautifully, if much faster than she wanted. It was fitted and covered in flat red sequins. A square neckline gave way to sleeves that would stave off any chills from potential breezes, above a short straight skirt those winds wouldn't budge, with slits to the waist on either side for ease of movement. I wore a pair of leggings underneath and my best pair of slippers. With one last tug on the sleeves, I ran—glittering—through the RV.

"I'm coming! Let's go!" I shouted as I flew out the door, slamming it shut behind me.

"We thought you might need a ride," Mom said.

She was on Beauty, her favorite mare. Beauty was saddled with an ornate leather contraption, a shock of red and gold feathers shooting off the bridle at her milky forehead.

I would have sworn Mom's eyes were shining with tears. Which I did not want. I was already crackling with nervous energy. I believed I could do this, but what if I couldn't? What if something went wrong? What if there was truth to what Nan said, and old magic that might put me in greater danger *did* exist?

There isn't. It doesn't. You're going to prove it.

"All right," I agreed, not thrilled about it. I did need a ride, just not this particular one.

Mom smiled. She knew I wasn't good with horses. She'd tried turning me into a rider when I was a kid, but all I'd done was kick and scream whenever she made an attempt to lift me into the saddle. It might have broken her heart, for a day or two, when I climbed onto the wire for the first time.

"How far behind schedule are we?" I didn't want Thurston to think I'd changed my mind.

I put my foot in the stirrup, and Mom helped pull me on behind her. "We will be right on time." She clicked her tongue and gave a command in Russian. Beauty bounced into a trot across the field. Mom's ponytail swished in my face. We hit the sidewalk, the horse's hooves clattering on concrete. Mom called back to me, "*Solnyshka*, you do not have to do this to make us proud. You know that?"

My answer was light. "But you *will* be proud, right?"

I was glad I was behind her, because I could hear the shiny tears in her answer. "I am always proud of you, my brave girl."

"Mom . . . I'll be fine. I promise."

"If anything happens to you"—she paused, then—"I'll kill your father."

We both laughed, though she probably wasn't joking.

The parade lineup came into view beside the river. Orange traffic cones blocked entry to the bridge connecting this side of the waterfront to the city. A couple of police cars were parked sideways to send a message: No Admittance. The herd of performers waited on this side, so bright and wonderful in the full sun that I almost regretted I wouldn't be crossing into downtown among them—even if they were probably glad to have one less Maroni in their number.

There was the silver-haired older lady ironically named Kat, wearing her epauletted uniform and surrounded by a half dozen of her dogs, barking and running around everyone's feet in excitement. The Chinese acrobats wore their dragon-covered costumes, holding long streamers to wave in the air when they weren't doing flips or when they were walking on each other's shoulders. The clowns, diamonds of red greasepaint on their faces, stood near them on stilts covered by ballooning white silk pants. They towered over the Garcias, decked out in their pink and red and black. I scoured their group and finally picked out Remy, standing next to Novio and clearly making the blonde twins laugh. Dita wore a bow tie with her costume. The fact that it clashed with her skintight sequined number made me think that her mom probably didn't approve of it any more than she had Remy's quad attempt.

And there was Dad, striding out of the pack toward us, with Thurston in full ringmaster garb at his side. I'd already seen Thurston earlier, when he met Dad and me in the morning to discuss the wire setup with the crew. Since then, Dad had been here supervising.

Thurston outpaced Dad to meet us, a wireless mic clipped to his collar. "Good timing," he said to us. "One of those cops is getting nervous. I'm afraid he's going to call someone. Vonia." He nodded at Mom in greeting.

"We'll be right here the whole time," she said, quietly.

"I know." I slipped off Beauty as Sam, wearing the fringed ensemble he donned to assist with getting the horses in and out of the ring, clopped over on another of Mom's mares.

Thurston rattled on, "I was almost afraid our star here had decided not to—"

"Do I look like a chicken?" I interrupted. When Sam opened his mouth to give a smart-ass answer, I gave him a good-natured dose of Bette Davis dragon: "Not a real question, Sam." I made sure Thurston was listening before I went on. "This was my idea. We're late because I *just* got my costume. No other reason."

"I was going to say, 'No, you don't look like you just came from a henhouse,'" Sam said. He grinned. "It was supposed to be a compliment."

I met Dad's eyes, gave him a nod to let him know I was solid. He gave me one back that said he'd never questioned it for a second. It did more than anything else to make me feel ready.

"Good," Thurston said, chastened. "Like I said, we have a nosy cop, and we need to get things moving. I had to pretend we have a helicopter that's going to fly over and drop a banner onto the wire."

Sam snorted. "What moron would believe that?"

"That's what I'm saying. Eccentric rich guy only goes so far. Let's get a move on." Thurston motioned toward the colorful crowd. Dad put a hand on my shoulder, squeezed, but that was it.

None of them bothered with questions, with last-minute good lucks or be carefuls or offers to stay with me until I went up. Maybe we were all too superstitious to do it. Or maybe it's just wiser not to consider the worst-case implications of anything we do, not right before we go on. I knew Nan was watching from the other side of the bridge. Maybe she'd keep her chipped fingernails crossed for me.

The bridge was painted a vibrant blue. A steel structure made up of crisscrossing beams stretched in a long arc over the deeper blue waters of the Saint Johns River, the two towers rising on either side of its middle section like some giant's Erector set.

As we approached, the circus's band arranged themselves at the back of the pack. They had brought the horn section and a portable drum along. When Thurston lifted his hand and signaled, they began to play. The sound was bright, horns blazing.

We surged forward with the parade onto the four lanes of pavement, blue metal beams crossing over our heads, a large chaotic group under control for the moment. The switch into performance mode was complete in a blink.

Thurston shepherded me to the front of the pack. He was talking, but I wasn't absorbing a word he said. Someone jostled against my other side, and there was a tug at the low knot of my hair at the base of my neck. But when I turned, no one was anywhere near me. I caught Remy's eye over my shoulder, and he gave me a slight frown. I resisted the urge to wave.

Thurston and I sped into a jog to outdistance the others. They'd crawl along until I was in position and couldn't be stopped, the better to prevent any interruptions by the authorities. We stopped below the first of the towers.

The tower began well above the roadway, poised on the sixteen-foot metal "ceiling" of the bridge. The innards of the column were full of levers and cables, equipment for its actual purpose—to raise the entire middle section so tall ships could pass underneath. A nylon ladder the workmen had left for me dangled at eye level. There'd be a match to it on the opposite tower.

And I'd be alone once I reached the top. The workmen, Thurston, my dad—they had no place in what was coming next. That was all on me.

Only then did I really stop and look up through the metal bars at the wire itself. I knew it hung at exactly 170 feet, attached to the bottom lip of the tower's top portion, instead of at the very top. That positioning offered more insulation from the wind without affecting the jaw-dropping visual that would be enjoyed by people watching from downtown. Thick braces punctuated the wire at three places, and guide wires clamped to the sides of the bridge below to keep the line stable.

The main wire was steady, with the slightest, unavoidable sway from the gentle spring wind and the length of it. I just had to be steady too.

"My PR team is the best in the country," Thurston said. "You're going up Julieta Maroni, but you'll come down one of our biggest stars."

Cottonball clouds drifted in a blue, nearly windless sky, and the sun shining through the gaps in the structure traced a dappled pattern over the pavement, my arms, my face.

"You know just what a girl wants to hear." No use telling him I was mostly interested in how the people at the Cirque would treat the Maroni family after this. The general public was the last thing on my mind.

I took a breath and motioned for Thurston to give me a boost. He lifted me at the waist, and I grabbed hold of the highest rung I could reach, pulling up until my feet found the bottom rung.

While I climbed, I concentrated on trying to find the calm place inside. It was a long way up, and I listened as the front of the parade passed beneath me, felt the nylon rungs straining against my fingers. Finally I levered myself off onto the flat lip of the ledge. I shook out the stiffness in my hands, did my best to shake off tension.

The moment of no turning back: I reached down and unclipped the edges of the ladder, letting it fall to the waiting arms below.

Needless to say, the platform hadn't been constructed for a picnic. It was sturdy but small, and I walked cautiously to reach my balance pole, which lay nestled inside a metal lip along the back. Dad had also left me a towel and gym chalk. I recoated my palms and the soles of my feet and dusted the bottoms of my slippers clean with the towel before I put them back on. Then I hefted the long pole carefully, letting my arms become accustomed to the weight.

I didn't usually use a pole. But for a walk this high, it was pretty much a requirement. This one was standard size, twenty feet long and forty pounds. That might sound too long or too heavy, but those are the things that provide the extra stability. I wasn't Bird, able to do this with a parasol and a smile. At least not yet.

I eased back to the edge of the platform, directly in front of the wire. The joyfully blaring horn section passed below. They nearly drowned out the shouting, which I'm sure was their intention. I caught sight of Thurston arguing with a police officer. The cop gestured angrily up to me, yelling, "You! You up there, stop!"

There was nothing for me to do about that, except hurry.

Still, I took a moment to mess around with my grip on the pole, shifting my palms an inch this way, an inch that, until it felt solid. Until my center of balance did too. Only then did I examine the flat horizon in front of me, the one I intended to walk into.

The world usually seems small from high on the wire. But from that height, it seemed enormous, like it could swallow me in an instant. Maybe it was a trick of the sparkling blue river water below—I'd only ever seen solid ground underneath me. The increasing volume of the shouts below told me it was time. It was now, or not at all. Once I got out on the wire, we didn't have to worry about cops interrupting. We didn't have to worry that I'd turn chicken.

One more breath, and I took my first step, letting my foot learn the feel of this wire. And then slowly, slowly, I placed my other foot in front of it. Lightly, lightly as a butter-fly, I moved forward, the platform left behind. One step, and another. And another.

Everything faded into the background except the weight of the pole, the easy sigh of the wind, the nothing scent of the air, and my feet, one in front of the other, one in front of the other, smooth and steady. There was no skyline, no tall buildings reflecting light beyond, no choppy water below. No clouds. No birds. No music. No nerves.

There was nothing but the wire fixed to the opposite platform. One I had to reach, by going steady and smooth. Smooth and steady.

And that's how it went, me feeling like time had vanished, that the only thing that marked the passing seconds was my forward movement, my progress toward the other side. The walk was going exactly as planned, and the bigness of the moment surrounded me.

I was doing this. I. Was. Doing. This.

I'd reached the homestretch, a good two-thirds of the way across, when I noticed the slight tremble in my arms. It wasn't the pole's weight—sure, it was heavy, and I didn't practice with it that often, but I was strong enough to hold it. There shouldn't have been a problem.

A rivulet of sweat ran down my forehead, dripped into my eye. I blinked at the burn, and I paused. I stopped where

I was, and the tremble became all I could notice. Except the sweat. And the wild pounding of my heart.

The wire under my feet was still stable, but I felt the opposite. Then I made a mistake. I shifted my focus away from the platform. I looked down, and everything swam for a moment, like a picture coming into and out of focus.

It's not like you can take a break in the middle of a high-wire walk two hundred feet above a river and not risk freaking people out. But I had to do it anyway.

Breathing the dizziness away, I made sure my back foot was stable. I couldn't slip. Once I was sure of it, I picked up my other foot and held it off the wire, an inch. Maybe two.

Then I bent the leg I still stood on, dangling the foot that was already off the wire. I resisted tightening my grip on the pole as I lowered myself to a crouch. I eased my thigh onto the wire, knee bent at a slight angle, and rested there for a moment.

My head felt woozy. There were shouts from far away, from somewhere below. My family would wonder what I was doing. This was an acceptable form of showing off on an open air walk that was going well, as long as I didn't take too long. They wouldn't immediately assume a problem, but they'd be worrying. I saw my mom's face, remembered her vow to kill Dad if anything went wrong. I heard Nan's warnings echo in my ears.

I didn't know what was going wrong, but something had definitely thrown me off balance. And that was the most dangerous thing that could happen, all the way up here, with no way to be rescued.

I had to get back under control. Maybe they'd believe I *was* just performing if I—

I laid back, reclining on the wire, my one leg on it, the other dangling off. The pole I kept flat on my stomach. I closed my eyes and breathed. Breathed.

I opened them. Lazy clouds. More shouts. Sirens in the distance. I had to get up.

Except getting up from this position, on this kind of wire, with its slight sway, well, that was harder than the lying down had been.

That was when I heard a voice, shouting.

It was Remy. Still far off, but nearer than the others. My curiosity was strong enough to get me back into a sitting position. I let the bar find my balance for me, and I scanned down the tower.

Oh no. He was climbing the ladder up to the second platform. There were more police down there, and the rest of the parade was barely visible, almost across the bridge.

I *had* to get up.

Remy looked at me then. We were too far from each other to make real eye contact, but he held up a hand to me. He called out, "You'll do this." And he started climbing again.

Of course I would do it. I was just taking a break. Letting the wooziness pass.

I brought my body into a crouch and drew my dangling foot back onto the wire. Then I straightened, rising dramatically, wishing there was a way to wave or flourish. But I couldn't risk releasing the pole with one hand to try. I needed it too much.

The only way I could show how okay I was involved finishing this walk. So, one foot in front of another. My breathing found its rhythm again, my heart no longer a flutter in my chest. I held my head high, and smiled, and I went on smoothly, but not so slow as before.

Remy had made it to the platform, and he had the nerve to look relieved. "You're okay," he called out to me.

I wanted to hit him over the head with the pole. *Of course* I was okay.

Smooth and steady. Steady and smooth. Smiling, managing not to grit my teeth by willpower alone, and the platform was two feet away, then one, and then Remy's hands darted over the pole, grabbed my waist, and lifted me onto it. For a moment, I might have been weightless. My breath came in gasps, and I wasn't sure if it was from the close call or relief at feeling Remy's strong arms bracing me. Pulling the pole from my grip, he put it down behind us. He clamped his hands onto my shoulders, holding on like he thought I might fall.

It took me a moment to be able to speak. "What . . . in the name of Barnum . . . do you think you're doing?"

He released one of my shoulders and reached behind me, messed with my hair, even as I slapped his hand away. Before he could do anything else, I straightened to my full height and folded forward into an elegant bow, in case anyone was watching. The shouts and sirens below assured me plenty of people were. I flourished, my hands happy to not be gripping the pole so tightly it felt like the bones in my fingers might break.

I could never admit to my family how close that had been.

Remy said, "Look," and he held up something I didn't recognize right away.

It was a long feather. A black eye at the end and a fringe of bright colors along the shaft.

A peacock feather.

The one thing that was absolutely banned from a performer's costume as bad luck.

The wind kicked up, plucked it from his hand, and we watched together as it twisted along the air currents to the river, and vanished beneath the deep blue water.

"You can thank me any time," he said.

nine

I could guess what Nan's reaction would be if she learned about the peacock feather. I wanted to excuse its presence away, but given what she'd said about someone planting the elephant hair . . . it seemed impossible that this was a random prank.

"It's just a feather. Right?" I asked Remy, feeling off balance again and wanting him to steady me.

Especially after I took the opportunity to look down. Dad stood at the bottom of the ladder with his arms crossed over his chest like a fatherly skull and crossbones.

"I . . . I don't know," Remy said. "I saw it on you before you went up. I was trying to get your attention." I flashed back to the moment I'd caught his eye in the crowd, and nodded. I hadn't realized then, but now I could imagine that, yes, he'd been trying to tell me something.

"But it's still just a feather." I straightened my skirt, pulled at my sleeves. Fidgeting. My wooziness returned stronger than ever when I thought about Nan's claim that the elephant hair had made me fall. I could have fallen much farther this time.

"A *peacock* feather," said Remy. "Don't leave out the details."

"Fine," I said, wanting to change the subject. "Did you give me that rose the other night?"

"What? No." He frowned. "Why did you even think of that?"

I frowned back. "Please tell me what's going on. Why did you come up here?"

"I *can* explain," he said. "Well, I can explain some things. Why I was worried. But I swear it wasn't me."

"Julieta!" My father's call was a command. Not a good sign. Below us, Thurston stood beside him, smiling nervously.

I motioned to the dangling ladder. "There's no time now. We have to get down there."

"I should go down first, in case—"

I interrupted. "So you can look up my skirt the whole way down? Not happening."

He smiled, unexpectedly, and stepped back. That smile should be registered as a deadly weapon. He moved aside so I could reach the ladder. "You go first then. *I* don't mind *you* enjoying the view."

I lowered myself onto the ladder, glad I could duck my head to prevent him from seeing me blush. He followed suit once I'd made enough progress, swinging his legs around to the opposite side so he was climbing down facing toward me. That balanced the ladder so it hardly twisted in the air.

"Jules," he said, when we were about halfway to the street. His tone was serious.

"Yes?" Next rung.

"Stop for a sec."

I did, reluctantly.

He came down a few more rungs, stopping when our faces were inches apart. His hands gripped the rungs on either side of mine. "There's more, but . . . I came up because I was afraid something was going to happen to you. I'm glad it didn't."

I tried to ignore the stupid thump of my heart. He'd saved me, but he could hurt me too. The only thing that determines the success of a performance is whether the audience thinks the performer carried it off. I didn't think anyone else would have noticed the peacock feather—besides whoever put it in my hair when I was in the crowd—but my family couldn't know about it. Nan would tailspin. I had to find out who was doing this, and why. Yes, I'd freaked out on the wire, but I still didn't believe it was because of magic.

Fears are what cause falls. That's all it was. Dad had been right. These ideas were the dangerous thing.

"You won't tell anyone about the feather?" I asked. "My grandmother . . . she's not what you think, but she believes in this stuff. You said your parents and grandparents did. You understand why she can't know?"

Our eyes caught, held. Sun and shadow raked across his features as the nylon ladder swayed with our weight. His eyes were so brown, the pupils small in the brilliant sunlight. He didn't answer.

"You don't believe it could really have hurt me?" I pressed.

"I don't know, but I know it shouldn't have been there. We need to talk," he said. "But I won't tell."

"Then I will say it. Thank you." I went back to making my way down. Hands gripping nylon, then lowering feet to next rung, repeat. At the bottom, I jumped to the pavement. Dad caught my waist. When he let go, he put a hand on my arm. Like he needed convincing I'd made it.

Remy leapt off and landed next to us. Dad gave me a narrow stare that made me want to flinch or curl up into a ball. Then he turned it on Remy. I still couldn't believe Remy had climbed up onto the platform during my walk—no matter what his reasoning. More, I couldn't believe I was grateful. I had been in trouble.

To his credit, Remy accepted Dad's regard without cringing or fleeing. He said, "Sorry. I was afraid"—he paused, shrugged in my direction, and I *was* afraid of what he'd say— "that she was about to go down in flames. And if that was going to happen, I wanted the credit to go to a Garcia."

In flames. Wanted the credit. Reminding Dad he was a Garcia. He was pretending he'd tried to wreck my performance, or maybe take credit if it was going poorly already, by interrupting. My dad bought every word. The rest of the Cirque would too.

"You could have caused her injury," my dad said, a murderous glint as he stepped toward Remy.

But I put a hand on Dad's arm to stop him. "No, he couldn't have. I was fine."

"Oh well," Remy said.

But he was smart enough not to linger. Maintaining the cocky façade, he sauntered away past Thurston and a couple of cops. And two men in fancy suits who were talking to the cops at warp speed, waving documents.

Dad was more skeptical of the explanation than I expected. "Have you been . . . fraternizing with that boy?"

I scrambled to reassure him. "Oh no—we're not . . . No. Is that what you thought?"

He didn't answer, only became more intent. "You are to stay away from that boy." He gave my arm a shake, hand firm. He meant it. "Promise me. You will stay away from that boy. The Garcias can't be trusted. Not by us."

Nothing less than total and convincing agreement would satisfy him. But I didn't want to flat-out lie to my father either.

"Dad, please. You saw. He almost ruined my walk. And enjoyed it."

He released my arm, satisfied. "You're okay?"

I wanted to sit down. I wanted to find out what Remy knew about all these superstitions floating around. Did he have answers about the rose landing at my feet, the feather in my hair? I gifted Dad with my best worry-free smile and said, "Never been better. The truth is, being on solid ground feels nice for once."

He looked only half convinced.

The lawyers stopped talking, and one of them held out a hand to the cop to shake. The cop's partner was talking on a cell phone, serious and deflated. Thurston left them and came over to us.

"Welcome back to earth," he said.

"Am I going to jail?" I asked. "I'm really not dressed for it."

"You'd be amazed what you can make happen by offering the mayor's office a few truckloads of new computers for local schools and a commencement speech by one of America's leading entrepreneurs—especially in an election year. I believe our friends are about to have it confirmed that our permit was to do whatever we felt like on that bridge."

"I want to be a billionaire when I grow up," I said.

Thurston laughed. We watched as the cop with the phone hung up and nodded sullenly at the lawyers. I could see them resist high-fiving each other. One of the cops said, "Free to go."

"Your public awaits," Thurston said.

The crowd gathered at the end of the bridge was large and only growing when we reached it. The circus parade had been entertaining them with tricks while they waited for us, but quiet spread among performers and townies alike at our arrival. Beauty's head stuck up over the crowd, and Mom waved to me from her saddle, her smile tight, but no less real for that. Nan stood beside the horse, patting its nose absently while she paid close attention to something in front of her.

Make that someone. I followed her line of focus to Remy, standing with his family. Novio and their mother were both scowling at him. Remy didn't wave to me or even look up. By all appearances, he didn't even notice I was there.

Thurston switched on his wireless mic and held up my hand above our heads. "Ladies and gentlemen, I present America's new Princess of the Air!"

I accepted the cheers, the shouted handful of questions from reporters, the smiles of my family. It was the spotlight I'd always wanted. But the walk hadn't magically transformed me into a princess or rehabbed the Maroni name.

The bullet had missed, but our family clearly still had a target on its back.

ten

During our first few days, whether the afternoon show or the evening one, I hid behind one of the dressing curtains in the corner of the bustling backstage tent for privacy before I went out for my act. There, I checked over every inch of my costume in a full-length mirror for unwanted additions. I never found anything suspicious, though, and the performances went off without a false pirouette. No one would ever guess I was beginning to have more questions than confidence.

Fake it until you make it. Or, in this case, until I figured out whether the danger was real and who it was coming from. I'd been waiting to talk with Remy since our moment on the nylon ladder, but that was proving impossible under my dad's watchful eye.

I was determined. Garcia or not, I wanted whatever answers Remy had to share. And maybe something else too. I couldn't forget that weightless feeling when he'd lifted me off the last inches of wire onto the bridge platform and to safety.

So after taking my bows at our last show in Jacksonville, I decided to linger backstage in hopes of bumping into him. The open floor plan of evenly spaced makeup tables and warm-up areas, punctuated by costumer, snack, and first aid stations, was usually filled with people. The grand curtained entrance out to the center ring was given a wide berth, however, with two costumed crewmen in charge of pulling and lowering the flaps.

Other members of the crew ensured the way was clear as Mom and her horses thundered past me to make their entrance. She shot me a wink as she ran by in her bright-blue jacket and riding pants. Sam came at the back of the herd of seven, clicking encouragement. The horses loved him almost as much as Mom.

I maneuvered through backstage to the side entrance near the edge of the stands. No one would think anything of me watching Mom's act from here. If I was lucky, Remy would turn up.

Mom was in top form as always, her adoring mares and stallion lifting their hooves high in the air to paw on command as they stood on their back feet. They lowered their bodies, raced in a circle around her. She let them make the rounds a few times, while she transferred herself from one horse to another. She stood on one's back, only to jump in a sideways blur and end up sitting backward on another, or to spin in the saddle while the horse was in motion.

Sam waited outside the ring, ready to help if any of the horses got distracted. They rarely lost their focus on Mom, her control of them so complete that it looked easy. But I knew that any one of these powerful creatures could cause a terrible accident in the smallest slice of time, in the wrong circumstances. It was good Sam was there, in case.

The act ended with all seven horses kneeling to Mom, and her flipping onto Beauty's back to ride them in one last circle and out of the ring. Thurston boomed his praise over the crowd's loud applause.

I waited for a while longer, but when Dad came for me, I hadn't seen any sign of Remy.

I dreamed a chorus line of elephants, vast and lumbering. They wore headdresses made of peacock feathers. They rose onto their hind legs as one, massive front feet swaying in a dance. And then I was in an ornate saddle on the back of one, clutching at the harness in an attempt to stay on, feathers coming apart in my fingers . . .

Just what I needed: bizarre nightmares.

We moved on to our next city, Charlotte, where our first three shows were already sold out.

My picture had been on the front page of the Sunday paper, along with my new "Princess of the Air" tag. The attitude of our fellow performers toward us remained chilly. I hadn't managed to talk to Remy yet, and I was getting impatient. The bad dreams didn't help.

At least I could watch him at work. I'd been taking every chance to catch the Garcia act over the last couple of days.

It was incredible to watch him up there. Yes, I'd seen him practice alone more than once, but there was no substitute for seeing the real deal in front of a live audience with the ringmaster's patter, with the lights and music going gangbusters. His charisma was undeniable.

Dad was busy preparing to go on after the Garcias, so I went to the side curtain to watch Thurston introduce them. His patter built up the excitement, and truly made their act come alive. The Garcias didn't perform as "The Flying Garcias" exactly. No, it was way more over the top than that. Thurston boomed, "Welcome the best flyers anywhere on Planet Earth or in the heavens of Olympus—the Love Brothers and the Goddesses of Beauty, featuring the Flying Garcias!"

I listened to the swelling melody that, I knew, would fade out to drumbeats for the biggest tricks. High above, Remy and Novio were doing their partner swing, putting a little extra zip into it for the adoring audience, while Thurston's voice told the oohing crowd, "Casanova and Romeo, timeless scoundrels, noble knights interested in slaying only the hearts of ladies . . ."

I didn't know if their stage names were their real ones, but I suspected they were. I'd go by Novio and Remy too, if those were my choices. Regardless, there was always a gaggle of women waiting for their autographs at the end of the night.

"And their sister, the lovely goddess of love herself, Aphrodite." Dita swung out and then up into her tight triple somersault, a spinning ball of pink and red flame, her hands extending for Novio to catch her taped wrists, her hands gripping his. Next came "the Sirens," the twins, twirling on their swings and flirting with Romeo until he gracefully leapt from his trapeze to land on their platform.

"Wherefore art thou, Romeo?" crooned Thurston. "With the Sirens perhaps?"

On the platform, one of the blonde twins fake-swooned into his arms. When we'd studied mythology, I hadn't gotten the appeal of the sirens. Why couldn't the sailors resist the empty promise of their song? I sensed rather than heard someone join me, checked over my shoulder and found Sam.

"It's too bad we're their ancient enemies," he said.

"Why's that?"

"Because it prevents us from mocking their names to their faces." He raised his eyebrows for effect. "*Romeo* and *Casanova*? Seriously?"

"And don't forget Aphrodite. But we can mock them from over here."

"That's what I'm doing, but what about you?" he asked, mischief in his eye. "Looks more like admiring."

I didn't bother with an answer.

A moment later, Thurston started the lead-in patter to the quad, explaining how Romeo was about to attempt one of the circus's most dangerous feats. Remy began to swing back and forth, back and forth, his body churning to build up power. Sam was focused on me, not the act. "Your dad told me to keep an eye on you," he said.

The band was doing its *drumroll drumroll drumroll.* "Because of Remy?"

"He wants me to tell him if I see you together. Just be careful you don't get caught. All they need is another reason to freak out. Especially Nan."

Nan had interrogated me about my pause on the bridge, but Dad had stepped in.

"Agreed."

I stared overhead, willing Remy to make it. But when he completed the fourth somersault, Novio's hands slipped past Remy's. They were heartbreakingly close to a catch. But not quite there. They hadn't mastered the quad yet. Down, down, down Remy went into the net.

When I looked back to Sam, he was headed toward the snack table. I decided to wait through Dad's act. The band played as he ascended to the platform, then stayed silent through his walk. The audience followed suit, at the edge of their seats, afraid to breathe.

My back warmed as someone came up behind me, taking my hand before I could turn to see who it was. A folded piece of paper pressed into my palm, and Remy murmured, "Take it," into my ear.

I closed my hand around the note, intensely aware of his fingers sliding against mine. By the time I whirled around, all I could see was his back as he crossed the tent. He laughed as he raised a hand to catch the bottle of sports drink Novio tossed to him. A quick skim of the people around told me no one had noticed anything.

I put off reading the note until I was back in my room, a delicious secret for me alone. The paper was a square torn from a notebook, ragged-edged and blue-lined. Printed in black ink was:

We still need to talk. Come to our trailer during dinner tomorrow. A good spy would destroy this message.

I stuck the note under my mattress instead. And smiled. Tomorrow, there'd be answers. Tomorrow, I'd get to talk to Remy.

Another nightmare.

I was back on the wire above the bridge. I was sweating, struggling to breathe, trembling, and, finally, shaking too badly to stay on. Remy stood on the platform and watched me as first one foot slipped off into thin air, then the other. I fell, down and down, toward a net made of peacock feathers. A thousand staring black eyes.

I woke before I hit.

eleven

Goosebumps covered my exposed arms the next night as I navigated the maze of vehicles in the lot behind the big top. The cooler temperature reminded me that our current stop in North Carolina was a long way from humid Florida. Even in May, evening brought a slight chill here, and the Garcias' home-on-wheels wasn't anywhere near ours. But I knew right where to find it. I'd stretched my legs earlier, and paid close attention to where everyone was parked.

As I approached, I was reminded again that their RV was much nicer than ours. Newer, bigger, shinier—a reminder of the years of top engagements they'd played while we toured in obscurity. The lights were off, except for the back right window. The same side as the door, but I went for it instead.

I'd dressed casually to discourage suspicion, and now regretted it. I wanted to be wearing something that would give me a boost. An eye-catching outfit, more like a costume. But, no. This was perfect. Remy wouldn't get the impression I'd dressed for him from this ratty-for-me look of jeans and a faded vintage blouse. I wanted us to be on as even ground as possible. That was hard when he'd essentially rescued me on the bridge, and I was coming to him for help again.

My hand clenched in a fist, and I tapped my knuckles to the window glass once, then twice. I moved my palms up and down my arms to warm them, and blew out a sigh when nothing happened. I raised my fist to the window again, about to give it one last tap, when the curtain moved and the window snicked to the side, revealing a screen.

And Remy behind it. He was silhouetted against the light inside the room, and I had to move closer to get a look at him. His jaw was shadowed with a day of not shaving. His eyes were shadowed too, but they crinkled at the corners as he spoke.

"You planning on climbing through the window? Because getting this screen out won't be easy."

I molded my lips into a smile. "I'd prefer the door. But make it quick. Someone could see me out here."

"Right." He slid the window shut and the curtain dropped back into place.

I walked over to the door. If someone did bust me, I could always claim I didn't know whose place it was. Well, that *might* have worked if the side of the RV hadn't been decorated with giant overlapping murals featuring the previous generations of Flying Garcias *and* the current Love Brothers and Goddess. Fake Remy grinned out, flying across a background of fake spotlights.

Why didn't we have murals? Right. Because we'd never been able to afford them.

Remy opened the door. "Come in."

He turned sideways, so I had to slide in past him, our bodies brushing against each other as I moved up the stairs.

"Nice place," I said.

It was immaculate. Pristine granite kitchen counters, longish dining room table attached to the wall, a large flat-screen mounted from the ceiling in the living room area, and a couch covered in satiny pillows that would've fit right in on the set of *Cleopatra*. According to one of Nan's favorite tabloids, Elizabeth Taylor's ghost made frequent appearances. If she needed a place to recline, she'd be right at home here.

Remy was watching me with an unreadable expression. There was nothing I hated more than an unreadable expression.

"So, what do you have to tell me?" I asked.

"I want to show you something."

"Okay," I said.

"It's in my room."

"I'll bet you say that to all the girls."

He shook his head. "I don't. I mean . . . I'm not like that."

"You're telling me you're not a Romeo?"

"Funny," he said. "But yeah. I can't stand guys like that."

Who can? But I shrugged the most casual shrug I could manage. A total lie, since there was nothing casual about my being here or the way I felt when I was around him. "Good to know. Lead on."

He angled by me, and I followed him down the tight hallway. Some family photos were hung along the short hall, which reminded me the Garcias were a family more like mine than most. Sure, they had more space than we did, but not *so* much more. An RV was an RV was an RV. I notched my envy down a peg.

Then we were in his room. His and Novio's, by the looks of the twin beds opposite each other. One was unmade, its built-in headboard shelf packed with a chaotic stack of paperback books with numbers on the spines. I picked one up and saw I'd guessed right—it was a mystery series. The other bed was neatly made with military corners, and a roll of wrist tape on the nightstand was the only personal effect.

"I thought maybe you wouldn't come," he said.

"You knew I'd come."

"I didn't." He ran a hand through his short hair, making it a little messy. The movement told me he was nervous, even though he was decent at hiding it. He gestured to the made bed. "Have a seat."

Have a seat on his bed. *Okay.* I did.

There were only a few feet between us.

"This room isn't big enough for the two of us," I said.

He countered. "Some people would say this circus isn't either."

Leave it at that. "What was the first show you worked on?"

He blinked. "Big Apple, I think."

"And straight to the Greatest after that?"

"I'm sure my mom has a scrapbook, if you want to see my baby pictures and relive my first catches. We worked all those shows, yes. But it wasn't what you think. The performing was fine, but our training schedule sucked. It was brutal." He paused for a second. "What you told me about learning to wire walk outside, pretending to be your hero? It sounded fun. More fun than any training we ever did when I was a kid."

"Really?" I was fascinated by the glimpse at Garcia life. "You seem pretty close with your brother and sister."

He nodded. "We grew up in the trenches together."

"Come on. It couldn't have been *that* bad."

"My grandfather was our trainer until he died," he said, as if that was enough explanation.

I sensed this was not the time to ask what that had been like. And silently thanked the universe that if my dad was a hard teacher, he was never a harsh one.

"Tell me why you came up on the bridge," I said. "What made you notice the feather and think it was a problem?"

Remy dropped onto the unmade bed opposite me, and there we sat, so stiff we were more like marionettes than the latest generation of two circus dynasties.

He watched me closely as he spoke. "When you were up there"—he raised his hand—"you were in trouble, right?"

My dad had drilled it into me for many years: weakness was the one thing I could never show. Not to someone who was my competitor.

Remy waited.

I stood. It would be a mistake to admit anything had gone wrong. I tried to tell myself to walk away, to not mention Nan or the doubts she'd planted in my head. My plan was to walk back through the Garcia RV and out the door, never to return. But my feet were glued to the floor.

He said, "I swear I'll never tell another soul, but I need to know. Were you in trouble?"

GIRL ON A WIRE

I knew I should leave. Everyone in my family, with the possible exception of Sam, would be telling me to make my exit right now. Instead, I sank back onto the bed. He'd already promised not to tell anyone what happened up there.

"I was in trouble," I said. "Nan—my grandmother—has been off since we got here. She's convinced someone is out to get us . . . with magic. Trust me, I know how it sounds. My dad believes her way of thinking is dangerous. He'd say that her doom and gloom must have affected me, and I think he's right." Now for the main question, the reason I was here. "But someone did plant that thing on me. Do you have any idea who?"

Remy held my gaze for a moment, and then he bent beside the unmade bed and pulled out a drawer beneath it. His white T-shirt showed off shoulders and arms as well formed as a sculpture. "I should just show you. It'll be easier to explain that way." Folded clothes filled the drawer to the brim.

So I was sitting on Novio's bed, not his. I got up again, asked, "You're going to show me your shirts?"

He ignored me, rummaging beneath the stacks of folded clothes. "Granddad passed away last year."

"Roman Garcia. I've heard of him." Legend had it, he'd been one of the best male flyers ever to work in the business.

I felt a pang of sadness for Remy that he'd already lost his grandfather. I couldn't imagine losing Nan, but then again, I didn't really have any other grandparents. Nan had never married, and Dad's and his brother's father took off before they were born and never came back. Mom's parents had both passed away young. All I knew of them came from stories and photos. Mom had been raised by distant relations who'd come over to work with circus horses.

Remy held the clothes up with one hand while he carefully removed a corkboard from the bottom of the drawer with the other. The board was almost too big to fit the space, and he lifted it out awkwardly. The first nonsmooth move I'd ever seen him make.

"Our house is in Sarasota." He held the board to his body so my view of the things hanging on it was blocked. "When we got to winter quarters to officially join the Cirque, I found this near our trunks and the other gear we brought across town from home. I'm almost sure I'm the only one who saw it. I don't know if it was my mom's or if it was my grandfather's and she had it with her. Or if someone planted it with our stuff. I found it right on top, like it had been left there for us to discover. I . . . I snuck it away and hid it, as fast as I could. I didn't want anyone else to see it. And no one ever acted like anything was missing, which means it could have come from anywhere."

"What is it?"

In response, he laid it on his rumpled bed, a few of the photos and clippings pinned across the surface fluttering before they settled. I couldn't make out the details from where I stood.

"Cops would call it a murder board," he said.

"A what?"

"Sorry. That's how I've thought of it. Too many mystery novels on the road." He glanced over at the stack of books. "The trusty detective always cracks the case. And Mom watches *Law and Order*. All of them. I just mean evidence. It's evidence."

"Of what?"

"That's what I don't know. But it can't be good. Murder boards never are."

I stepped next to Remy. My shoulder brushed his. I dreaded seeing what was on the board, but couldn't keep myself from looking.

The largest photo was of Dad, looking so light on the wire that it was as if his feet weren't touching it. My semi-blurry face and blonde hair were visible behind him. I must have been on tiptoe, doing one of our occasional duo sets. The picture couldn't have been more than a year old.

Much of the rest of the board was taken up by black-and-white snapshots from decades ago, clearly taken long before the age of digital cameras. All of them featured performers. Two tiny girls, one standing on the other's shoulders so her hand was high enough to rest on the flank of an enormous elephant wearing a fancy headdress. The girl highest up had a familiar-looking rose pinned to her chest. In another picture, a ring girl for Barnum wore an uneasy smile and a hat with a tall peacock feather. A third featured a group of clowns standing next to a leather steamer trunk that looked old and beat-up, with a distinctive pattern of gold studs embossed on the top. One of the clowns was mugging for the camera, holding up a square scarf with an exaggerated eyebrow raise.

The rose. A peacock feather. My breath caught in my throat.

There was also a faded newspaper clipping with the head-line "Clowns fired after malfunction blinds three, kills two." Another clipping read, "Elephant, 'Tiny,' kills two performers in escape." And one more: "Ring girl dies in fall at 19."

Remy reached out and tapped a washed-out photo I hadn't noticed yet. It was creased at the edges in a way the others weren't, like someone had handled it often. "This is an old picture of my grandparents," he said.

A handsome young man with broad shoulders easily held a smiling beauty perched on his forearm, while his other hand extended forward with the palm open, something in it glint-ing in the camera's flash or the sun.

I turned from the board, my breath still caught. I released it. "What do you think this means?"

"I saw the feather in your hair when we were in the crowd, walking toward the tower. I thought it must be a joke," Remy said. "I wasn't going to say anything to you, even after I saw it. I didn't think any of this meant anything. I assumed the board was someone messing with us, or maybe something my grandfather would have kept. But . . . now, I don't know . . . These photos are like proof of some of the stories people tell about your grandmother. Proof that the accidents happened."

Anger rose up in me. "You saw the peacock feather. Why didn't you tell me on the bridge that it was something you thought was linked to my grandmother?"

His expression was pained. "I wasn't trying to keep it from you. I didn't want to talk nonsense. Because the thing is, I don't believe in magic either—it seems crazy. But my grandparents always did. My mom does. And then, I saw the feather, and you were up there and you stopped. And I thought, What if the board does mean something? What if that ring girl died because of the peacock feather? Or the others? That picture of you and your dad . . . I didn't even know who it was for sure until you guys showed up in Sarasota. That's why I came over to dance with you during the masquerade party. To see if you knew us."

"I'd heard of the Garcias, that we . . . didn't get along," I said. "But I knew almost nothing about you." I examined the ominous collection of items on the board again.

"My mom was beside herself when she heard the Maronis had been hired. I thought maybe she could finally let the past go after Granddad died. He was her dad, and he was as hard on her as on us. But your family's name brings out the worst in her."

"Do you think she would . . ." I didn't want to finish the accusation, and I didn't have to.

"No. I can't imagine my mom *doing* anything to you, besides being unhappy you're here. But somebody made this board, and whoever it was might. So before I knew what I was doing, there I was, climbing that bridge tower. Just in case."

"Remy . . ." I wanted to tread carefully. "This *is* sounding a little crazy. What are we talking about here?"

His face hardened, the stubble adding to the effect.

"You admitted you were in trouble up there," he said. "Is there a logical explanation?"

Sure. I could explain it lots of ways. The wind, the height, my nerves. But what Remy was talking about, well, the only word for it was magic. I couldn't make myself believe that was the answer.

"If someone is out to get my family, they wouldn't need magic to kill us. We're in a dangerous line of business."

Remy said, "There's something else." There was an envelope pinned to the bottom of the corkboard, and he unfastened it. He handed me the letter inside, handwritten on fancy paper and addressed to Roman Garcia. I read it, shaking my head.

I'm starting a new circus and I hear the most fascinating stories about the Amazing Maronis and what they are capable of, why they were cast out of the community. I'm told you are the one who can tell me the truth of things. Please contact me at your earliest convenience with any guidance you can share that will help me bring them back into the fold. The circus needs all its old magic back. Don't you agree?

It was signed Thurston Meyer. The date at the top was from last year.

"From Thurston to my grandfather," said Remy.

"He never comes right out and asks if Nan is magic . . ."

"But I bet he did when they talked."

My hand trembled. Remy noticed and lifted the sheet away, folded it carefully, and gave me a moment to collect myself.

"Remember at that first party, I had a rose after the lights came back on?" I asked.

"The rose you asked me about on the bridge?" He looked chagrined. "Like I said, I had nothing to do with it. But . . . I am sorry for coming on like such a jerk that night."

"Well, you're gifted at it for someone who doesn't want to be a Romeo." I paused, deciding how much to tell him. I might as well say it all. "Anyway. I wore it the next day to rehearse, and I fell. I hadn't fallen since I was four years old. When I got home, Nan saw the rose and freaked. She unwrapped this gross strand of hair from around the stem. Claimed it was an elephant hair."

I hesitated.

"What?" he asked.

"She said someone had left it to rattle her, and that *it* made me fall. Then she burned it. I caught her."

"Do you think the stories about her are true?"

He said it softly. Like he didn't want to ask.

"No." I wouldn't believe that. I couldn't. "There must be some other explanation. When she burned it, she told me she was making sure that it couldn't hurt anyone. I don't know what happened in the past, but I know somebody wants revenge. I can't let anything happen that could ruin my family's future. I've worked—we've *all* worked—too hard to get here."

"I understand." Remy reached out to touch his grandfather's photo. "Before he died, he started talking constantly about how he'd lost his luck, how it was stolen from him, a long time ago. How he'd lost our family's place on top."

"But your family is on top. Always has been." It was the Maronis who'd shuffled off into the shadows. It was me fighting to get us back in the spotlight. It was Nan who'd suffered. "It's not been as easy as it looks from the outside."

Before I could say anything else, he went on. "We were raised to think the Maronis were awful. And, like I said, my mom has been extremely weird since you guys arrived. Wanting to know where we're going, what we're doing. Climbing up on that bridge—I might as well have asked for them to watch my every move. That's why I gave you the note."

"Similar story here." Though, in my case, Sam was charged with the watching. "Remy, is it possible—just possible, I'm not saying I think this—that someone in your family planted these things on me? I know you said it couldn't be your mother. But . . . could anyone have had access to these . . . bad luck objects?"

"I've looked everywhere, and found nothing. I don't think so. I hope not."

"But then where does that leave us—Thurston?" I asked.

"I don't know, but we need to find out. You could have died on the bridge."

I swallowed. "We could always die."

There was no way to dispute it. "There's one other thing I have for you." He took my arm, and even though his grip on my forearm was light, I felt his touch as acutely as a burn. He tugged me along behind him, up the hall toward the kitchen. He stopped at the low dining table attached to the wall, plush chairs dotting its edges.

His hand left my arm and he pulled out another drawer, this one on the side of the table. I saw a jumble of candles, matches, and place mats.

"This isn't going to be another murder board, is it?" I asked.

But I recognized what he removed from this drawer immediately. The painted faces were as familiar as my childhood. Nan's deck of cards. I hadn't seen them since we arrived in Sarasota.

Remy laid them on the table. "The night you got here, after the fight, I brought Novio back home, and my mom was sitting at this table with those in front of her. She shoved them in that drawer and hasn't touched them since, from what I can tell. Everyone knows your grandmother used to give readings for people from her one-of-a-kind hand-painted circus tarot cards. Even me. This is hers, isn't it?"

I stared. Did that mean someone in the Garcia family *was* behind the break-in? But that wasn't possible. They were all accounted for. Nan had visited Maria Garcia and her husband that night, and Remy, Dita, and Novio had been at the party. And Nan hadn't said a word about the cards being missing . . .

"Yes. They're hers," I said.

He frowned. "Does she know they're here?"

"I don't know."

The front door banged open, only steps away, and I almost jumped out of my skin. Over his shoulder, Remy said, "Dita, give us one more minute."

She was breathing hard. "That's all you've got. Everyone else is on their way back."

But she left us, back out into the night chill and grass to wait. I jerked my head back toward his room. "Does she know about . . . ?"

"You're the only one besides me who does. I told her you were in love with me."

"You what?"

"It was the most believable story I could come up with on short notice." The corner of his mouth lifted. "There's no time to be mad about it."

"There's a little time," I grumbled.

He picked up the deck of cards and pressed them into my hand. "Take these. See how your grandmother reacts to them."

"She's not guilty of anything," I said, automatically defensive. "I don't want to upset her."

"Jules . . . it's a good first step. Just see how she reacts."

I took them. "Fine. I'll give it a shot. How will we talk?"

"Thirty seconds. Hurry," Dita called from outside.

"I can text you. What's your number?" he asked.

"I don't have a phone." I was against them on the grounds that text speak was inelegant. Plus, I'd never needed one.

He lifted his eyebrows, but said, "The school trailer, then. I get there a little early for afternoon classes. Say you need to use the computer. And be careful."

"You too."

"I'm not the one being sabotaged." He lifted his hand, trailed his fingers along my arm. "Take care."

He was already dashing back to his room to conceal the board. I banged down the stairs and out into the night with a heavy sigh.

Dita raised her eyebrows. The sleeves of her shirt were rolled to her elbows, and she raised an arm in good-bye. "See you around, Jules."

"You will."

"Oh, and tell Sam hi."

She was inside before I could ask why she wanted me to do that.

I had believed Remy's answers would make things clearer, but they were only getting more complicated. Now I officially had suspects, plural. Not to mention a suspicion that something was happening between the two of us—and that I wanted it to.

twelve

I couldn't put off showing the tarot cards to Nan forever, but I'd decided to try another tactic first. One that took me an extra day to arrange, given our travel to the next stop in Raleigh and, once we arrived, my walk between two buildings that were a mere few stories tall. What that added up to was two nights of restless sleep after Remy's murder board revelations.

And when the morning of truth came, I wasn't sleeping, but waiting for Nan to wake up. As soon as I heard her stirring in the RV kitchen, I bounded out of bed.

I walked in to find Nan, with her red dressing gown wrapped around her, sitting at the table, her hand resting on a white coffee mug. She claimed her morning caffeine was the "threshold between being asleep and being me."

Schooling my face into its very best helpful, solicitous, adoring-relative expression, I eased down across from her, leaning my elbow on the table. I hadn't run my new approach by Remy, because he couldn't understand what she'd be like with the tarot deck back, and able to make grand pronouncements again. Pronouncements that might be enough to sway Mom or Dad into listening. No, I needed more intel first. And the more I thought about Thurston's letter to Roman Garcia, the more I was sure it had to come through the billionaire himself.

Nan could help, without realizing what she was doing. I batted my eyes at her.

She gave me a small smile. Wary, but real. "Yes, Jules? Don't you have your next stunt to rehearse?"

I wasn't doing a bridge or building walk in every city, and she knew it.

"You're finished with coffee?" I asked.

"With round two of coffee. This might be a three-round day."

"But . . . do you have any other plans today?" Before she could answer, I added, "We haven't been spending enough time together. I know you're mad at me, but I miss you."

It was true, and the attention pleased her. I knew it would. In this way, all Maronis are alike.

"We just watched Hildy and Walter the other night, and you've been busy. You're becoming a star. Just like you wanted. And you've managed to stay safe. So far."

She sounded approving, but there was still worry beneath it. I couldn't put the corkboard out of my mind. I'd had a nightmare about that ring girl, her mouth stuffed full of peacock feathers, smothering her . . . one of my worst dreams ever. The sheets had been soaked when I'd woken up in the middle of the night. I'd lain there trying to picture Roman Garcia, wondering whether he'd spent his life wishing for bad things to happen to us. Someone out there was picturing *me* and wishing for them now.

"Plus," I said, "you've been staying in way too much."

"Jules," Nan said, "what are you after?"

"I made us an appointment."

She drummed her fingers on the table. The perfect red nails on each tip were a relief. "For?"

"It's a surprise."

Her lips pursed. She picked up her cup of coffee, took one last swallow, and handed it to me. "You're not going to tell me, are you?"

"I learned from the best. But I think you'll enjoy this."

No reason for her not to, depending how our visit to Thurston went. He could be charming, no matter what he was up to, and maybe it would even have the side effect of making her see our presence at the Cirque in a better light. I'd get to watch him with Nan and look for any sign that he believed in the "old magic" he'd mentioned to Roman Garcia in the letter.

Nan sighed. "Get me round three and I will begin the necessary improvements to go out."

Nan's preparations took a good hour, but I'd factored that in. She'd already been beautiful sitting at the breakfast table without a speck of makeup on. There was something quietly incognito about her in the mornings, yet her star power was always intact. Seeing her was like spotting Katharine Hepburn dressed down and hiding behind sunglasses. For people like them, it was impossible to pretend not to be exceptional.

But I understood her need to wear armor. She emerged from the back in a calf-length silk dress with a swirling pattern of black and white stripes and black heels. Her lips were Monroe red, as usual.

"Now *I'm* the one who's underdressed." I adjusted the maroon bandeau I wore with jeans and a Chinese-style silk jacket I'd liberated from the cast-offs corner in the costumer's trailer. The dragon on the back was missing a wide swathe of gold detail, but it was still pretty.

"Youth never has to worry about being challenged by the beauty of age."

"You don't believe that," I scoffed. "Plus, it's not true."

"You're right," she said. It was her turn to bat mascaraed lashes.

My heart seized. This was my Nan. I hadn't realized how much I'd missed her, since we got here. She *hadn't* been herself.

"I don't mind being overshadowed once in a while. Not by you, at least," I said, and stepped aside so she could exit first.

The day was all blue sky and shining sun without too much heat. We ran into Sam outside on the grass, weaving toward the trailer to shower off after his morning routine of mucking the stalls and learning a few tricks of the trade. Mom had begun to teach him some Russian voice commands, after she caught him trying them solo.

"I don't know what this is about," he said, taking in Nan, "but I'm all for it. Carry on."

He mock-saluted and gave me a look that said, *Well done,* and went inside. He and I had talked over our concerns about Nan more than once in the past couple of weeks. I hadn't told him about Remy and me teaming up yet, but I would when the time was right—when we had enough info that I was sure it wouldn't result in Sam picking a fight with a Garcia.

"You're still not going to tell me where we're going?" she asked.

I looped my elbow through hers and started us across the grounds. "It's a surprise."

Heads turned as we passed, and the whispers reminded me there was a reason Nan had been holing up in the RV. I glared at everyone whose reaction was visible.

We stopped at Thurston's massive personal trailer, or, rather, at the semi-massive trailer *behind* that, which housed his mobile office. The crew jokingly called it Air Force One. Someone had hung a sequin-studded American flag inside one of the long windows, above the Cirque's painted logo on the outside.

"Here we are," I said. "I made an appointment with one of your biggest fans." Before the prospect of us working with the Garcias at the Cirque had come up, Nan had tended to enjoy reminiscing about her glory days. And Thurston had mentioned to me that he would love to get her autograph on his posters of her, when she had time.

"I have a bad feeling about this," she said.

"Too late to back out." I knocked.

Thurston's office door popped open immediately. He beamed at us. "Come in, come in."

The steps up into the behemoth were wide enough for us both to walk aboard. But when I moved forward, Nan stayed put. She had a hand at her throat.

"Jules . . ."

Nan never started sentences without finishing them. Not for anything other than effect. She was as spooked as one of Mom's horses during a thunderstorm.

"Nan, don't be shy." I reached out and laid a hand on her arm. "Thurston has a collection of old posters, including some of yours. You love this sort of thing. When you were the world's favorite Maroni."

Thurston had picked up on the tension. "I wouldn't want to impose. Jules didn't think you'd mind, and I am an eager fan . . ."

His pause let me know that he was not happy this was a surprise to her. I didn't care. He'd sent that letter about us to Roman Garcia. I wanted to know why.

Nan relented. "I suppose I'm protesting too much," she said. "I never used to overdo it. Nothing worse than false modesty in a performer."

Thurston laughed. He reached past me and took Nan's hand. I released my hold on her, and he guided her up the broad stairs.

"I was going to offer you coffee," he said, "but that dress merits champagne."

"A man after my own heart," she said.

There was nothing Nan liked better than an excuse to have champagne during the day. Not that she was a heavy drinker; she wasn't much of a drinker at all. But she'd explained to me years ago that champagne was an exception. Drinking it is simply telling life that its finer moments are appreciated.

"I'll have some too," I said. We hadn't had much call for celebration in the past few years.

"You have a show in three hours," Nan said.

"And the owner tries not to directly break laws. Unless it's to put you a few hundred feet above a city," Thurston said.

I shut the door behind me. "Woe."

The office had a comfortable seating area in what would have been the living room, with a buttery leather couch and chairs and a polished coffee table in between. A big desk covered in papers took up the rest of the cabin. It was outfitted with state-of-the-art computers and phones and gadgets, and there was a kitchen with a fridge and a coffeemaker beyond it.

Thurston waved Nan onto the couch, and I noticed a heavy leather valise on the table. He made his way to the fridge and selected a bottle of champagne. I sank into a chair as the cork sighed open. He filled a glass for Nan, and carried the bottle over with him to hand the glass to her.

Nan took the flute, and a sip. Her eyebrows lifted. "This is a nice vintage."

Thurston waved, embarrassed. "I'm honored to have you here. The amazing Nancy Maroni. You are a legend—not least because you retired well before you had to."

Nan downed more of her drink instead of answering. The bubbles rioted in the glass. I frowned. Thurston knew at least a little about why she'd left.

"Nan has many gifts. For my whole childhood, people lined up before our shows to have her read their tarot. Very popular."

"To tell the future is definitely a gift. To be able to influence success or failure," Thurston said. "The businessman in me is jealous."

Nan took another drink.

"I don't think I ever heard what made you decide to start your own circus," I said.

"Me either," Nan murmured.

He shrugged. "I've always been a circophile, and when you've made as much money as I have, you can afford to indulge a few dreams. I wanted one of my own, and I want to make it the best in history."

"A modest goal," Nan said, dryly.

Thurston leaned forward and picked up the portfolio. "It's why I started collecting the old posters and other memorabilia in earnest when the idea first occurred to me. What better way to learn my competition? We're up against the golden age and its epic performers." He looked at Nan. "Like Nancy Maroni and all the other greats of the past. Do you want to see?"

"Of course we do," I said.

I stayed on high alert, listening closely to see if anything might implicate him in a vendetta against my family. But so far all he'd admitted to was an obsession with circus history. That wasn't enough to prove anything.

Thurston unzipped the case to reveal posters in plastic slipcases. It was quite a collection. He flipped past the first several posters, some of them faded with age and probably rarer than any baseball card.

The poster he stopped at was one I'd seen before—a painting of several flyers and, in big letters at the bottom, the act name, The Soaring Sloans, and the circus's name beneath, The Chapman Brothers Circus & Menagerie. A blur of audience was dabbed into the background, and two trapeze artists with yellow and red feathered costumes passed each other in midair, having just released from their trapeze swings. The artist's style wasn't anything special, but it was nice enough.

Nan's face softened and her fingers went to the poster's edges, a light touch. "That's me. My first big job. Well, it wasn't that big, but it seemed like Broadway and Ringling and Hollywood all rolled up into one at the time. I was only sixteen. Do you want me to sign it?"

The young version of herself she'd tapped was a bottle blonde and feathered sketch on the platform. She hadn't been well-known enough to be anything more than roughed in, but it was the first time she'd been included on a sell sheet. Nan was in her seventies now, and these were from more than fifty years ago. An eternity.

"You'd have to put down your champagne," he said. "Let's say you can sign them next visit, okay?"

Nan tilted her glass. "Happily."

I didn't want them to get too chummy. I still had my suspicions that Thurston might be the one so determined to keep rumors of Nan's magic circulating—maybe even the one behind trying to upset her with the returning objects.

Thurston turned a few more pages. "What was it like back then?"

Another sip. "Not like now. People knew us. We were the last of your golden age. My mother and great-grandmother, they were the best of it, but we were the last. The audience was starting to get distracted—cars, TV, the war du jour, all of it." She waved a hand. "But they still paid attention for a while."

"Was it a close community? Sometimes I wonder if I'm doing things right here. Everyone seems to stick to their own. I apologize for the snubs your family has received."

Nan grew serious. "Performers compete. Families do too. That's the way of things. But it's closer-knit than you think. People get bound up with each other, when they spend so many years bouncing around the same circuits. You may not see it every day, but the ties are there. That's part of why they treat us the way they do. We went our own way a long time ago. We don't belong anymore."

"Ah," he said, "I have to disagree. The Maronis are my stars. You do belong." He flicked to another page. "I bet you remember this one."

Even I nodded. A print of it hung in our hallway back home. Nan had gotten bigger billing, just two years later. Her face was the focal point of the poster, and radiated a swoon-inducing beauty.

"Yes. My mother knew these half-crazy flyers from Bohemia. She used to read the cards for them. She signed me with them, the year before she died, when one of their girls broke her leg in a missed catch. I was watching them rehearse—I'd been doing a solo swing act—and I remember the bone sticking out of her shin. This guy"—she pointed to a barrel-chested catcher—"was quite a charmer. Or thought he was. The chemistry between us gave a little extra to the performance, so I suppose I owe him."

"You must have been quite the heartbreaker."

"Careful," I said, "you'll make it sound like she isn't anymore."

Thurston inclined his head. "You've got a smart girl here."

"Don't I know it," she said, her tone considering.

Thurston kept going. They chatted pleasantly through three more posters from giant Ringling Brothers and Barnum & Bailey tours, which had featured Nan in various famous flying acts. Those were the shows where she'd really made her name, in the early 1960s. I stole a glance at Nan. She was finally relaxing, and had polished off her second flute of champagne. Thurston hadn't given away anything else.

"This was a pleasure," Nan said, and I understood she was making her good-byes.

"Oh," Thurston said, "the pleasure is mine entirely. But we're not quite done. I have one more to show you, the rarest in my collection."

He turned to the final page in the valise.

I stood. There, on the most dazzlingly beautiful poster I'd ever seen, was Nan in a silver-sequined white costume draped in folds, like a goddess, only with bared legs. She was sitting on the trapeze in the center, and on swings around her were men outfitted in Roman soldier–style garb, with short Caesar-style haircuts. Men with somehow familiar faces. One of them, with a fake breastplate sewn onto his costume, towered above Nan, standing on the trapeze above her. They were all smiling. The script proclaimed them *The Roman Warriors and Their Goddess*, and after studying the poster for a few more seconds, I finally understood what I was seeing: Nancy Maroni starring with none other than the Flying Garcias.

My gasp was audible.

"I bet that brings back old memories," Thurston said, perhaps to help cover the shock reverberating from me. Or was he motivated by something else? Was he trying to goad Nan into speaking out against the Garcias? Explaining what the old feud was about? Or did he want to discover the truth behind the rumors of magic that swirled around our family?

"Too many," Nan agreed, with an undercurrent of anger.

I couldn't stop myself from leaning forward, holding the page up to get a closer look at the poster. Which let me see the contents of the plastic slipcase behind it: a flimsy white envelope addressed to Thurston. I barely got a glimpse of the return address before Thurston reached in front of me to pick up the valise and close it.

The letter was from Roman Garcia. Thurston had kept his return correspondence.

"My apologies if seeing that poster made you uncomfortable, Nancy," he said. "Truly, that's the last thing I intended."

Nan nodded, but didn't speak.

"The things ancient history has to teach us," I said. I lifted the empty champagne glass from her hand and set it on the table. "We'd better be going."

I held Nan's shaking arm as we descended the stairs to the outside. I had found only more questions. I couldn't point the finger at Thurston for planting the magic objects at this point. But I wasn't entirely convinced he was innocent either—not without knowing what was in that letter.

All I knew for sure was that my plan to keep from upsetting Nan too much had accomplished the exact opposite.

thirteen

After our early show the next day, I plopped Sam's laptop on the kitchen table and started making loud noises in my mother's general direction about how our wireless network was down, some trouble with the satellite provider, "I hate this stupid thing," and so on. The usual noises I made when I couldn't get Sam's computer to work.

Mom and I were alone. Dad had already left for a walk, and Sam was out helping give the horses their rubdown. Nan was home, but in bed, claiming a migraine. Our visit with Thurston really had upset her. I'd found out enough that I needed to talk to Remy about next steps, but I still felt guilty.

"What's your trouble with that thing?" Mom asked. She didn't like computers.

"Someone told me there's a video of me online. I want to watch it."

"A video doing what?"

"Walking." I mimicked holding the balance pole. My fingers twisted as I snapped them. "I know. I can use the schoolroom's."

She frowned, but only for a second. "They probably won't mind. You can get Sammy to fix that later."

I was already on my way out the door. "Back in a few."

I knew exactly where the schoolroom RV was parked, despite the fact I hadn't been inside of it yet. Before we'd even arrived, my parents had decreed that Sam and I would stay separate from the other under-eighteens, clocking our time with Nan to get enough school hours for work permits. That was fine with me. I had no need to spend hours with the teacher Thurston hired, a perky PhD student from the Ivy League. I guessed she'd taken the gig for résumé color or as research for some long-winded essay about how wacky circus culture was. Nan was a great teacher, and I liked getting the extra time with her anyway.

The small trailer was more battered than most of our fleet, but a fresh coat of red paint made it less of a scrap heap reject. I was jumpy approaching the door. Not because of seeing Remy, I told myself, but because of what I had to tell him.

The schoolroom was cramped inside. Old desks crowded around the edges, and I spotted only two computers. In contrast to everything else, they appeared to be state-of-the-art, with huge flat-screen monitors. Thurston's doing, no doubt.

I almost smiled with relief when I saw Remy at a desk, scratching away with a pencil at a notebook, a book open flat in front of him. But I stiffened when I realized that he wasn't the only other person in the room. Novio was occupying one of the computer stations.

Clearing my throat, I stepped forward. This was my best opportunity to talk to Remy, and I didn't want to miss it. But what would Novio think? Remy had told Dita I was interested in him, but that didn't mean Novio had been given the same story.

Novio said, "What are *you* doing here?"

His tone made it clear he'd be happier if it turned out he was hallucinating. Great. No cover story.

Remy said, casually, "Yeah, to what do we owe the honor? You need to borrow a dictionary or something?"

Novio laughed as if this was funny.

I studied my surroundings, like I was ignoring them both. *C'mon, Remy, help me out here.* The wood-paneled walls were dotted with "art" done by children. Near me was a messy, many-hued drawing of a cigar-smoking clown, colored way outside its lines.

"Where's your teacher?" I asked.

"She ran over to the mess to grab coffee before the others get here," Remy said. "Caffeine addict. You need something?"

Novio tossed his brother a frown. "Why don't you just roll out the red carpet for her?"

Remy shrugged. "What does it matter?"

Novio stood. "I think I need some coffee too."

"Suit yourself," Remy said.

I braced like Novio was going to punch me as he went past, but couldn't resist a quip. "Don't bother to bring me a cup. I'm not staying long."

"I wasn't going to," he said, "and good."

With that, Novio left. But he didn't shut the door behind him.

"Hurry," Remy said, getting up. "He could change his mind and come back."

Remy sat down at the computer station next to the one his brother had just been working on. "Come on," he said.

"Why?"

"In case they come back. I'm helping you, remember?"

"Right." I pulled over a chair so I was next to him.

Remy punched a button and the screen flared to life.

"I don't really need to see anything."

"Appearances," he said. "Other people will be here soon. What did you say you were coming here to do?"

"Look up a video of myself. But I just made that up."

He launched the browser and started clicking around. I took advantage of the opportunity to look at him without having to meet his eyes. He was clean-shaven today, his hair still damp from a shower. It was yet another of the unfair things about life that he was this appealing.

His head shifted toward me, brown eyes seeing far too much. *Busted.* I waited for him to tease me. Instead he leaned in, and I did the same, before I even understood why. Our lips met, tentative at first, then less so. Far less so. Remy caught my upper lip softly with his teeth and my mind blanked.

Then he pulled back, and our eyes skated away from each other.

"What'd you find out?" he asked, his voice a little shaky.

That you're too attractive for your own good. That I just had my first kiss. "What?"

"You wouldn't have come here unless you had a reason. Though . . . I'm glad you did. But did you show her the cards?"

Oh, right. The reason I was here. I straightened, and laid my trembling hands on my knees to steady them. "Not exactly. Has anyone ever mentioned an act your grandfather did where he dressed like a gladiator?"

Two small furrows appeared on his brow. "Yeah. It was actually part of the inspiration for our act now. He had the idea because of his own name—*Roman*, get it? At some point later, he suggested to Mom that she give her kids names along the same lines, so they'd end up with a ready-made act."

"Wow," I said. "So Romeo *is* your real name. That's . . . wow."

"Why are you asking me about this?"

"I took Nan to see Thurston's poster collection. There's one of her as part of that act."

"No way." Remy shook his head. "A Maroni in a Garcia act? And we never heard about it?"

"I know, right? Might be worth asking your mom. See what you can find out."

He frowned at me again. "You didn't find out the deal from your nana?"

"Nan," I said. "Never nana." I bit my lip. "She flipped out a little when she saw it. Went quiet. But I discovered something else. Remember that letter from Thurston on the murder board? Well, I'm almost positive he still has your grandfather's response to him. I saw a letter when he was showing us his poster collection. It's in the leather portfolio, right behind that poster that shows Nan and your grandfather together."

He blinked. "You risked bringing it up with him? On your own?"

"I didn't take any risks or say anything outright," I said. "I just happened to see it. And Nan was with me the whole time. I wanted to feel him out. I definitely think he knows more than he's saying."

"We need to read that letter," Remy said.

"But how? We're going to break into the owner's office? Because that's definitely something that won't get us kicked off the show."

Remy sighed. "Have a little faith. We'll figure out a way. Now, what did your . . . Nan say about the cards?"

"I haven't exactly shown them to her yet."

"Jules, you have to."

I knew that, but, "You can't tell me what to do."

He gave me a wry grin. "I know that. We're too much alike. I saw that about you when we met. It was a useful thing to notice. Or it was until now. You love doing what you shouldn't."

"I do not." Though I remembered, with slight mortification, how I'd stepped between Sam and Novio during their fight. And how much I'd enjoyed the kiss we'd just shared, even though a romance with Remy Garcia was probably the worst idea in the world.

Wasn't it?

He was visibly biting the inside of his lip to keep from laughing, and it made me want to kiss him again. I was doomed.

But his smile vanished. "We don't know when something else might happen. There've only been two objects, and there were more photos on the board than that. You have to talk to her."

"I'm not sure how she'll react to having the cards back." *Or if it will incriminate someone in your family besides your grandfather.*

"Well, show them to her soon. Or Jules? I will. There is danger in waiting. We need to figure out who's behind this before someone gets hurt. Before you do."

Before I could growl at him that *he* was not to talk to Nan about this, no way, no day, he started clacking away at the keys and examining the monitor. Noise blared from the computer speakers all of a sudden, the tinny sound of wind blowing.

On the screen, there was a blurry video of a girl in red walking across a wire. It was from my bridge walk.

A cough sounded behind us. "Ego Googling?" The teacher stood inside the door, coffee cup in hand. She rolled her eyes behind heavy-framed glasses, but her smile was friendly. "You're the one whose grandmother teaches you. Did you want to sit in today?"

"No, I'm good. I have everything I need." If only that was true.

"Okay, then, it's almost time for our class," she said.

Remy stayed focused on the screen, where the shaky camera made it appear that I was wobbling across the wire. He reached forward, flicked the monitor off. The image of me disappeared, fading to black.

"See you around," Remy said.

I'd been dismissed. It shouldn't have stung. He had no choice, with the teacher watching and Novio due back any second. "Sure. I've got important things to do."

The teacher smiled again, like she almost believed me.

But Remy was right. I needed to give Nan her cards while we decided how to get the letter from Thurston. I might have growing doubts about what was causing the mayhem around me, but I still couldn't swallow claims of magic.

I also couldn't forget that our families were enemies, even if Remy and I were becoming something else. The two of us couldn't keep meeting like this, not without solving the puzzle first. No good would come of it.

fourteen

Sam and I walked back from dinner together, an hour and a half before that night's show. He was rattling away, beyond excited, about how Mom had promised to let him give a command in the middle of the act soon. The schedule was tough now that we were in the thick of it, hitting a new town every three to five days. June was already here. Our shows weren't all sellouts, but some were, and the rest drew more than decent crowds.

"You better shine your cowboy boots," I said. "It's all about the glam under the spotlights."

He shook his head, sand-colored bangs so long they brushed his eyebrows. "It's different for me. The horses are the stars. And your mom."

"So modest. Why, I'd think you wanted to stay hidden on the sidelines forever."

"No," he said, oddly serious for once, "I'm proud to be part of the family tradition. Like you. I'm paying my dues. I can't believe I get to be a part of this, or that I might get to share the ring with your mother."

I smiled at him. Throughout our arrival and frosty reception, and discussions about magic and stunts, Sam had been a grounding presence. He'd been like a brother before we came, but he was even more like one now. I couldn't imagine not having him to talk to.

Which is why I felt guilty I hadn't told him everything yet.

"Shine those boots, I'm telling you. We Maronis have a reputation to uphold."

Sam laughed. "I am *not* putting sequins on my boots."

I shrugged. "Fine. Smudge the family name."

"Like we could, either of us," he said.

A clown already in full makeup tipped the ashes from his cigar as we passed. Not many clowns were smokers at the Cirque, so the drawing I'd seen in the school trailer must have been modeled on this guy. "Evening, Sam," he said. He blew a smoke ring overhead.

Sam nodded at him.

"Look who's making friends and influencing clowns," I said, once we'd left him behind. From Nan's old stories, I could barely think the word *clown* without also thinking, *Debauchery.*

Sam said, "They practice their gags behind the stables. They've all been nicer lately." He paused. "Jules, you've been hanging out with Remy some, haven't you?"

I kissed him. I nearly blurted it out, but pulled myself together. "You're not spying on me for Dad, are you?"

He snorted. "Like I would. No." He stopped and pushed his hair out of his eyes again. "Can you keep quiet?"

I mimed locking my mouth and throwing away the key, intrigued.

"Dita told me. She likes the horses. I've been teaching her how to ride a bit. Only when no one's around," he said. "Nan won't find out."

"Sam," I said, "who'd have guessed we'd both be hooking up with Garcias?"

"We're not hooking up," he said, in a way that was not convincing. "Yet. Are you?"

"No," I said, not sure if it was true or a lie. "We're just both interested in what happened between our families back then."

Sam nodded. "The Garcias, our ancient enemies. Nan hasn't mentioned them lately. Maybe she's mellowing."

I couldn't help thinking back to the way she'd spoken of bad blood before we came here. She'd been avoiding me ever since we visited Thurston. Her migraine resurfaced every time I was home.

"Maybe," I said.

"I know, probably wishful thinking on my part," Sam said. "I told Dita we should be careful, at least for now. But do you think Nan really might mellow out some? If she did, then we could tell her. If and when there's something to tell."

"We'll see." I didn't want to discourage him from hoping for the best, no matter how unlikely it was.

Sam opened the door to the RV, and held it for me. The first thing I saw inside was Nan, reclining on the couch.

Remy had been serious when he'd threatened to tell Nan about the tarot cards if I didn't. And seeing him turn up at our front door would make Dad's head explode. The possibility was a clock *tick-tick-tick*ing in my ears.

It was time to present the cards to Nan and see what she had to say. After tonight's performance, I'd be able to catch her alone. With this plan in mind, I changed into my costume, pulled my hair back, and put in some small black pearl combs that had once been hers. I tried to channel calm as I layered on mascara.

My nerves didn't have anything to do with the wire. They were about the confrontation that was yet to come.

I pulled on the cast-off Chinese silk jacket over my blood-red tutu as I left backstage and made my way across the grounds. A fat pumpkin moon hung over the horizon, pale orange and low. A hint of wind worried the loose tendrils of hair around my face. The forecasters had claimed clouds would move in soon, buckets of rain with them.

We were to roll out later that night to Norfolk, as soon as we could get the show torn down and packed up. The local meteorologists were fortune-tellers when it came to our travels. A circus never wants to wait on a turn in the weather, not if it can be helped. It's bad luck.

The living room light in our RV was on, the window bright. Mom was going on now, and she and Sam would be busy for a while after. Dad had taken to watching my act and then Mom's from the side curtain, and returning to our makeup table to wait for his finale spot to roll around.

Once inside, I saw Nan had the TV on mute. A black-and-white Western I didn't recognize was playing, while Nan flipped through the new *People* that Dad had picked up for her in town. Her eyebrows lifted. "I wasn't expecting you back so early."

She wore her red silk dressing gown over a pair of pajamas. Minimal makeup, but enough to be what she would call "presentable." She had a scarf patterned with black and gray roses tied around her head, tail hanging over her shoulder.

"Headache better?" I asked.

"Some."

"Any afterlife messages from Elizabeth Taylor reported?"

Nan let the magazine close, her hand holding her spot. "Not in this one. This is reputable journalism."

"Right. My mistake."

I went back to my room, debating whether to go through with this. I'd risked catching Remy's eye backstage. His look had been a question, and the question was, *Well, have you told her?* What is it they say about pride? Lots of things. Fear too.

In my room, I noticed Bird commanding the city from her framed photograph, which reminded me to be brave. This was Nan. This was a conversation with Nan. I'd had a million of them. I smoothed my hair back and wedged my hand under the mattress. The edge of my finger brushed Remy's note as my hand closed around the deck.

I took a breath, and left my room.

Nan looked at me over the magazine, and I held the stack of cards high. "Look what I found," I said, as casually as I could manage. "How about a reading?"

For a long moment, she stayed fixed where she was like a statue of herself. *The Lady on the Couch*, the piece might have been called. Then she folded the magazine shut and tossed it onto the floor. It slid, stopping at an angle that turned some actress's face into a sleek funhouse curve.

She rose to her feet, pulled her dressing gown straight. "Did you steal those?"

I was supposed to be asking the questions.

"Did you steal them? *Answer me.*"

Lying had no point. Not when the idea that I'd taken them disturbed her this much.

"I didn't steal them. I . . . found them at the Garcias'. Were they taken the night of the break-in?"

I watched her face change as she puzzled through what I was saying.

"No," she said, after a pause. "They weren't taken. They were given. They were a peace offering."

I didn't know what I'd expected, but that wasn't it. "These were handed down to you from your mother. Why would you give them away as a peace offering? Does it have anything to do with you and Roman Garcia being in an act together? Did he accuse you of doing something to him too? Before he turned against you and started the rumor mill?"

She didn't respond right away. Finally, her voice strung tight as a wire, she said, "I won't talk about him with you. You know all you need to. The Garcias hate us. They always will. Don't kid yourself that family won't come first in the end. Blood is always thicker than water. But if a reading is what you want, who am I to refuse you?"

Before I could react, she grabbed my upper arm, her fingernails biting into the muscle through my jacket. She yanked me through the living room to the kitchen table, levered me down into one of the chairs. "Sit."

I'd lost control of this, and I wasn't sure how to get it back. "Nan, I—"

"Stay here." She hurried back toward her bunk, the robe flaring behind her.

I laid the deck on the table, no longer wanting to be the one with the cards. Wishing I'd left them in that drawer in the Garcias' kitchen, refused to take them from Remy.

Nan returned with a candle and positioned it at the table edge. It was fat and white. Odds were it was the same one I'd seen her with that night, burning the elephant hair. The lighter sparked to life and she lit the wick. Smoke streamed toward the ceiling. She stepped around me and flipped the overhead light off. The TV was still running. The flicker of the black-and-white movie combined with that of the candle made me feel dizzy.

Nan pulled out the chair opposite me and lowered herself into it.

I asked, "Why are you so angry at me?"

"No," she cut me off. "No, there is only one thing that can happen now. You want a reading, and you will have one."

This wasn't how I'd meant for the conversation to go. There was something almost possessed about her face. Some harsh force motivating her. But her readings had never caused me any harm. There was even a chance that doing one would remind her of how close we'd always been.

"Fine." I nodded, and her eyes narrowed. Candlelight writhed across her cheek and the scarf above it. She picked up the deck.

"Why did you need to make a peace offering to the Garcias after what Roman told people about you?" I asked.

She didn't answer. The painted faces on the cards shifted in the dim light as she shuffled, thumbing the edges as she sorted. She set more than half the deck aside, and I could guess from experience that she had kept only the Major Arcana in her hand. They're the cards most people picture when they hear the word *tarot.* She always consulted them on serious matters. I'd never been sure if she did it that way because people wanted to see cards that seemed the most important and powerful, instead of the more anonymous ones, or because she thought they gave a more accurate picture.

She shook her head at me. "No," she said, "your questions are going to be answered by the cards. You don't know what you're playing with. It's time you understood the danger you're in."

"I want to understand, so I can stop it. That's all I want."

"No," she said, like that was the only word she had for me. "No, you only think you do."

She stroked the cards, fanning them out and then bringing them back into a tidy stack. "Time to glimpse your fate. It's the only way we can see what's ahead. Three cards. Draw them."

No, I echoed her in my head. *No.* "A Three Fates reading? But you always said that the Fates are too powerful to mess with."

I'd never believed tarot readings amounted to anything more than superstition from the old country, handed down like the cards had been. These cards had been custom painted by Nan's mother to feature circus-themed figures and scenes, and she'd added her own twists to the usual fortune-teller bag of forecasting tricks too—or so Nan claimed. I wasn't sure if the Three Fates reading was one of them or not, but Nan had always been consistent in telling me how potentially dangerous it could be.

She nodded toward the cards again. "You want the attention of the mother, maiden, and crone, don't you? You want the universe focused on you? You said you wanted answers. Now you'll have them."

Nan did many different spreads of the tarot, from incredibly complicated arrays to the more common Celtic Cross, but I'd never seen her do this one. When people at our shows asked for it specifically, she always refused. According to Nan, you couldn't argue with a Three Fates reading. The future it predicted could not be changed.

She shoved the deck closer. "Three cards, from anywhere in the stack."

So much had happened since we'd come here. I still didn't believe Nan could do magic or tell the future. But I was no longer so sure what might be possible.

Uneasy, I removed the top card, laid it down. The hand-painted swirls on the back seemed to crawl in the candlelight, a black and red and white nest of snakes and shadows, shifting end over endless end.

"And again," she prompted.

I selected the next card from the middle. When I went to lay it down, she tapped to the right of the first card. "Here."

"I know."

The third card I barely touched, holding it with my fingertips the few seconds it took to drop it at the end of the line. I blinked, trying to blot away the blur, the snakes, the twist, the heat from the candle. My cheeks were hot. The painted backs of the cards kept shifting, swirls moving, despite my blinks. This didn't *feel* like any reading I'd ever had before.

Nan studied the backs of the cards like they were already speaking to her. Then, she reached out and touched the back of each, briefly.

She turned the first card over. Then she grunted, but said nothing more.

I bent forward, the heat from the candle warming my face as if it were a much larger fire. The first card I'd chosen was the Magician. A sexless figure, possibly a man, possibly a woman, dressed in robes covered by stars and suns. A red moon hung in the background, over a black sky. Though outside, the magician was on a stage. In one hand was a snake, in the other a wand.

"That's you," she said. One red-tipped nail touched the table just above the card. "The Magician, the performer, the traveler, the trickster."

"That's not so bad," I offered.

"I'm surprised it wasn't the Fool or the Hanged Man." She sighed. "The fact that you are represented so clearly means this is your story, Jules. Whatever the next cards represent is going to happen to you. You started it when you tricked us into coming here."

"But that's not so bad?" I tried again.

"Maybe if there weren't two more cards still to go."

She tapped her nail at the top of the third card, skipping over the middle.

"Why are you—"

"Let me speak," she said. "The cards do not tell a linear story."

She flipped the card, and I saw it was Blindfolded Justice, perched atop an elephant, a grand set of scales painted on its side. Her sword was extended down, the point tipped toward a nude weeping man covered in heavy tattoos. The audience at the edges of the scene was mixed, some smiling and some sobbing.

"The Fates are weaving a different picture, one of converging points. You on the one side, and on the other, Justice," she said.

"I haven't done anything wrong," I said.

I was only trying to stop the sabotage, and find out who was hanging on to old grudges.

"The weight of the past is behind you always, Jules. You don't recognize it because it has always been there. You were born with it when you were born a Maroni. It doesn't matter what *you* have done, right or wrong. The sins of your family over all time are balanced against you now. It's a balance that can't hold. We should not have come here."

She turned the middle card. The Tower.

I shivered, despite the heat from the candle. The wick flared, as if the flame were participating in the reading too.

As if the fabled Fates—the mother, maiden, and crone Nan had mentioned—sat at a fire, getting warm off my future.

On the card, tongues of flame licked at the sides of a large striped circus tent. But people were fleeing the exit flaps, running into the fire. At the top of the tent was a crown shaped by fluttering rags of canvas.

"The Tower is a shattering of illusion. A sudden shift that will change everything. I only hope this change comes soon enough to prevent you from doing any further harm. Or, worse, you coming to harm. Once your eyes are open, you will see."

I continued staring at the card, mesmerized as I realized that the rag crown was angling down, plummeting to where it would burn and be destroyed.

I bit my lip. I couldn't believe she hadn't seen the other obvious interpretation. Me. The Princess of the Air. The cards were saying I was going to fall. Justice was going to make me fall.

"And Jules? Try to be careful with that boy."

I didn't bother asking who she meant. I should have noticed that she'd said *try*, like she already knew I'd fail. Like she already knew I was falling for him.

It was a good thing I didn't believe in the cards.

fifteen

When I emerged from a deep sleep the next morning, what was visible of the Virginia fairground out my tiny bedroom window was blanketed in thick fog. The gloomy view perfectly suited what I was thinking about: my tarot reading from the night before. I sat up slowly, trying to snap out of it.

One thing you learned early in the circus was that hesitation could be just as dangerous as acting rashly. You must keep moving or the audience has nothing to follow. With motion comes purpose. With motion comes discovery.

No one had ever accused me of holding back, and I wasn't about to start. I chose to keep going. There were still answers to be had. I wanted them.

Within minutes, I was dressed and in the kitchen. I expected a question, since I was rarely up and moving at this time of day, and I got it.

"Where are *you* going?" Dad asked.

He and Mom were both at the breakfast table. Sam was already gone to handle the morning feed. Nan wasn't even up yet, but that wasn't unusual. I was relieved not to see her at the table.

My plan was to tell Remy that we had to leave Nan out of this from now on. She'd spooked me, and she'd do the same for my parents given half a chance.

"I asked Thurston if I could clock some wire time this morning."

When Dad frowned, I added, "To fine-tune that arabesque I'm adding."

"Do you want me to go with you?" he asked.

He was two seconds from standing up.

"Nah," I said, "I'm sure it won't take long. I don't want to mess up your morning routine."

I hated having to lie to my parents, but I didn't have another option.

"She'll be fine, Emil." Mom put her hand on his. "She's growing up. Leaving us behind."

Dad's scowl said what he thought about that, but his only comment was, "Don't lift your leg until the other foot is completely stable."

I covered my relief that he hadn't insisted on coming along. "Ahem, did you think there was an amateur here or were you talking to me?"

Mom patted his hand again when he started to protest. "She's teasing you."

"She's right," I said, and left before he decided to punish me by tagging along.

The Garcias had an obscenely early rehearsal every day, I knew, so that they could add another later if they missed their marks. Their mother had a reputation as a tough trainer.

Postrehearsal was my best shot to pull Remy aside early in the day. And I was curious whether his mother was as hard on them as I'd overheard people saying she was. After all, Nan had felt moved to give her a peace offering, even if she wouldn't say why. It made me wonder.

The tent was completely different this early than during shows. I pulled the flap aside and stepped into the quiet, dark backstage area. The only noise was muffled, coming from inside the main tent.

In it, a few spotlights were trained on the rigging where the Garcias were practicing their trapeze act, while other lights shone down on the center ring. To one side, Kat and her dogs were practicing their act, facing the main stands. Two of the larger mutts sported costumes that made them resemble elephants, and two smaller dogs dressed as tigers were riding the backs of their compatriots. Kat waved her arm and encouraged them to trot in a circle. I stepped closer to watch.

"All you need is to add a monkey," I said, taking a chance at making conversation. She hadn't been incredibly pleasant to me, but she had said hello once, which was the closest thing I'd gotten to a warm welcome.

She turned. "Monkeys aren't naturally obedient creatures like mine."

Reaching down, she scratched the ear of a scruffy brown dog brushing against her knee, and her gaze drifted over and up, to the Garcias. "What brings you here so early? They won't be happy about your presence."

"Thanks for the reminder. I wanted to try out something new after they finish."

"Best stay out of the way until they're done." She clapped, and called, "Form up!" The dogs raced around in a twist, weaving by one another until they were in a perfect half-moon around her. They sat on their haunches, tails visible and wagging despite the costumes.

I took her advice and went toward the stands, and then slipped into the shadows underneath the bleachers. No need to have an awkward confrontation, at least not with *all* the Garcias. I could wait.

I generally avoided the tent outside showtime, except for the occasional practice round—a side effect of being one of those late-arriving, much-gossiped-about Maronis. Even though most people were no longer actively rude to my face, possibly due to Sam's unexpected ability to charm clowns and Garcia girls, we remained apart. I wasn't going to start hanging out in the common areas joking around anytime soon.

Which was a shame. The big top floor, the grounds—even backstage—looked wildly different depending on the time of day and what was going on. There were so many ways to see the circus. From under the stands was a new one for me.

I stopped when I was at a good vantage to see the net. Remy's mother was watching the troupe perform with narrowed eyes and a pinched face. She shouted up to them, "Sloppy! Novio, the grab must be crisp, but look soft—she's supposed to be a goddess, not a beach ball! Your grandfather would turn over in his grave if he saw you do a catch like that."

I couldn't help but half smile. Roman was still guilting people from the afterlife. Remy had made him sound like pretty much the worst as trainers went, but his mom was clearly no picnic either.

Peering up through the slats at the trapeze, I watched the goddess in question, Dita, swing back to her platform, release her grip, and jump onto it. She raked a hand through her short hair, and then a body stepped in front of her, blocking her.

"Mom, it was my fault—my speed was off," Dita called down.

It was Remy, stance more tense than usual. He touched Dita's arm, supportive.

"Yes, I know it was," her mother called up. "But that doesn't mean Novio gets to practice bad form. Do it again."

Remy called down, "I thought we were done."

"Do it once more. We're never getting the finale if you don't get this act perfect."

The finale decision's already been made, lady, I wanted to say.

"But fine," their mother called. "Just do your foolish attempt, Remy, and we're done for now. This morning isn't going to get any better."

"I can do it later," Remy said.

"No, you wanted this in the act so badly you didn't bother to consult anyone else, so you can do it now. And we will watch your failure, like we do every morning."

Yikes. But Remy must have been used to it, because his face stayed exactly the same, as if she hadn't spoken. My dad respected that my performance was mine. Mine to make final decisions on, mine to shape.

Novio had settled on the swing opposite for a break during the back-and-forth, and now he swung out, knees over the bar. Remy squared his shoulders and took his own bar, began to swing, building up speed. Not enough speed, though. This wasn't one of his better attempts—how could it be after his mom's lead-in? In fact, it was the weakest I'd ever seen him do. He only completed two revolutions, and missed Novio's grab by a mile, then spun into the net. If it was possible to land sarcastically, he did.

He stood, shaking his head, and glanced over. His eyes were gleaming, and he stilled for a moment midmotion. Had he seen me? I assumed I was well hidden in the shadows. He turned his back with no indication that he had or hadn't caught me there, and said, "Happy now?" to his mom.

"No, I'm not happy. The act was perfect before you started this with the quad. You need to keep doing your extra practice at night, so you can finally make it one of these days during a show. The Garcias won't be known for failures."

"Of course we won't," he said. "The sky would fall first."

The others were vaulting into the net behind him now, the twins draping arms over each other's shoulders and heading out. "See you at the mess," one of them called.

Dita stopped to talk to her mom, and they walked out together with their heads close, Novio trailing them. No one seemed to notice that Remy lingered, unwinding the tape around his wrists. After they disappeared through the tent flaps, he turned back toward the stands.

There was no doubt he'd seen me now. He cast a glance at Kat, who wasn't paying any attention, then headed for the edge of the bleachers.

I hadn't really thought this part through. I figured I'd leave the safety of the darkness and call to him, that we'd talk at the edge of one row, in the light. But Kat's presence complicated that, and here he was, coming toward me in his snug black practice clothes. He moved silent as a jaguar that had escaped the cage.

"My mom might have seen you," he said.

"I'd pretend to be spying."

"She'd love that." His cheeks were a little pink, and I didn't think it was just from the exertion of practice. He was ticked at his mother.

"She's not a fan of the quad, huh?"

"Now I *have* to do it and soon. I was just messing around that night and then you . . . I can't let them down."

"I get it." *Kiss me again.*

He leaned one firm, rounded shoulder against the side of the bleacher. "Why are you here anyway? Did you find out something?"

Nan's tarot cards say I'm going to fall. You should kiss me again just in case.

"Sort of," I said.

His eyebrows arched in question.

"That we need to leave her out of it. But she did admit that she gave your mom the cards."

"Weird."

"I know. Can you ask your mom if she remembers our grandparents' act together? If we knew what caused such a public break when they were working as a team, maybe it would give us something to go on."

"No." He shook his head. "But I can give a shot at asking my dad. He might know."

"We still need the letter from Thurston's file, I guess."

We stood, awkward and silent. We weren't supposed to be friends, just partners in figuring out whatever these strange objects were, whatever weird family history was between the Maronis and Garcias. But I didn't want to leave.

"We do," he agreed. "You know I come practice here almost every night?"

I hadn't. But it made sense. In Sarasota, we had our own practice buildings. On the road, the only space for real practice on the wire or the trapeze was the big top. "On your own?"

"After everyone's gone," he said. "Mom insists—she only lets me attempt the quad once in our practices. My night sessions are a punishment."

"Do they feel like a punishment?"

Remy considered. That was something he did often, I realized. He didn't just answer when I asked him something important. No knee-jerk response. He took time to roll the question over in his mind. Not like a hesitation, but in respect. He was giving my question respect.

"No," he said, "I like it. There's less pressure than when Mom's watching, when everyone else is. Just me and the shadows." He waved his hand at the pocket of darkness that

159

surrounded us. "Or, like in Sarasota, the occasional spy." He didn't say it accusingly, more with a slight challenge. He added, "You could join me tonight, and we could come up with a way to get the letter."

There wasn't a sensible way for me to do it. I couldn't justify it like I had this morning visit. My family would freak out if I asked to practice late at night when Remy did.

My father's voice interrupted us, calling from the ring, "Julieta?"

"I'll see you later then," Remy whispered. He hurried toward the far end of the row.

"Coming!" I called, before pausing to decide on a cover story. Whipping off my silk jacket, I dashed to the closer side of the bleachers and darted into the light to find Dad frowning at me.

I steadied my breathing and held up the jacket. "Dropped this while I was waiting my turn."

Dad reached out for the jacket, peering up at my wire and then over to the far side of the ring, to the trapeze swings. His gaze searched the tent, but it was only us and Kat. Remy must already have left.

"Best head up before it gets any more crowded," he said.

I raised my hand to signal whatever crewman was staffing the rigging that morning to lower the ladder.

Whew. He bought it.

Guilt nibbled at me, but the attraction of being in the big top after dark with Remy to make our plan was stronger. I'd find a way to meet him. He was expecting me, after all.

sixteen

Leaving aside my experiment with hitchhiking to force my father's hand in joining the Cirque, I'd never really run away or snuck out or done anything remotely like it. That night, I lay beneath the covers dressed in my jeans and slippers, and waited for any hint of noise to die down. The blanket was stifling, since I'd cracked the window before I got in bed. June had brought full-blown summer weather with it.

There was a fan in my room, and it blew the curtain as I watched. I wanted to turn it off, but would be grateful for the noise later. It made hearing movements in the main cabin difficult, but it would cover whatever noise I made too.

I waited longer than I probably needed to, then stole out of bed. I'd already decided the door was too risky. Someone in my family might be up. The window slid easily the rest of the way open, and I was grateful for its size, if not for the five-foot drop I was about to make. Standing on my bed, I eased one foot out and leapt, landing in a crouch.

No lights came on. No flurry of sound. And there didn't seem to be any witnesses.

Excellent.

Remy was in the big top waiting for me—or he wasn't, actually. He was already rehearsing. There were a few lights on the trapeze, the net stretched safely below. He was jack-knifing through the air when I entered, the only thing in motion in the deserted tent.

I was a little disappointed he wasn't waiting. Which was stupid. This was mainly his rehearsal time, and there'd been every possibility I wouldn't show.

I could see right away he was in better form after that night's performance, and he'd been better than at the morning's practice then. But he still hadn't come close to making it.

He went faster and higher, flung himself into the air, and began turning, turning, turning, *turning*—

The rotation was far too fast this time. His hands would have been way too high for Novio to catch. He was overcorrecting.

Remy landed in the net and lay back in it, reclining with his hands under his head like someone lazing in a hammock. I made my way over.

"Well?" he asked, when I got close enough for him to see me.

"You're speeding up too much now." My knees touched the edge of the net, and he looked up at me. My heart was pounding in my ears. Leftover adrenaline from sneaking out collided with all-new adrenaline from being alone with him.

"Yes, I am," he said. "But why?"

He scooted forward and then he was on his feet beside me.

"Trying too hard," I said. "Desperation setting in?"

He didn't agree or disagree, just said, "You mind if I go once more before we plot?" I nodded and he jogged over to the ladder. He paused, gestured at it. "Do you want me to show you how to operate it? So I don't have to climb every time?"

"I'm fine here. I like watching you climb." Okay, I didn't mean it like that, but he laughed.

I took a seat in the dust of the ring a few feet away from the swaying net, hugging my knees. It's not like there was anything else *to* watch than his climb. When he grabbed the bar, I called up to him. "Pretend I'm not here."

"What if I'd do better because you are here?"

I was glad he was too far away to see me blush. He *was* much better this time, the revolutions tight. But there was no way Novio and he would have connected. He was still that same half beat off he'd been when I'd seen him do the quad the very first time.

He bounced out of the net to his feet. "Better," he said.

"But still not there."

That might sound harsh, but coddling performers who know something isn't working will only make them angry. Empty flattery never pushed anybody into mastering anything.

"Still not there," he repeated. He eased down beside me, and my adrenaline surged again. He straightened his legs, and one of them touched mine. "You didn't say much about how your chat with Nan went."

"There's something you probably should know." I felt silly telling him. The cards said what Nan made them say, didn't they? But what they'd said most recently continued to haunt me at inopportune moments. "Nan gave me a reading that wasn't so great. More like, it was a terrible warning. And when I went up tonight, I couldn't stop wondering, Will the wire collapse? When will this danger I've been warned about finally knock me flat? For the first time, I'm scared of falling. I can close my eyes and see it happen. It feels real."

He put a hand on my upper arm, made sure I was looking at him. "Jules, you're not going to fall. I'm not going to let anything happen to you. We're going to figure this out. Because we have to, especially if it's bothering you this way. Now, about getting into Thurston's. We're doing it tomorrow."

"Together?"

"Yes and no. I asked if I could stop by in the morning and check out his vintage poster collection and talk to him about how the quad practice is going. We set it for ten forty-five. You'll interrupt us and provide a distraction—"

"Yes," I said, catching on. "I'll say I need to talk to him privately, and be all snobby when I see you in there and insist it has to be outside. I can keep him there while you read the letter. Except I want to read the letter. Maybe we should switch?"

"No," he said. "If he catches me, it's a letter from my grandfather. I don't want to risk Thurston finding out that you're part of it."

Sound reasoning. "Okay. You can tell me what it says tomorrow night."

And all day long I could look forward to us being alone together in the big top again. Even if he hadn't made any move to kiss me again.

"Mind meld," he said, and nudged his leg against mine. "That was my plan."

It got my hopes up, but he just brushed my shoulder as he got up to make another attempt.

I was dying to get there and play my part the next morning, but I waited until ten fifty before I marched through the grass to Thurston's trailer. At first, I'd obsessed over what I should claim I wanted to see him about. But in the end, coming up with a few items of business to take care of hadn't been hard.

Stopping at the door, I reached out and knocked three times. It didn't swing open right away, but just when I was about to knock again, it flew open. I barreled right past a surprised Thurston, inviting myself in. "Hey, boss," I said, breezily, "I wanted to talk to you about a couple of things."

At the sight of Remy, I drew up short like I'd discovered a vampire on the sofa. I considered making the sign of the cross, but decided that would be going too far.

"I already have some company at the moment," Thurston said. "But I'd be happy to discuss whatever you like later. Give us half an hour?"

The leather portfolio was unzipped on the table in front of Remy, who, while Thurston was fixated on me, shot me a wink.

"Don't mind me," Remy said. "I hear the Maronis are temperamental, but I have the patience of a saint."

I pulled a face at him. "That's what's required for anyone else to be around you."

"Now, now," Thurston said. "Peace. Do you mind if I talk to Jules for a moment?" he asked Remy, who nodded. Thurston then turned to me. "This will be quick?"

"As a shooting star," I said.

"Fine," he agreed.

I cleared my throat and spoke in a stage whisper. "But outside in private, please?"

Thurston led the way to the door with a put-upon sigh. I returned Remy's earlier wink. We made nice partners in subterfuge.

Once we were safely on the lawn, buying Remy his chance, I came to my first point. "You shouldn't have shown that poster to Nan the other day. She had a migraine afterward."

Or she'd faked one to avoid me, but he didn't need to know that.

"I'm so sorry to hear that. I would never wish any ill on her, you must know that. I'm a huge fan of your grandmother's."

By all appearances, he was sincere. "Have you heard the rumors about her?"

That much was common knowledge, and not risky to mention.

"I don't put much stock in rumors. I require proof." He saw I was on the brink of interrupting and rushed on. "And from what I have seen, your grandmother is a class act who was a victim of rumors at a time when they were rich currency."

"She still is." But I did feel slightly better about him.

"If that's all?" he asked.

"One more thing," I said. "I've been thinking we need to up the ante on my walks. We need one that will top Jacksonville."

"I'm listening," he said.

"We have the big Fourth of July weekend in Chicago. Why don't you get your guys to send us some options and work your permit magic and the like?"

"I love this idea." Thurston grinned at me, a happy billionaire. "It really is too bad your grandmother still gets the whispers she's bad luck, because as far as I'm concerned, you Maronis are my lucky charm."

The door of Thurston's trailer swung open, and Remy appeared in it. "Pretty sure shooting stars are faster than this. I had a question for you about one of these, Thurston?"

Thurston apologetically left me standing there. Remy waited until he'd passed to go inside, then gave me a slight shake of his head and lifted his hands in frustration.

No dice on reading the letter, then. So much for the luck of Thurston's lucky charm.

seventeen

Almost a week later, I still hadn't managed to talk to Remy to confirm that we'd struck out. I was almost crazy with the need to see him when I dropped out of my bedroom window and crept across the grounds by the riverfront in Cincinnati. A whole city's worth of dates—in Richmond—had passed since our try at the letter. June was flying by, and unfortunately my dad had taken to staying up late and drinking Chianti while I stared at the ceiling and willed him to go to bed. Finally the late nights must have caught up with him, because he headed to bed early and left the coast clear.

I picked my way through the damp grass, heading for the big top. Nan's reading was still on my mind. It kept returning again and again, both in dreams and on the wire. The cards' verdict was like the blade of Justice herself pressed against my neck. I felt it there, sharp and cold.

Not that everything was bleak. My outdoor wire walk here had been one of my favorites yet, between two ten-story buildings downtown, with streets in the distance curving up steep hills. Cars crawled along those streets while I walked. From the wire, I'd seen the crowd gathered to watch the parade. It was the biggest so far, and four shows had sold out in advance. After my performance, Thurston had glowed with the satisfaction of someone who had gambled—yet again—and was winning.

When I reached the big top, I double-checked to make sure no one was around, then ducked inside. Remy was just finishing a somersault.

He landed, and bounced out of the net. He started talking as soon as he saw me, before he was even on his feet. "I thought you'd decided it was too painful to watch me fail over and over," he said, moving toward me. His tone was pitched so I wouldn't think he was serious.

"Miss me?" I quipped.

"Maybe a little."

I rolled my eyes, crooked my head toward the trapeze. "Are you getting any less sucky at that?"

A hand over his heart. "You wound me."

But he was grinning.

I'd been strangely not nervous during this exchange, which made me 100 percent nervous. "You're in an awfully good mood for someone I'm assuming did not find the smoking gun letter from your grandfather the other day?"

The grin vanished. "I didn't. The slipcases in the back were empty, so he must have moved it. But I did find something else—and it was from the posters. I really did have a question for Thurston when I called him back in. I thought I recognized someone in one of them, and so I asked if he knew who she was. And I was right. It was Kat, way back when, but in an act without her dogs. She was helping her older sister with tigers. Apparently the sister was the next best thing to the great Mabel Stark, and Kat was her assistant before she retired to get married."

People who ran tiger acts tended to end up mauled or dead. Marriage was a better fate. Maybe the tiger costumes on the dogs in Kat's act were a nod to her sister. Kat certainly was old enough to be one of Nan's contemporaries, with her thick wrinkles and silver hair, and a dog act was one where age didn't matter much.

"But what does this have to do with Nan?"

"The date on the bottom of the poster. I checked. It was the same as the one from the summer in the sixties when our grandparents were in that act together."

"Nice job, boy sleuth." He smiled at that. "So, Kat might know something."

This was an encouraging development. Kat had deigned to speak to me, which was more than most people around here had done. Though I doubted that meant I could count on her divulging all.

"I did mention to Dad about how I heard Nancy Maroni once did an act with Granddad. He grabbed my arm and towed me down the hall so no one else would hear. Even though we were the only people home. He said not to ever bring it up around Mom, no matter what. That it had all happened when she was a little girl."

"What all happened?"

Remy raked a hand through his hair. "Dad didn't know the details. He said it was the summer Nancy Maroni left, and that whatever went down upset my grandma—and by proxy, my mom too. I bet if we could see the dates on the newspaper articles on the murder board, they'd all be from that same summer."

A chill ran up my spine, down my arms, out through my fingertips as I thought of the stories about the "accidents." I joined my hands together, to prevent trembling. We'd discussed how the gossip about Nan might have its origins in those articles. Articles that described people not just getting hurt, but killed. It was a logical conclusion that the dates would match up, but it also put faces and facts to the rumors about Nan, which made me feel sick.

"I bet you're right," I said.

"Nothing else weird has shown up?" he asked.

"No roses wrapped in elephant hair or peacock feathers, or . . ." I had to think to picture what else had been in the photos on the board. The clowns standing around the battered old steamer trunk with gold studs, with one of them holding up that square scarf. "No clown trunk. Or scarf."

He said, "I went ahead and told Kat I was going to stop by her place sometime soon, but she doesn't know why."

If I told Kat or anyone else I was dropping by, the reaction would probably be along the lines of asking what was wrong with me and why I thought I was invited. "She didn't think that was weird?"

"We've been on a lot of the same shows over the years. She's circus family, feels like a great-aunt."

No way I was missing out this time. "I'm coming too."

"But what if someone sees us together?"

He had a point. Not that I was willing to concede. "I can meet you there, as long as you can trust your not-really-a-distant-aunt to not tell anyone we paid her a visit. Together."

"I trust her to if I ask." He shrugged. "She likes me."

I envied that sense of a big, extended community he could count on to have his back. But I had a closer-knit family than most. I batted my eyelashes innocently. "But why?"

He gave me some fake affront. "Most people like me, Jules. Don't you?"

Embarrassed, I resisted telling him to shut up.

But he saved me. "I stop by and hang out with her dogs sometimes. We never got to have pets, and I always wanted a dog."

"Me too." Mom was scared of them. Ironically, since giant horses spooked her not in the slightest. I asked him, "What would you name your dog?"

He grinned, making fun of himself a little, in a way that made him even more attractive. I could tell he had an answer, but he hesitated.

"Don't you dare say Jules," I joked.

The grin widened. "Okay. Dragon."

"You'd name your dog Dragon?" Before he could get offended, I rushed on. "I think that'd be a great name for a dog. Dragon." What dog wouldn't feel somehow more impressive wearing it? Not what I'd expected, but I liked it more because of that. I liked him more because of it.

"What about you?" he asked.

"Oh," I said. "Asta." And when he tilted his head in question, "It's from *The Thin Man* movies. That was the name of Nick and Nora Charles's dog."

"Of course," he said, and started backing up, heading toward the ladder to rehearse. "By the way, I missed you more than a little, First of May."

I pretended consternation by whirling like I was about to stomp out, but it was just to hide the wattage of the smile on my face.

The next day after dinner break, Remy and I met outside Kat's small trailer. The only outside adornment was the painted logo of the Cirque. But if it was visually quiet, the racket coming from inside was loud. Barks sounded in a thousand—or at least a couple dozen—registers, tiny delicate *arf*s to outright howls.

If someone spotted us, our cover story was "just friends," and I couldn't help crossing my fingers that it was a lie. Friends was fine, but I wanted more.

I wanted another kiss.

"The dogs like me too," he said, by way of explanation for the howling.

"And they're not shy about it."

The door swung open before we could knock, and Kat was beaming until she spotted me at Remy's side. "What's this? Why is Jules Maroni with you?" she asked, forehead wrinkles deepening as she frowned. Despite it, she made way to let us in.

Kat's dogs surged around Remy—big ones, small ones, the barks and yips not necessarily matching up with the size—and he bent to scratch at ears and endure a few face licks.

"We're, um, checking into our grandparents' pasts a little," Remy said.

I interrupted. "Think of it as an ancient history project. We'd really like it if you didn't mention that we came here. Together," I added, in case she was unclear on my point.

Kat glanced at Remy, and he nodded. "Fine," she said. "I don't imagine anyone will ask. I won't volunteer the information. What kind of ancient history are we talking?"

I bent to pet a blonde dog with a big fanning knife of a tail that beat back and forth in approval at the attention. She had long, soft ears. A mutt. Beside her was a brown dog with odd eyes that resembled a fox—he could have been named Dragon, though I imagined Remy would probably prefer one bigger and fiercer.

Kat was watching me, and apparently my petting the two dogs had earned me a pass. The blonde one followed me as I trailed Remy to the couch. We sat down and were immediately covered by several more dogs, but when Kat took an armchair for herself and said, "Off," they all moved, settling down on the floor in complete obedience.

"Impressive," I said.

She shrugged one shoulder. "What kind of dog act would mine be if they ran it instead of me?"

"Good point."

"What history?" she asked.

Remy leaned forward. "You were on a show with my grandfather, Roman, one summer."

"More than once. We were on the same circuit for a long time." Kat measured each word.

"But you weren't on that many with Nancy Maroni, were you?" I said. "There was a summer when she and Roman performed together."

Kat sat back in her chair. I worried she might deny it, but she said, "I was fourteen that summer. A pest. That's what my big sister called me. That's what everyone called me."

"She was a tiger trainer?" I asked to keep her talking. "Was she crazy?"

"As the day is long," Kat said. "She quit not long after that. I couldn't manage the tigers, so I did other things instead. But you don't care about that. You want to know about Nancy."

I nodded.

"I don't know anything for sure. Just rumors. Although these rumors are about things that are true. Things that happened."

"There were accidents, deaths," Remy prompted. "We know that. What did people think caused them?"

"They thought Nancy caused them," Kat said, sounding regretful that she had to say it in front of me. "Times were different then. Everyone was anxious. You think we're competitive now? Back then people were clinging to what they had. It was worse. Nancy and Roman—their chemistry was unmistakable. I was only fourteen but everyone knew what was between them. His poor wife . . ."

I swallowed. Remy's face revealed nothing of what he must have felt.

"But were any of these rumors specific?" he asked.

"Well," she said, hesitating. But then, "The thing is, the people that were . . . affected . . . they weren't any competition for Nancy. Roman had eyes only for her at the time. But he had been involved—Remy, are you sure you want to hear this?"

Remy gave a tight nod.

"Roman was an old-school ladies' man. He loved his family, but he got around. There were rumors. There was a ring girl who died—who happened to be Roman's girlfriend before Nancy. And there were others. Some sisters that people said had both been with him at different times. A clown he punched out one night, for dating one of his girls. People noticed, so it wasn't a stretch to assume Nancy did too."

"You're saying my grandmother hurt people because she was jealous?"

Kat didn't flinch. "I'm not saying anything. Only telling you what I remember. I also remember that Nancy Maroni's mother gave tarot readings that were scarily accurate. I hear your grandmother can do the same."

It was my turn to nod tightly. "I think I'm going to go."

Remy reached out and caught my wrist in his hand, and the light, comforting pressure held me there when I would have left.

"There's nothing else?" he asked.

Kat shook her head. "Roman was the kind of man who inspired obsession in people around him. Always the center of attention. He encouraged it. He loved admiration, especially from women, no matter how young or old. His wife was no exception, but it must have gotten old, being married to him." She turned to me. "Even as a young girl, I could see how much your grandmother was in love with him. Her passion, it wasn't healthy."

"Do you think they had an affair?" I asked her, point-blank. No use in leaving with only vague ideas.

"Yes, I do," she said, with regret. "And the truth is, it all stopped—the accidents, the rumors about some kind of mystical voodoo—all of it stopped after Nancy left. I'm sorry. But it did. That's what happened."

I wondered if their affair had been based on obsession or love. Because none of that sounded anything like love to me. I had to admit, though, it certainly sounded like something that would provoke a response—even if I still couldn't believe in Nan's magic, or that she'd use it to hurt others. Crazy in love or not.

I wrapped my arms around myself like I was cold. And I was grateful when Remy made our good-byes.

Right up until we were outside. I wanted to say something, to process what we'd just heard together, but the sound of nearby laughter reminded me that we couldn't say a word to each other. Not out in the open where someone might see.

eighteen

Another week of late Chianti nights for Dad followed, mixed with a busy itinerary for the show. We did a few days in Indianapolis, followed by a few more in St. Louis, and all Remy and I'd been able to do in the meantime was exchange looks. I even chanced dropping by the schoolroom to see him, but only got out a furtive hello before almost getting busted by Novio.

Today, the Cirque had paraded through Kansas City, Missouri. I had done an outdoor wire walk in some tourist-revitalization-type district. It was only about five stories above the sidewalk, so I'd used a parasol and chanced a single pirouette in the middle. Wild applause had drifted up to me, but I'd felt wobbly. I'd think twice before trying it again outside. The problem was just from wind or unsteadiness from too much momentum, though. Of that I was *nearly* certain.

After the evening performance, my parents went to bed early. Thankfully. I snuck out wearing my own practice clothes, a black leotard under a petal-pink tunic covered in tiny black polka dots. I was hoping to get in a little time on the wire. I'd never gone up at night, when the tent was deserted, the stands in shadow. And . . . I wanted to show off for Remy. I was at my best when I was performing, never unsure and awkward like I was sometimes with him off the wire—and what we'd learned from Kat definitely landed us in the territory of Totally Awkward.

When I arrived, Remy wasn't practicing for once. He was sitting outside the edge of the center ring, legs sprawled in front of him. His back was to me. Probably because turning your back on the ring was the same as turning your back on luck. No one did it. Another superstition.

I toed the ground beside him with the point of my red slippers. "Running late tonight?"

"I was waiting for you, hoping you'd show up," he said, and I watched him take in my clothes. "*You* want to learn some trapeze?"

My laugh rang out way too loud, loud enough that I quieted. I didn't want to tempt fate *that* much, and risk our discovery in here.

"No way." No way I'd try something like that for the first time with him watching. "I thought I might get in a couple of turns on the wire tonight."

"I don't know why the idea of trapeze is so funny."

I patted his shoulder as he rose to his feet. "Of course you don't. You like nets."

"It's almost like you don't want me to turn some lights on for you."

I poked him with the end of my parasol. "*Pleeeaase?*" I added a dose of eyelash fluttering.

"Not because of that," and he fluttered his own entirely too long lashes, "but because I owe you."

I could have asked what he meant, but I didn't need to. He'd come the closest ever to making the quad during that night's show. The adjustments to his form going into the somersaults—some of which I'd suggested during these nighttime rendezvous—were finally paying off. At least, I thought that was what he meant.

Remy jogged into the stands and disappeared into the control booth where the lighting and mechanical team manned the switches and boards. As far as I was concerned, the ladder rising and falling was akin to magic—the delightful kind you could see, not the kind that supposedly brought bad luck and rumors. But someone was still responsible for it.

Lights splayed over my wire as everything except it and the trapeze faded to dark. My ladder lowered. When Remy didn't return right away, I went over and put my hands on the rung to start climbing. It immediately started to rise.

The ladder's progress paused. I used the second to get a better grip, shaking my head since he could obviously see me. When I was settled, the ladder started again.

He wasn't making me climb. It was Cary Grant-esque.

I stepped off onto the platform, and waited. Remy jogged back out of the corner, the grace of his movement unfair to regular people. I couldn't believe I'd thought he didn't move effortlessly enough to be a flyer when we met at the masquerade.

He jumped up into the net beneath the trapeze, lay back, and waved his hand.

"Go on," he called. "I'm ready."

Did he think I wanted him to critique me? The idea made me squirm. *Too late now.* I did a couple of stretches to warm up, and set a foot on the wire. I went cautiously at first, in case he startled me by calling something up to me, but I should have known better. He was no amateur.

I went through the act, doing the version that had a little extra. The new arabesque, some elaborate motions with my free hand. I added a curtsy at the end. There was no applause when I finished and crossed back onto the platform. Remy was standing, gazing up. He called a question: "You want to go again?"

Not if I wasn't getting applause. "Nah."

"Excellent," he said, "because you don't need the practice like I do."

What was that supposed to mean? "Hey, I practice hard."

He gestured for me to get on the ladder. I did. He vanished and it lowered me to the ground. In a few seconds, he was coming back toward me.

"I'm not saying you don't, just that you make it look so easy," he said. "Did you always know the wire is what you wanted to do?"

That was such a compliment coming from him that I almost missed the question. I snapped back to attention. "What, the wire? You've seen my dad—he's better than me. I wanted to achieve that. Still trying to."

"I prefer you to your dad."

"It'd be a little creepy if you didn't. Despite the fact our grandparents apparently preferred each other at one point."

There it was. The first mention of what we'd discovered. Saying it made me feel vulnerable, and I was even more aware of him, standing in front of me, close enough to reach out and touch.

"True." Remy nodded, but didn't look uncomfortable. That was a relief. "I've been doing trapeze since I could walk. But I didn't choose. It was chosen for me—for all of us."

"But you love it now, don't you? You wouldn't work so hard, if you didn't."

"It's one of the reasons I started trying the quad. To add something *I* wanted to do in our act. I wish we'd grown up training with the same freedom you did."

"Remy," I said, and reached out to him before I could stop myself. Before I realized it was a risk, I had his hand in both of mine. "I'm sorry about what Kat said about your grandfather the other day."

Remy's head gave a slight shake. "Don't. You shouldn't be." He put his other hand on top of mine. "You know I told you I didn't want to be one of those guys?"

"You aren't."

He waited, his eyes on mine, and I was quiet.

"It's a choice. Not that I ever could be, but . . . Jules, none of that was news. I grew up with 'Roman Garcia: Roman Gladiator.' You know, he used to tell us the stories of his conquests—of the women he slept with, led on, screwed and then screwed over—while my grandmother was right there. She could hear every word. I would *never* want to be like him."

I clutched his hand like it was the ladder soaring up to the wire. "I'm so sorry."

"But I would never wish for a different family," he said. "Dita, Novio, my parents. I know how lucky I am. I would never wish it different, even the bad parts. Never. But I wish he had hurt people less. And I wish you didn't have to listen to all this stuff about Nan."

"What if she *was* jealous? It's still crazy, right, the idea that she could have used magic for it?"

He didn't answer right away. "Yes," he said. "Still crazy. And we're going to find out who *is* behind this."

And that was the truth. I could tell he meant it. He was hanging in there with me on our search. It made me want to fall into him, into *us*. But I was still too afraid.

He grinned, like he sensed the need to lighten the moment. But what he said next wasn't funny. "I wish our families didn't hate each other."

Before I could respond, he was pulling his hands away and backing toward the light booth, saying, "Enough of that for tonight, though. I'm getting closer. Have a seat and tell me if you see anything else I can adjust."

So I did.

By the time I made my way back to the RV, the grounds were silent. Even the last carousers were in for the night, so I took my time, wondering whether I'd missed my opportunity to let Remy know what I wanted. If I had the guts to officially want it. Our first kiss had been almost an accident. The risk to both of us if it happened again seemed much bigger now.

Grass tickled my feet, crickets singing loudly in the darkness. Remy was going to make that catch, one night soon.

And I'd know I had a part in it. But no one else would know—they might never know. As it should be. We acted as each other's invisible nets these days, supporting and saving with no one else the wiser. Without him, I'd have been on my own, digging into the past, trying to decide if magic was real. Or, much worse, I'd be in the river in Jacksonville.

I stopped at my window. I'd pull myself up and shimmy quietly inside until I was safe in bed. There were benefits to the kind of strength you get as a performer that were a major help at sneaking out and back in.

A low cough sounded, and I turned. Sam stood at the door to the RV, his palm on the handle. We looked at each other.

"Sam?" I whispered.

But he didn't answer, only lifted a hand in greeting. He opened the door and went inside, silent as a thief. A silent, happy thief. There'd been the hint of a smile on his face, and bumping into me hadn't budged it.

I made my way back through the window and waited for him to come in so we could talk and I could find out if he'd been with Dita . . . or somewhere else altogether. I'd been neglecting my snooping duties as his surrogate sister. But he didn't visit, and after a long time, I went to sleep.

I'd get the dirt tomorrow.

nineteen

Sam always got to the mess tent before me at breakfast, and I spotted him at our usual exile table as soon as I entered the tent. I was on a mission to talk to him. Grabbing the last glistening cream cheese Danish from the deluxe catering table, I started his way.

Only to be nearly plowed down by Thurston's pixie-small but high-energy admin assistant as she waltzed in to make an announcement. She clapped her hands for attention, and shouted, "All Call in twenty minutes. All Call in the big top in twenty. Everyone—crew, performers—should be there. Orders of the boss. Spread the word."

Someone was getting to like the lingo. And she left the tent buzzing in her wake.

An All Call was rare once the season got under way. Announcements tended to be minor and spread by word of mouth or flyers tacked onto a board at the back of the mess. Getting a message to everyone was easy enough; the circus was an efficient place to spread news . . . and gossip. As I knew firsthand.

Sam's eyes met mine, and he got up and ambled over to me. "Wonder what this is about?"

Wonder where you were coming back from last night.

"Hopefully we're not both busted," I said, low.

Sam didn't appear to see the humor, which wasn't like him. "That wouldn't require an All Call."

He was so serious this morning. Interesting. I snagged an orange juice and managed a bite of the pastry from heaven as we walked outside. "Sam, slow down."

"We don't want to be late," he said.

I stepped in front of him, making him stop. A few people behind us grumbled with irritation as they were forced to go around. Sam could've ignored me and kept going, but my breakfast would have ended up all over both of us.

I handed the juice to him. "Hold this. We've got a few minutes. Now, over here. You know when you're evasive it just makes me want the details."

We stepped out of the leisurely stampede of performers heading for the big top. I steered us to an uninterrupted stretch of grass in the morning sun along the back of the mess tent. Then I gave Sam my best *I'm waiting, explain yourself* expression.

"You know, I'm not interrogating *you* about where you were last night," he said.

"I know, and I'm shocked. That doesn't mean I don't want to know where *you* were. They hardly even police your whereabouts. It's one of your boy perks. So why were you sneaking?"

Sam stared over my shoulder like he was deciding something. I ate some more pastry while I waited.

"Okay," he said. "I'm only not asking you because I know where you were. You've been hanging out with Remy when he rehearses at night."

I froze. Completely. I had no idea what to say. Whether to bother denying it or try to explain.

"I'm not going to rat you out, Jules. Give me some credit. I don't care who you date, and your parents'—and Nan's—thing against the Garcias has nothing to do with us."

I was reminded that he didn't have the whole story of why Remy and I were meeting.

"And you know about my activities because . . ."

"Because I was with Dita. We've been seeing each other. Quietly."

"Not just riding lessons!" I shoved the rest of the Danish into my mouth and swatted Sam's arm with a sticky hand. "Shut up!"

"No, this is where you have to shut up."

I was offended. "I'm not going to tell either. We have to keep all this secret or Mom and Dad will *flip*."

Sam shook his head. "No. That's not why I haven't told anyone. This is still new. Jules . . . She's not sure of me yet. I'm waiting until she is. But I don't care if they disapprove. I . . . I really like her. They'll have to get over it."

"Sam, I apologize. I never figured you for a romantic."

He rolled his eyes. "Stop reminding me that there are other benefits to keeping this secret."

"I think she's great," I told him, seriously. "I can't wait to get to know her."

"She is," he agreed. "But don't scare her off."

He and I exchanged a conspiratorial smile.

"There's something you should know," I said. "Something Remy and I found out. Nan, well, she had an affair with Roman Garcia."

Sam gave a low whistle. "You think that's why he spread all that stuff about her? So he'd come off like the innocent, misled lamb kind of cheater?"

I nodded. "And maybe it's why she's so determined to cling to this idea of being able to do magic. I'm thinking maybe it's that she's still hurting from that after all these years. Maybe he even helped convince her it was true that she could do magic in the first place. He sounds like a real piece of work."

"You're right about that," Sam said. "Dita told me about his reaction the first time she borrowed one of her brother's suits and wore it. She was just a kid, and he threw it away. Told her she was born to wear sequins and be a fantasy for boys, not dress like them."

He was angry when he said it, and so was I. Roman Garcia wasn't fit to date our Nan, let alone break her heart and leave her with a delusion that sent our family out into the cold for decades.

"How did you find out?" he asked. "And why?"

Oh. It wasn't that I'd been keeping it a secret from Sam for any real reason. I knew he'd agree with me about the importance of finding out the real history—so we could explain away the "magic." But it felt like the mystery belonged to Remy and me. The rose with the elephant hair, the peacock feather, the articles pinned to the murder board . . . all of it.

"Just curious," I said. "Don't worry about it."

There'd be plenty of time to share the rest when we had answers. If I told Sam now, there was no way he would be patient enough to uncover Thurston's secrets on the sly. He could be as unpredictable as Nan, in his way. Especially if he thought there was a threat to the family. Or to his new girlfriend.

I hoped he didn't see the flash of jealousy I felt. I didn't want to feel it. Hearing from his own mouth that he and Dita were an item, unofficially but officially, drove home that I wasn't sure how to describe Remy and me anymore. Were we friends? Were we more? I wanted it to be more, but I had no idea.

"*All Call!*" one of the clowns bellowed somewhere not that far off, and Sam and I started back.

A group of stragglers came into view. The Garcias, including Dita and Remy, happened to be in front. Dita had on a man's loose white button-down, and gave a casual little wave to Sam while pretending to smooth her cropped hair behind her ear. His smile turned into one for her alone. Remy and I exchanged a look, one that I wanted to interpret but couldn't quite. Novio gave Sam and me a mini-sneer, and I blinked first.

If something else happened between Remy and me, something besides one stolen kiss and looking into circus voodoo.

If we became the more I longed for, I still couldn't imagine telling my parents and Nan we were together. Not yet.

We joined the tail end of the herd. Sam slipped his phone out of his pocket, and I peeked to see him send Dita a quick text: *Good morning*, it said, *I can't wait to talk later.*

"Sam, I wish I had your guts," I said.

"You don't need them," he said, with a familiar Sam shrug. "You're the Princess of the Air, as brave as it gets."

I chose a seat on one of the bottom rows beside Dad. Sam took a spot on Mom's other side, and they began discussing the horses.

"What's this about?" I asked Dad.

"Bosses like to remind everyone who the boss is from time to time," Dad said, and added, "And we let them believe it."

Well, he was in a good mood. Probably because he didn't know his two youngest family members were traitors. Definitely because, unlike me, he had no reason to harbor any mistrust of Thurston.

I surveyed the crowd of performers and crew settling into the stands. Once people had stopped coming in, and a low hum of conversation buzzed, the center ring spot came on and the owner in question strode in like he was performing. He was dressed in a T-shirt though, not his ringmaster's tails.

With a wave of his hand, the crowd quieted. He had gotten better at commanding the reaction he wanted, and with him right in front of me, it was hard to believe he was up to anything except doing his job.

"I thought it was time for a meeting, now that we've been on the road for more than five weeks, and we're hitting our stride. As you all know, we have five days of shows in our biggest city yet coming up at the end of next week: Chicago."

This earned a few catcalls and whistles from the crowd, and he brightened, clearly encouraged to go on.

"It's the big marker at the middle of our season. We'll have some VIP guests, but more, we'll have an opportunity to truly make that national splash we've all been waiting for. We've come close, but this is when we cement our story. When we convince the world we're a success." He paused. "Trust me when I say the spotlights will be brighter than ever. I want you to pull out every stop. Anything you've been holding back, let it go." He lightened his tone to add, "Garcias, make that quad and there's a significant bonus in it for you."

I cringed on Remy's behalf. They were at the bend on the other side of the stands from us, so we had a decent view of them. Remy set his arm across the back of his mother's shoulders, nudging her with his own shoulder, getting her to smile at Thurston's challenge. Hers was a worse false smile than Dita's. Remy was better at it than both of them.

"And Jules . . ."

I startled. Thurston scanned the crowd until he found me, then went on.

"You're the other half of my victory plan. The city has asked us if you'd hold off the building walk until their Fourth of July festivities. It'll be the day after our last shows, but in the same location we'd discussed."

My pulse jumped at the news. The Chicago site was going to be the biggest and best of my outdoor wire walks since the bridge in Jacksonville. Doing it over the holiday meant an even larger crowd. The idea was exciting, but tackling another stunt this high profile did scare me a little, with our culprit still unknown. I once again had the feeling I was on a ship before a storm, that the stands and the earth were rocking beneath my feet.

Thurston gathered his hands in front of him, then swung them out, palms opening with a flourish. "This is it, guys. This is when we will make or break the Cirque American's future. It's been a pleasure coming this far, but from here until our last show in August, there's no letting up."

Since the season started, I hadn't given any thought to the Cirque not continuing on next year. But beneath Thurston's showman was a businessman. He'd walk away if this wasn't as huge a success as he expected. Of course he would. He could do it and not look back. It was up to us to make it worth his while not to. The earth was *definitely* shifting beneath my feet. I had to stay upright, no matter what potential saboteurs lurked in the wings. Even if the boss giving us instructions turned out to be behind it all.

And I thought the stakes were high before.

twenty

Our next few dates, in Des Moines, passed in a blur, with everyone full of anticipation for what came next. I'd been stuck, unable to sneak out, this time cursed with an insomniac Nan. Even Sam had been trapped at home for a few nights. At least I had someone to commiserate with.

But this was the last night before we traveled to Chicago, and I decided to go for it anyway, even though Nan was awake and watching a movie. I didn't bother asking if Sam wanted to leave together. Sharing this secret didn't make it any less risky for me. Like I'd said to him: boy perks, he got them. And if he and Dita took their relationship public, those boy perks—and him being my Dad's nephew instead of his son—would protect him from the full Maroni wrath and being locked in his room until age one hundred.

No such protection existed for this *solnyshka*, the precious only daughter. That status had its perks too, but getting away with private time with Remy—who I'd been expressly warned against—wasn't likely to be one of them.

So I took even more care than usual passing through the shadows to the main tent. I waited, watching the entrance. Once I was certain I was alone, I darted across the green and inside the darkened backstage area—

Where hands grabbed me and spun me around. I squeaked in surprise. As soon as I processed that someone had jumped out to scare me, I expected it to be Sam. But it was Remy. He was laughing, turning me in his arms to face him. "Wow, I got you good."

I shoved at his chest. "Not funny."

His arms stayed around me, holding me loosely in front of him. "Funny from where I'm standing."

Our eyes met, and his laughter died down, faded into a heavier moment. I realized this was the *if* moment. The possibility for *more* moment.

I exhaled, shaky. "Remy."

"Yeah?"

I really shouldn't watch his lips so closely.

Biting my own lip, I lifted a hand to his bicep. I resisted the urge to hold on, to see where this would go, and instead patted his arm. "We'd better get you up there. When you make the quad in Chicago, that'll show them all."

"Right." He didn't move for a long second.

My heart *beat beat beat* and I wanted him not to let me go, even though I'd as much as asked him to. But he did, releasing me with a shrug of his shoulders. He gave me a sideways glance. "After you," he said.

I followed him through the nearly dark entryway and into the better-lit big top. I was such a coward. I'd never felt like a coward before. But what if he didn't want the same thing as me?

"So," he said, as we approached center ring, "Dita told me she's been seeing Sam. He a good guy?"

"What did you tell her?" I asked.

He kept on track toward the ladder, already down in wait for his first attempt on the swing. The spots lit the trapeze and the net below.

"About us? Nothing," he said. "Just that we were hanging out sometimes."

There was a strain to the words. We were usually so easy together. This night wasn't turning out to be anything I was prepared for.

"He's a great guy," I said. "And he told me he really likes her."

"Good." He stopped and focused his full attention on me. "Dita is special. She knows who she is, but that just means it hurts her more when she's rejected. A lot of people can't even see her, because their own garbage is in the way."

"Spoken like an excellent big brother. She's lucky."

He gave a small bow, and when he straightened, our eyes caught again. "I have my moments."

Yes. Yes you do. I smiled at him. "Let's see what else you've got."

"Fine," he said. "I'll impress you yet."

There was an edge to his voice that made me shiver. With fear or anticipation, I couldn't say.

He climbed the ladder with an economy of motion borne of the hundreds of times he'd done it. I sank down into my usual vantage spot just this side of the net, worrying that I was ruining things. Was I imagining our chemistry? I didn't think so. But I also didn't know if most of his connection to me came from wanting to make sure I was safe on the wire, and atone for his grandfather's bad karma. I sighed. I hated when girls in movies did this, went back and forth, back and forth, about whether someone was into them.

As I looked up and watched Remy chalking his hands on the platform far above, my perspective on everything suddenly shifted. Because wait. Why was I worrying about his intentions, anyway? The question was what *I* wanted. He'd offered me an opening, and I'd shut that door in his face. I'd *patted* his *arm*. I'd sent a clear message. But I wasn't sure it was the right one.

Sam had told me I didn't need his guts, but I was having trouble locating my own backbone. This wasn't a trouble I'd ever had before. My family's approval was important to me, but was it the most important? I already knew Sam's answer to that question. But what was mine?

Remy stepped off the platform and grabbed the swing with one strong movement. He swung out wide, slicing into the air. He was in optimal form, swinging powerful and high, gaining speed quickly. But not too much speed, and not too quickly. And then it was time.

He tightened his body, released the bar, and curled into his first spin, hanging there in defiance of gravity through his second, his third, his fourth, and then he came out of it, dropping fast—

I don't know when I stood, but I was on my feet.

He was dropping with his hands extended—

There, right *there*. He'd done it. Novio would have caught him, no problem.

One of his hands tightened into a fist and pumped the air as he spun down into the net.

I was jumping up and down when he hit. Powered by pure joy, I raced over to meet him. We were both laughing. "You did it!" I shouted.

"I know!" He tipped forward out of the net, reaching out and pulling me toward him, reeling me in closer and *closer* until his lips were against mine—

I hesitated for the length of one heartbeat, and then, then I was kissing him back. Our lips fit together like they were made for it.

I leaned into him, and his arms circled me. My arms slid around his neck and my hand tangled in his sweat-damp hair. There was nothing tentative about either of us this time. He made a noise and tugged me forward and we fell into the net together.

"Swoon," I said.

I had. Practically. We were both laughing again. The net swayed under us. He'd made sure his arm was under my side to keep the mesh from biting into my skin. Cary Grant-esque. Better. Cary might have been in vaudeville, and even learned trapeze, but he couldn't have ever pulled off a quad like that, now could he?

Remy shifted so we were curled toward each other. Face-to-face. Our laughter vanished. But the heaviness didn't return. We were floating.

"You're sure?" he asked, his mouth coming closer to mine.

And I was. I was also watching his lips again. "Sure as sure gets."

Slowly he tilted his head, and we were kissing again. It was like this was the taste of victory, the best sort of madness. Addictive.

It wasn't until I made it back into my room later and crawled under the covers, my heart still pounding, my lips kiss-swollen, that I worried how we'd ever manage to keep this particular madness under wraps.

I shrugged.

Maybe we wouldn't. Sam was right. Parents got over things. It was one of the things they were best at. And those kisses? *Those* had been pure magic, and there was no mystery to that.

twenty-one

The city of Chicago felt as blazing hot as the surface of the sun as our pack of Cirque performers hiked alongside Grant Park on the way to our parade. Heat rose from the sidewalk in waves. I stayed with Dad in the middle of the pack. Mom and Sam were riding off to the side on tall white mounts.

The setup here was way more complicated than normal. The big top was at the far southern end of the park, with baseball diamonds around the wide grassy space where it was erected. Sawdust and earth topped a thin layer of material to help protect the ground. The waterfront was close, just a crossed highway and some sidewalk away from where the tent was staged. The park hosted plenty of festivals and tromping feet for other events, but Thurston had to sign papers promising there'd still be grass under there when we left.

I scanned the pack until I spotted the Garcias. I could make out Remy's black hair about fifteen feet ahead of us and to the left. I felt almost dizzy and nearly delirious every time I replayed our last night together in my head, but I couldn't stop. Yesterday's travel day had been a logistical nightmare, which meant I hadn't seen him face-to-face again yet. I was filled with butterflies about it. I wished there was someone I could talk to—about how fast or slow I should be taking things, about when it made sense for kissing and touching to turn into something else.

Broaching the subject with my old confidante Nan was out of the question. And it wasn't like I could grill Sam about whether he was a virgin and, if not, the details. The very idea of the expression on his face if I did made me crack up.

Remy must have heard my laugh, because he turned, and our eyes met. My heart backflipped at the connection, even with a crowd of people in the way. I was definitely still swooning.

Dad rolled his eyes affectionately at me, because as far as he was concerned, I was laughing for no reason. I vowed to enjoy today as much as possible. If Remy agreed with me that we should come clean, then my dad would be mad at me, maybe for a long time. Nan would definitely freak.

The idea of disappointing my family was the lone dark cloud that hung over my impossibly sunny mood. But then I heard Sam's voice in my head, talking about Dita: *I don't care if they disapprove. They'll have to get over it.* He'd been so confident that I was brave too. I wanted him to be right.

When we reached the corner of Michigan Avenue, Thurston summoned Dad and me up front. Like always around him these days, my thoughts gravitated to the letter in his valise of old posters and why he'd moved it. What was he up to? But I was distracted when Remy caught my eye again. He gave me a hello with a subtle tilt of his chin. My toes curled. I gave him a big grin, not caring if I looked goofy.

Next to him, Dita scanned the crowd, then looked down as if disappointed. I was sure she'd been searching for Sam. So I checked to make sure Dad was occupied talking with Thurston, and hooked a thumb to point behind the horde of performers. She nodded, mouthed a silent *Oh*. She was wearing her costume, customized with her usual bow tie.

I realized too late that our minor exchange had drawn Novio's attention. He was now staring at me. Remy jostled Novio to distract him, and to my relief it worked. I played dumb and swung into motion and around the corner before he could look again.

Thurston kept me on one side of him and Dad on the other as we waved at the more than decent crowd lining the sidewalks. We'd come to Chicago often enough when I was a kid, but I'd never imagined playing here with a gig like this. Not being advertised as a big attraction for a major holiday. Never in my best and wildest dreams.

But so much for my vow to enjoy the day and how special this was. I just wanted it to be late at night. I was determined to sneak out and see Remy again.

After the parade was over, Dad and I went with Sam and Mom to "stable" the horses on the green in a temporary paddock that created a wandering space backed by trailers lined with blankets. A couple dozen feet away, the red and white stripes of the big top made the slightest sway in a welcome waterfront breeze.

Sam removed Beauty's plumed headdress, which the horse appreciated. She lowered her head so her cheek was alongside his.

"True love," I said.

He stroked his hand down the middle of her long nose. "She's one of mine, no doubt."

I could guess who the other love would be. But it wasn't the right time to say so.

Or was it? I was desperate to tell *someone* about what had happened between Remy and me. I could tell Sam. But he probably already assumed we were romantically involved . . . and what was he going to say? Congratulations? He still didn't know about the weird objects and the murder board, the magic and the threats that had pushed Remy and me together. I wasn't sure he needed to. Now, with my thoughts wrapped up in romance, all that seemed far away. I thought about Nan's ominous tarot reading, which no longer made me feel as nervous as it once had. Maybe there were different kinds of falling. Maybe a fall didn't always have to be a bad thing.

When Sam and Mom finished settling the horses, we started the long, hot walk back to the RV, weaving our way to the cramped museum-complex parking lot everyone was calling home. It was much farther away than usual, and the trailers were forced into rows with only a few feet between each. The poor work crew had even more of a hike, and were already exhausted from the back-and-forth.

Finally, after what felt like a sweaty eternity, we neared our spot. I asked Sam, "You want to check out the Batman building with me?"

The site in question was several blocks away, the bor-
ingly named but excitingly designed Chicago Board of Trade
building. It had been dramatically wrecked in the movie
Transformers, but Sam cared more about its famous role in
The Dark Knight, which was his favorite Batman movie. The
building was where the superhero had gotten into elaborate
fisticuffs with Heath Ledger's Joker. Neither was my kind of
movie, but the building was my kind of building—a perfect
setback at twenty stories to stretch a hundred-foot wire across
from one side to the other, with art deco loveliness above and
below. The street in front would provide an ideal view for the
spectators.

"All I want to do is sit in front of an air-conditioning vent,
with a fan," Sam said, his hair plastered to his temples.

"Come on," I wheedled. "It'll be fun. It's the Batman
building."

Sam gave me a look. "I need to be around to check on the
horses. And things."

Oh. Maybe he had a rendezvous with Dita. "And things,"
I said, poking his shoulder.

His look morphed into an unmistakable *Shut up*, so I did.
He was right. Just because I wanted to tell the world everything didn't mean he and Dita were ready to. But my parents
gave no sign they suspected a thing. They were holding hands,
despite the heat. I didn't know what he was worried about.

Sam had a point about the pleasures of fans, though. The
day was only supposed to get hotter.

Our RV wasn't visible until we were practically at the front
door, and we all stopped at once in front of the large item that

had been left there. It was an old-style steamer trunk, covered in creaky aged brown leather.

Sam took a step forward.

"Wait!" I said, too loudly.

I tugged on my lip while my family frowned at me. And then it connected, where I'd seen it before. In the black-and-white photo on the murder board hidden in Remy's room. In it, clowns had been standing next to a trunk identical to this one, right down to the distinctive pattern of gold studs across the top. I'd focused on the scarf, but maybe the trunk was supposed to be the threat.

The door to our RV swung open, and Nan appeared. "I thought I heard you—" she started, and blinked with shock at the trunk. She stepped down and carefully around it, wearing a simple black tunic that flared as she hit the pavement.

"We'll have to get rid of this." She held my gaze. "I told you there was still danger." The effort it took her to keep her voice calm was obvious by the wobble at its edges. "But first I need to see what's inside."

There was a large brass buckle on the side nearest us, and she reached out with immaculate, red-polished nails to prevent anyone else from opening it. "Let me."

None of us appeared to know what to say. My parents and Sam were probably too confused.

Nan worked her nail beneath the buckle until it popped free. She didn't object when Sam eased in to help her lift the heavy lid.

The trunk was filled to the brim—with *my* things from backstage. They were mostly spares, since I tended to get

dressed in my room, but they were *my things*. Stuffed in.
Tights. A tutu and bodice. Hair combs and extra slippers.
Wadded and balled and heaped.

Nan stilled, not moving or even seeming to breathe. The
stinging heat made the moment even more surreal, as if we
were all being baked into stillness, standing over my things
crammed into this mystery trunk.

But then she bent forward and pawed through the trunk,
tossing my clothes and hair ties and shoes out onto the hot
pavement. She made quick work of emptying it.

Once she'd stopped, my father spoke. "What is the meaning of this?" he demanded.

Nan exhaled. She was breathing hard from her exertion.
"You know the superstition about wardrobe trunks. Once
placed upon arrival in a new city, they must not be moved
again until the circus itself moves on. It is extremely bad luck,
especially if a performer goes against it and wears the items
inside a trunk that *has* been moved. Accidents can happen."

"Why are you so worried?" My father looked perplexed.
"This trunk isn't ours. It must be a mistaken delivery. But,
then, why are Jules's things inside?"

Nan didn't shrink from the questioning. "I know this
trunk. Someone is not willing to forget the past. I know you
don't believe me, but I told you I could work magic, and
magic lingers. We have to get rid of this now, in just the right
way. If we do, it won't cause any harm. There's no other danger here, and nothing that I cannot dispel."

"Then get rid of it," Mom said, and removed her arm
from mine so she could make the sign of the cross.

Dad insisted I stay behind with Mom while he and Sam carried the trunk somewhere they could get rid of it, under Nan's direction. When I'd started to walk with them, she'd given me a stern look and added a "Please" that told me I'd have a battle on my hands if I wanted to go. So I stayed, helping Mom clean my things off the pavement. There was no slipping off to talk to Remy, either, not with Mom watching me.

When it became apparent the trunk disposal wasn't going to be that quick, since they still weren't back, I took a shower and changed clothes. Mom and I ended up back in the living room. We sat, waiting, in front of a large round fan that boosted the efforts of our old air-conditioning system. Cool air whirred toward the couch. The wet ends of my hair dripped onto the shoulders of the silk dress I wore, soaking the thin fabric through.

"Julieta." Mom's eyes were ice blue, trained on me so she wouldn't miss a thing. "Do you think your grandmother is telling the truth about this magic?"

Yes and no. Yes someone is clearly obsessed with the past and out to get us, but no, no on magic. Still don't buy it.

I had to be careful what I revealed to her. "I think she believes it, and I think she has enemies. I think *we* have enemies. That's all."

She was about to ask something else when the door opened and Dad came in. His face was grim. "Vonia, I'm so sorry about all of this," he said.

Mom sniffed, but she patted the vacant side of the couch. "Come get in out of the heat."

Nan had entered behind him, and stood in the kitchen. Sam stopped next to her, in front of a smaller fan on the counter. "Is anyone going to explain where that thing came from?" he asked, not sounding like he had much hope of it. His T-shirt, wet with sweat, clung to his skin, and his cheeks flushed red.

We were all looking at Nan, even Dad.

"There are lots of old superstitions," she said. "As I said, this particular trunk is familiar to me. I thought it no longer existed. I haven't seen it in decades. I don't know how or why it arrived now. But it doesn't matter. It can't hurt Jules anymore. Someone wanted to upset me again. They let us get comfortable. That's all."

"Do you really think that trunk had the power to *do* something?" Sam couldn't have been more skeptical. "As in *magic*?" At the last word his voice almost squeaked in disbelief.

"Yes," Nan said, firmly.

I knew what she believed, but I was curious why she'd been so intent on emptying my things out of it. "When you threw my stuff out of it, were you looking for something?"

Nan hesitated, and then said, "I was making sure that the trunk was the only threat. It was."

I conjured that picture in my head, of the clowns pointing . . . at the trunk. The scarf might have nothing to do with any of this. I had no reason not to take her word.

Mom said, "I don't like Julieta being involved in this. If you think it's the Garcias behind this, I'll go to them now and end this. Whether it's just meant to upset you or not, I have no idea. But it's not okay."

I was certain Sam felt the same panic I did.

"No," Nan said. "I don't know who it is, but I don't think it's them."

Dad spoke up then. "This is a good reminder. Not to trust, to be careful. We must all be more cautious. Our success makes us more visible."

There was a knock at the door, loud enough to startle all of us. Sam went to answer it. "Yes? Oh, hi, boss."

I glanced at the clock below the TV. Dad and I were supposed to have met Thurston and Remy's dad fifteen minutes ago for our scouting trip.

Thurston poked his head inside the door. "You ready? I figured I'd come check in case there was—" Seeing us so serious, he took a step up the stairs, pulling the door to behind him. Sam backed up to let him in. "Everything all right?"

I tried my best to look inside his head, see if he was surprised or checking up on his handiwork. But Thurston had some poker face.

Dad finally said, "Just some family business. Jules, why don't you—"

"You can go on and scout without me this time, if that's okay," I said to Thurston. "I've already been once."

Dad nodded, and I felt relieved. I still wanted to talk to Sam, and determine if Nan had anything to say that could help Remy and me get to the bottom of why the trunk had shown up now.

"I understand family business comes first," Thurston said. "All right."

Once he left, Nan clasped her hands together and said, "I'm going to lie down. Like a bad habit, my headache is returning."

After she passed us, Dad leaned into Mom, voice lowered. "Bad memories. All of this brings them. Makes her over-react." Mom nodded. He was offering her an explanation to grab on to.

"We're going to take a rest too," she said, though it sounded like she'd more likely be asking Dad questions than napping.

When they were gone I asked Sam, in a whisper, "What happened?"

"I've never seen her like that. It was scary, Jules," he said. "She told us we had to throw the trunk in the water, and when we told her we couldn't do that, she sent me to go get lighter fluid from the supply trailer. We carried that thing way back behind a bunch of Dumpsters. Where she made us torch it. The smell of the leather . . . it was awful. And she was chanting something weird under her breath. I guess in Italian. Or Latin maybe." He shivered in the fan's breeze.

"Wow." She'd burned the elephant hair too, of course, and even though I didn't swallow her "magic lingers" expla-nation, I said a silent thanks that the feather was gone forever, having fallen into the river. Just in case.

"Do you think Nan's okay . . . mentally?" he asked.

Trust Sam to bring the logical question. I was less and less convinced there was much place for logic in the reality we had apparently entered when we came to the Cirque.

"I think we have no idea what she's going through, what she went through back then. We have to cut her some slack."

"I guess."

He sounded about as convinced as I was.

twenty-two

Backstage was packed tight that night, since the parking complex was so far from the big top. It was the only convenient place to be for the first of what had been nicknamed our "Very Important Performances" by Thurston. I claimed my usual vantage spot by the side curtain early. At first, I planned to catch Remy and tell him about the trunk. But then I recalled how much pressure was on him tonight to get the quad. They'd just missed the catch at the last performance, and Thurston had promised a party after tonight's attempt— but only if Remy made it.

I decided he didn't need the distraction. The bad news that our saboteur had returned could wait until later.

So I contented myself with watching the jugglers balance atop giant balls and toss flaming knives to each other. Right before my act, I made my way over to our dressing tables. Dad sat there, quietly watching the hubbub.

I picked up the lipstick I'd brought with me to replace my stolen one, and reapplied. Then I asked him, "Dad, you're not sorry? That we came here, I mean."

He considered. "It hasn't been easy. I told you it wouldn't be."

"I know."

"But, no, I don't regret coming here. Performing in such a company . . . seeing you get your chance . . . I'm grateful you're so stubborn. Your grandmother had to confront her history sometime, and she'll get through this."

I inhaled to keep tears from coming. Dad reached over and gave me a little push. "It's your time. Knock them dead, my heart."

"I plan to." I gave a quick check to my costume, something I hadn't done since the first few days of the season—and found nothing unwelcome. I grabbed my parasol and scampered over to the curtain. Dad's answer had been more important to me than I'd realized.

From the second I took the spotlight, I was determined to let whoever left the trunk know that they hadn't knocked me off my game. Gripping the ladder with one arm, I twirled my parasol as I rose to the platform. Once on the wire, my pirouette sequence went *swirl snap swirl snap swirl*, every movement crisp. My arabesque was high enough that it risked overextension.

The audience clapped loudly as I came down, clowns circling the outer ring to entertain until I exited. As soon as I got backstage, I headed over to the side curtain to catch Mom's act.

She and the horses were at their best. She even earned a gasp from me with one of her gravity-defying leaps from horse to horse. About halfway through, she made a big show of leaning against one of the stallions and gesturing for Sam—a few steps outside the bounds of center ring—to come in and take over.

He was in his normal costume. No shined boots. She'd said he would get a chance soon, but . . . tonight?

I couldn't believe it. From his slight hesitation, it was clear he hadn't expected it either.

But he recovered fast and strutted into position, a pro born and bred. I wondered if he felt short of breath or like he was about to throw up or like he was on fire. They were all things I'd felt the first time I was allowed to perform for an audience.

The audience had no idea it was his first time, not with his confidence. He looked to Mom for a cue about what to do— something I noticed but they never would—and she must have urged him to Beauty.

Sam stopped in front of his—and Mom's—favorite mare, standing straight and tall. He raised his arms and barked a command I was too far away to hear, and Beauty raised on her hind legs, pawing the air impressively. He gave another shout and all four of her feet were back on the ground. He stepped back a bit and gave a louder command. Seven of the giant beasts whinnied and went down on one knee to him, a horse serenade.

Mom allowed the trick to set for a moment, then strode over and brushed his shoulder as she commanded the horses *up, up, up* with a series of quick motions. Sam left the ring to applause, and Mom finished the act to even louder accolades.

I glowed with happiness for Sam. So today hadn't been a total wash. I left my spot to meet Mom and Sam as they reentered backstage. Sam jogged alongside the horses, and I held up my palm to high-five him.

Mom said, "Enjoy it, Sammy. Good job for your first show," and shooed him toward me. She must have told the stable guys her plan, because one of them appeared to assist her.

Sam smacked his hand into mine.

"Welcome to being an official Amazing Maroni!" I said.

With great relish, he stuck his tongue out at me. I heard laughter and looked over to find Remy and Dita and a few others watching us. Grinning, Dita split off from her brother, distracting everyone as she rocketed past me to fling her arms around Sam. He caught her without a hitch. And then he kissed her. In front of everyone.

There was a moment of quiet uneasiness before someone wolf-whistled. Remy turned to speak to Novio, who'd stepped out of the crowd and was taking in the scene with an expression of dazed horror.

Dad appeared at my shoulder and demanded, "Did you know about this?"

Sam and Dita's kiss had ended, both of them pink-cheeked. Sam reached down to take her hand, and he walked her toward the curtain that led outside. He ignored the bait when Novio cursed loudly. Remy put a hand on his brother's shoulder, not letting him follow them to make trouble.

My response to Dad was cautious. "Dad, it's no big deal. I think it's nice."

He gave a curt nod, said nothing more. I sighed as he stalked back to the dressing table and retook his seat. His scowl this time was real. But at least he wasn't threatening to kill Sam or anything extreme.

It gave me hope I, too, might survive.

There was no way on earth I was missing Remy's act, worry about drawing Dad's attention or not. Sam came back in time to join the crowd at the side curtain to watch the last performances of the evening—and Dad made his way over too, which he'd never done before that I knew about.

Dad had always been a fan of the philosophy of not watching the competition. Noticing their achievements means having to acknowledge them, and this takes energy away from your own efforts. Better to stay focused on the act *you* have to do, he'd say.

There was logic to it, but I liked watching everyone else hitting their marks. Not to mention, I'd have been glad to lend my energy to Remy to help him make the quad. I felt like I was the one about to perform. He could do this. I'd seen him. But would he? Would this be the night he finally caught it during a performance? Was there going to be a party?

We were packed in tight, Dad on one side of me and Sam on the other, a crush of people around us. Mom had stayed outside with the horses, but I was certain that by now she'd heard about Sam's girlfriend. Dad had yet to acknowledge Sam.

I nudged Sam with my shoulder, and said under my breath to him, "That was subtle."

Sam shrugged one shoulder. "Painful but quick. Band-Aid approach."

"Didn't look so bad." I raised my voice for the next thing I said: "Have I mentioned how excellent you were tonight? That was a big deal, performing."

My intention was to remind Dad that the outing of Sam's relationship wasn't the only important event of the evening.

"It was just two little commands," Sam said. "Nothing major."

"Hear that. Nothing major, he says," I said to Dad.

Thurston launched into the patter lead-in to the Garcias' act, and they started to dash out into the ring from the main entry, one by one. Dad leaned in front of me, bringing his face close to Sam's. He said, "Please do not mention the . . . other thing to your grandmother. After the shock earlier today, I worry for her."

"Dad, don't be so dramatic."

"Promise you won't tell her. Not now," Dad said.

Sam didn't answer right away, and I could see an anger forming on his face that I hadn't seen since the night he fought Novio. I reached for his arm, discreetly, gave it a supportive squeeze. "Let's all be calm," I said.

"I live under your roof and we're family, I know that," Sam said.

I held my breath against the sure-to-come *but*. It didn't take long.

Sam was as serious as I'd ever seen him. And he did have guts, to look my dad in the eye and hold his ground. "I'll wait to tell her for now, but not forever. And I'm not keeping Dita secret from anyone else. I'm the lucky one here, to have her."

Dad nodded. Sam gave me a sympathetic look, and I knew what he was thinking. That I was screwed. Well, I'd have to burn that bridge when I came to it. Remy and I hadn't even talked about how . . . if, when . . . to tell anyone. The concept of *us* was too new.

Sam directed his still-tense gaze above the ring to watch his girlfriend. That was when I realized that the clowns behind us weren't just idly standing by. One was taking bets from the others about whether Remy would make the quad.

Almost no one was betting on Remy. I wanted to lecture them, but I bit my lip. And crossed my fingers.

Remy and Novio were flying in their first swing, exchanging trapezes, while Thurston did his well-rehearsed commentary. Dita was as good as I'd ever seen her, dazzling in her triple, spinning so fast her costume glimmered like an in-the-sky star.

"Such a flyer. She might as well have wings," I said for Dad's benefit, but he didn't react.

Sam smiled, smug. "I know."

She made a multiple-turn-in-midair fall down to the net, as graceful as any of the flying trapeze elements we'd seen so far. Making a fall appear effortless and under control at once was not easy.

After what felt like an age trapped between Sam and my dad, it was time for Remy's big attempt. My stomach gathered in a tight ball, and so did my hands. Keeping them in fists was the only way to ensure I wouldn't grab Sam's or Dad's.

Remy and Novio might have scrapped earlier, but they were in rare form tonight. Novio was as relaxed as I'd ever seen him. And when Remy swung out, his angle and speed were perfect.

He might just do this. My nails bit into my palms as my fists tightened.

Remy went back and forth, gathering speed, but not too much. Novio was swinging idly back and forth in wait, giving his brother space to prepare . . .

And Remy tensed for one breath, then released the bar, curling into his first spin—his second—his third—his fourth and—

He extended his hands, dropping out of the tight spin, as Novio swung toward him—

Novio's hands touched Remy's taped wrists and—

Touched and *held*.

Novio grasped tight, Remy dangling from his solid grip.

He made it. *He made it.*

In front of *everyone*.

I was jumping up and down, but no one noticed because—other than Dad—everyone else was too. The audience's cheering turned from enthusiastic to thunderous, while Thurston's booming voice made clear the rarity of what they'd just seen. Sam folded me in a hug, slapping my back like I'd done it.

Novio released Remy's wrists and Remy went down, knifing into the net. After he landed on the ground, he allowed himself one celebratory fist pump, before cooling his reaction and taking his sister's hand. Novio fell to the net and then was on Remy's other side and they were bowing, accepting adulation from the crowd, and finally leaving the ring at Thurston's cue.

When I turned, Dad had already gone. He was up next regardless of what happened before his walk, so of course he had.

I wished that were the only reason.

The performers who'd been watching with us headed off to mob the Garcias, the clowns grumbling about the money they'd lost. Sam went with everyone else, toward Dita.

I stood, torn. I could join the congratulations party, get *us* out in the open like Dita had with Sam earlier. But when I caught Remy's smile, that was all I got. A smile. And when I tried to read in more, I was *trying*. Did I see a slight regret there, or was I imagining it? And Novio was right next to him, slapping his back, bro-hugging away. Sam and Dita were leaving already, and Novio rolled his eyes in their direction to Remy.

Remy didn't respond, but he stayed in Novio's half embrace.

I could wait until later. This was one tiny moment out of every moment left to come. That's what I told myself, but it wasn't what I wanted. I wished I had the nerve to just go over to him, make it clear how proud I was, let him decide on the next steps. I moved closer.

Their mother streaked across the space to enfold both of her sons. Novio elbowed Remy, crowing at her, "Someone was channeling Granddad's luck tonight!"

I stopped where I was. It wouldn't go well if I interrupted them.

I'd just have to be content waiting for the party I *was* invited to.

twenty-three

The party was in the dining tent, which was near one of the park's baseball diamonds. I was smack in the middle of it, but it might as well have been happening in some other universe. Stepping around tables toward my parents, I located a mob scene around the Garcias out of the corner of my eye. Thurston was introducing someone in a suit to Remy and his mother. I didn't see Sam or Dita among the throng.

Mom appeared to be in a social mood, despite the tense afternoon. She broke off her excited conversation with the woman who hung from her long brunette hair and did aerial feats just after each intermission. The woman took off abruptly, after being favored with my father's dark expression.

"Emil, don't be so glum," Mom said, kissing his cheek as I came up. "It's not the end of the world. He's a good boy." So she *had* heard the news about Sam. "Will you get me some more champagne? And some of those cream puffs?"

Dad softened slightly and headed toward the refreshment spread. Mom pulled me down beside her. "Did you know?" she asked.

I wasn't crazy enough to try to lie to my mother when she was watching for it. "Not for long."

She tipped her head toward the corner. *There* were Sam and Dita, sitting next to each other at a back table. People gave them a wide buffer of space. They were the picture of adorableness. Her in a sharp men's suit, him in a T-shirt with an Avengers logo. They held hands on top of the table and talked, eyes only for each other.

"They make a nice couple," she said.

"I agree. But Dad doesn't."

"He's just worried about Nancy. He remembers when she left the circus. It was bad, Jules, and the Garcias made her life miserable. Bad enough that it kept him away too. But this may be good for her. Prod her into finally making peace with the past. Sam deserves to be happy, and so does she. So do all of us."

"You know I'm on board with that. He did great out there tonight."

She said, "He was ready."

Dad plunked down a full flute in front of Mom and—to my surprise—added another in front of me. "Just *one* for you," he cautioned.

I grabbed it before he changed his mind, and stood. "I'm going to circulate," I said, admiring the speed of the bubbles in my glass, "then turn in for the night."

Dad slipped into my seat, and Mom put her arm around his shoulders and tucked her head on his chest. I should probably have thought it was gross, but it was nice that they liked each other in addition to loving each other. Mom would take care of Dad—and she was going to be on Sam's side in this. He owed her, big.

Wandering the mess tent, I sipped my champagne, and wished I didn't feel out of sorts. The Garcia table was still mobbed when I casually checked. No one wanted to make chitchat with a Maroni. I was impatient to finally get a few moments alone with Remy. From the way things were going, it wouldn't be tonight. I decided to head outside, get some air.

It was selfish to feel jealous of Sam and Dita having their perfect moment in the corner. To feel this way after Remy's big achievement. I wasn't just upset because I needed to tell him something important. I hated that I couldn't congratulate him in front of people. Even worse, he didn't seem to want me to.

I ducked out of the tent, gazed up at the clear night sky, and took a drink.

The clown who'd been friendly to Sam was smoking by the entrance. He stubbed his cigar out when he saw me, and said, "Don't drink too much of that. You'll regret it tomorrow," before he went inside. I stayed out, almost enjoying my discontent in the night air with a glass of champagne in my hand. Under my breath, I said, "Nan says only bad champagne gives you headaches."

I tilted back the flute and finished what was left. And bit down on a squeal when a hand folded around mine on the glass as I lowered it.

"You didn't save me any," Remy said.

He plucked the glass out of my hand and set it down in the grass beside the tent, took my hand, and pulled me along with him.

Dizzy from the champagne, I went along after him, and when we reached the end of the mess tent, he steered us around it and pressed me against one of the swaying lines staked into the ground.

"Hi?" I said.

"I thought I'd never get away from them," he said. "Did you see—"

I pushed his chest, lightly. "Of *course* I saw. It was beautiful—you should be so proud."

"Even my mom's proud," he said. "And I may have saved Dita from possible excommunication."

He must have noticed my face fall, despite my best efforts to keep it firmly *un*fallen. "What is it?"

I lowered my head, so he wouldn't be able to see. He brushed my hair back, tilted my chin up. "Jules, talk to me."

"I'm being an idiot." Here we were hidden away, after all. *I know the rules, that we can't tell anyone. I just can't bear to hear them. I'm jealous of Sam, not having to hide.* "This is your big night."

He shook his head. "Wait." He held up his hand. "Let me think."

I did my best to get hold of myself. *Stupid, traitorous champagne.* The security light above revealed entirely too much of our expressions. I didn't want him seeing mine so clearly.

Then he smiled. That stupid—okay, not stupid—smile I was too susceptible to.

"Wait. I know," he said. "You think I'm ashamed of you. That I don't want anyone to know."

I straightened so our eyes were level. "Not exactly. But acting afraid to be seen with me is the same thing." I swallowed the sudden and truly stupid urge to cry. "I get it, though."

He was still smiling. Grinning, even. *Maddening.*

"Why are you smiling?" I pushed him a little in the chest. "You understand it's going to be worse for us than for them, don't you?"

"Jules, I don't care. We can tell the whole world whenever you want. Since when have I ever cared about making my mother happy? It'll help take the heat off Dita. Unless you don't want to—"

"Shut up," I said, "and kiss me already."

He came closer, and I added, "Congratulations. I just wanted to say congratulations. Earlier. Apparently I get cranky when I can't say what I want."

"Thank you."

His lips against mine were soft.

This kiss was different than our first ones, and not just because it tasted of champagne. It was like we were promising each other something, and sealing it with an actual kiss.

I was the one who broke it off, though I didn't move away. I snuggled against him, and he held me. It felt shivery nice. I tilted my head up and kissed the underside of his chin, his throat. He shivered too.

I hated to break the bubble we were in, but I had to. "There was another object today. It showed up outside our RV."

"Jules, why didn't you say so? What was it?" He pulled me in tighter for a second before he leaned back so we could see each other's faces.

"I didn't want to spoil your show."

"What happened?"

"When we got back from the parade, there was this trunk—the one from the board, with the clowns? It had to be the same one, because it had the same weird pattern of gold studs on the top. Nan recognized it too. She was in shock. Anyway, it was filled with my things. Nan emptied them out, and then went into magic mode. She took Sam and Dad with her to burn it."

His eyes narrowed. "The trunk . . . I never even really thought about it. We have a ton of old trunks. My grandfather hung on to them. I don't know if any are missing . . . and I've never seen one with studs like that. But I'll ask around, see if anyone knows anything. Jules, this does prove it, though."

"What?"

"That whoever planted those first things is still here, and that they want to get into your head—not to mention your grandmother's. Why act again now, I wonder?"

"Well, that's all the photos accounted for at least, right? Except the one of your grandparents. All the ones tied to news stories, at least."

He was bothered by it, I could tell. But he nodded. "You're right. Maybe it was their last gasp."

"But not ours," I said, not wanting to be talking about this anymore. Not wanting to be talking, period. He picked up on my cue, angled his head down to mine, pulling back only after a long kiss.

"We'd better get back if we're not telling them tonight," I said, a little hoarse.

"You're making an excellent case for telling them."

This time his lips were less soft, and so were mine. We were making a different kind of promise.

One that would have to wait. I found his hands with mine and held them as I stepped back. "We should wait on any announcing until tomorrow. Let Sam and Dita have their day." And let Dad recover and adjust. Let me make sure Nan was okay.

"I know it's more complicated for you," he said. "If you're having second thoughts . . ."

"I'm not. First thoughts only."

"Tomorrow then," he said.

I'd need to tell Dad and Mom before Nan, if Dad's reaction to Sam's news meant anything. "Tomorrow night," I said, deciding that was best. "We get through the evening show and then we'll tell them after. And if I'm grounded, we can sneak out after everyone's asleep and tell each other what a disaster it was."

"Deal," he said. "But it's going to work out fine. Our sneaking days will be over."

"Spoken like a boy. We'll still have to sneak to do this."

"This?" He slid his arms up, forming ours into a frame, so that we were dancing together. We swayed slowly. He raised his lead arm and twirled me beneath it, and I felt like the world, like *we*, were moving not too slow, not too fast, but at exactly the right speed. "An innocent dance?"

"Yes, this. This is what I meant."

"Until tomorrow night then," he said, and stole one more kiss before we parted company.

twenty-four

Because the RV was such a hike, I ended up coming back from the afternoon show the next day with my parents and Sam. But Dad and I could have disappeared without the equestrians taking notice.

Mom opened the door without pausing in her directions to Sam. "Just remember, when you're up, best if it looks like you barely have your footing at first," she said.

"You've told me all this once or twice," Sam said.

More like five times. But pointing that out to a coach was never wise. He was about to be in for it. Except Mom only said, "Ha," and climbed the steps inside.

Mom's act combined liberty elements with trick riding. Sam was a trick riding natural. And that night he was going to stand tall on the backs of two horses with one foot on each as they raced around the ring. While Mom did the same.

As we stopped in the kitchen, Sam said, "I wouldn't mind you showing me the hands again."

Nodding, Mom went to the living room. We stayed where we were. Nan hadn't been up that morning before we left, but now she sat on the couch watching an old movie. She muted the sound without being asked as Mom took over the floor.

Mom's feet were not quite shoulder width across, her knees the slightest bit bent as she raised her arms over her head. Her hands moved in a victorious flourish. "If at any point you feel your balance going or the horses become erratic, drop onto Beauty, halt her, and dismount. Safety first. Always. Understand?"

She waited for Sam's nod. It came quickly.

"But don't worry. Beauty's a pro. And you are more than ready. I've seen you do this like you were born in Russia."

She dropped her arms to reach forward and pinch Sam's cheek.

"Thank you for everything," he said. "I can't tell you how much I appreciate it."

"Dork," I said.

"From you? I'm flattered," Sam countered.

Nan was staring at us as if we'd betrayed her in the worst possible way. "Does this mean what I think it does?" she asked, standing and shifting a hand to her hip.

Dad passed me to go to her side. "What's wrong?"

"I mean, am I to understand Sam had his first performance and I wasn't invited?" Nan turned a gimlet eye on my mom, who suddenly appeared guilty.

"It wasn't a full performance," Sam said, jumping in. "Just a couple of commands."

"But tonight you're performing?" Nan prompted.

"Only a small part of the act," Sam said.

"Then I'm coming," Nan said.

Sam started to protest. "Nan, don't feel like you have to—"

"Nonsense," Dad said, using his patented *don't you dare argue* tone. "It'll be an honor for Sam to have you there."

Nan relaxed, no longer offended. "This way's better. Now I'll get you in your full glory. No first-time jitters."

Sam and I exchanged a look.

He didn't know I planned to tell my parents that Remy and I were seeing each other later, but he was no doubt remembering his promise to keep Dita a secret from Nan for now. He probably hadn't shared that tidbit with Dita yet. The night was going to be interesting.

"Maybe a *few* jitters," Sam said.

Nan scoffed. "Doesn't matter. Maronis are born with a talent for hiding them."

I hoped she was right.

My performance nerves were a tiny flicker in comparison to the burning candle of uneasiness about how the rest of the night would go. I could ask Remy if we should wait one more day. I was sure he'd understand.

But it wasn't like I could just pull him aside and discuss it. Not until my parents knew. The closest we'd come to talking so far tonight was a smoldering look across backstage as I made my way to the curtain. *That* was a flame I didn't want to douse.

I'd just have to be careful about my timing. Remy knew I worried about Nan. I had to keep Nan calm and let her carry on, blissfully unaware of me crossing what she perceived as enemy lines.

These preoccupations circled while I was doing my act, and it wasn't my best performance as a result. I still did everything I was supposed to, and the audience still applauded, but it was hard to believe they hadn't noticed I wasn't fully in it. Worse, as I left the ring, what I felt most was relief to be done.

Mom and Sam were heading through backstage with the horses, and I perked up at the thought of watching Sam's truly big moment. He was even wearing a spiffy costume for a change—black, knee-high equestrian boots that matched Mom's, and tight blue pants, with a classic black vest embroidered with various colorful designs.

I jogged over to tell him, "Now *those* are appropriately shiny boots."

"Thanks." He rolled his eyes at me, but he had the flushed happiness of a new performer in love with the spotlight.

The music picked up tempo, and Mom entered the ring with the first of the horses. Sam passed me, following with the rest.

The flash of emerald green on the back of his vest drew my eye because green was *never* part of a costume. It was another old superstition. The fluttering green fabric looked like it was attached to the vest somehow, not sewn into the fabric like the other designs. But Sam was already through the curtain. He didn't notice me stop.

Dad tugged on my arm, "Jules, let's go watch."

Frowning, I let him lead me away. I wanted to see the act, reassure myself I was imagining a problem that wasn't there.

"Dad, isn't green on a costume supposed to be bad luck?"

He blinked, but he didn't strike me as troubled by the question. "Yes, but I've always heard it's just an unflattering color under the lights. It makes your skin look green. Like a Martian."

"I guess." Something about Sam's costume continued to bug me.

The small crowd clustered at the side curtain made way for us. Dita stood where she'd have a good view. The rest of the Garcia troupe was behind her, showing support for her in a nice way—though Novio looked bored, like someone had twisted his arm to get him there. Maybe Remy had. He stood at his sister's side.

He smoldered at me again when our eyes met. I couldn't help but think of that last kiss the night before.

I forced my attention to the ring. Sam was waiting outside it, as usual. "Sam looks so dapper," I said.

Dad grunted, ignoring me and the Garcias, and watching Mom. Dita said, "He does," with a shy smile.

Recent developments might mean she and I could be friends. The thought was a happy one.

Mom took the horses through their first set of paces, circling the ring, kneeling, and raising on hind legs. They danced in circles in tandem, and she jumped from horse to horse. As Mom's act went on, I became increasingly convinced that the green I'd spotted on Sam's costume was nothing. It probably was just part of the design, in some other color that had just *appeared* green in the relatively dim light backstage.

About ten minutes in, Mom called Sam into the ring. The horses each raised one of their front legs, letting them hover six inches off the ground.

Sam commanded their feet down with a verbal cue, and drew a circle in the air with a short—ornamental only— whip. The horses began to trot slowly around the edge of the wide center ring. On their second trip around, Sam leapt onto Beauty, grabbing the thin set of gold reins she wore. All the horses had them. They weren't for control, but for slight guidance or to use as a steadying grip during tricks like this. He swung onto the pad on her back, crouching there, and the audience applauded. I could just see Mom get up on her horse on the opposite side.

Mom and Sam slowly rose to their full height as the horses sped around the circle. Sam looked to Mom, and at some silent signal I didn't see, they raised their arms into the stance she'd demonstrated earlier with perfect timing. They flourished to acknowledge the audience's applause.

After one pass, they each signaled a second horse to come alongside their current mount, and placed one foot on its back. They were riding the horses like waves, steady as the ocean.

When Sam passed our side, with his feet on the two giant horses, I saw it again. I blinked, but it was still there. A flash of green fabric waving off the back of the vest. I had to wait for him to come back around to focus in on it. I stared with all the intensity I could muster.

There.

He was moving, so I couldn't get a great look, but I saw the flash of green again, better this time. It was a square of emerald green fabric. Was it a scarf? Where had I seen a shape like that before? Why was it so familiar?

Oh God. No.

The old photos on the murder board were all in black and white. But now I remembered the clowns gathered around the old steamer trunk, how one of them had held up a square scarf.

I stepped out past the curtain, drawing murmurs from the stands nearby. The Cirque's clowns were also at the edge of the side ring, and one of them said, "What's she doing?"

Dad said, "Julieta, get back here."

There had to be some way to alert Sam. To stop this. But the horses were moving so fast, and they were big as buses in that moment. What if I interrupted for nothing? What if *I* spooked them? The act was going fine. But *I'd* been fine on that wire above the bridge until—all of a sudden—I wasn't.

"Jules?" Dita asked, curious.

Remy left the curtain for my side. "What is it?"

"Sam's costume," I said. Not caring that Dad was witnessing me talk to Remy.

Remy joined me in scrutinizing the ring, trying to see what had spooked me. "Where?"

What if the scarf really was part of the costume and not the one from the picture? There was no way to be sure, not when the photo hadn't been in color. But what if we'd been too quick to dismiss Nan's worries about the objects? What if it was one and we didn't do *something*.

I started forward, Remy alongside me.

My dad called, "Julieta! Come back here!"

I glanced over my shoulder to find him heading after us.

But it was too late. We were all too late. I knew it as soon as the audience gasped. Not in amazement, in horror.

When I turned to the ring, Beauty was rearing. Her hooves were the size of dinner plates, pawing the air. Sam was nearly horizontal, hanging off her back by those thin reins. If he didn't let go, he'd pull her over right on top of him.

My mother was on the complete opposite side. She dropped down, but I couldn't see what she did next.

Sam hung even farther back, Beauty continuing to beat the air with her hooves.

I screamed. "No!"

He released the reins and fell to one side, landing hard in the ring. I ran forward, hearing others join me. No one cared about the performance any longer. Sam's leg was twisted at a terrible angle.

Beauty was stomping, spooked, sending up a storm of dust clouds. My mother was in the middle of the ring, and she managed to command the other horses into stillness. She was walking slowly toward Beauty, barking a command.

But Beauty rose again on her hind legs, pawing furiously. We weren't going to make it to the ring in time to help.

The band stopped playing in one abrupt, off-key blast. I watched in horror as Sam clawed the dirt, trying to crawl out of the ring, away from Beauty. She lowered her hooves only to rear again over him, her feet about to come down—

Mom jumped forward to grab the reins, but costumed arms and pale hands knocked her aside. She sprawled in the sawdust, safe. The clown who'd saved her dove out of Beauty's path. And the horse's hooves landed on Sam, even as the creature whinnied in fear and tried to shy away.

On the ground, Sam wasn't moving. The gem-green scarf was just past him, the square of fabric unmistakable in the dirt. I lunged forward to grab it, but a hand closed weakly on my arm.

Sam's.

I sank to his side, the scarf forgotten. Blood trickled down his temple, and another thin line of it ran from his mouth. His pupils were shot through with red.

"Oh God," I said. *Not helping.* I sucked in a breath, then said, "Hang on. Sam, you have to hang on."

"I'm so sorry." Sam gritted the words out.

"No, it wasn't your fault. It wasn't—"

His head shook, the barest no. "Jules, don't let them . . . don't let them kill Beauty." Sam's eyelids fluttered, and his eyes rolled up and then closed. "Sorry." And he didn't speak again.

"Hold on, Sam. Somebody, help him," I cried out, and hands were pulling me up. The clown's.

I pushed him away. I had to get the scarf. I turned to where it had been moments before. And it was gone. Nothing but sawdust where it had been. The ring was too chaotic to lock on a culprit. Horses milled with disconcerting unease, and people dodged through them to help.

Remy appeared at my side, and I had a moment's hope. "Did you get the scarf?" I asked him. "It was green. From the photo with the trunk."

"No," he said, "I didn't see it. Is Sam . . . Oh no, Jules." He tried to pull me to him, but I dodged away. There was no time for comfort. Sam couldn't die. He couldn't. I wheeled around, trying to find Nan.

Dad helped Mom off the ground, and she shouted a command loud enough that it was audible over the noise around us. The horses stopped, just stopped. They lowered themselves to the ground and rolled onto their sides, as if they were the ones that had been trampled.

The trick would have been a showstopper during a performance.

Beauty was the only one who didn't obey. The white horse snorted softly and advanced on Sam. He lay sprawled in the ring. Dita, sobbing, knelt beside him now. Thurston was just behind her, calling into his microphone, "Medics! We need medics out here now—"

Thurston stopped talking, trying to pull Dita's shoulder to get her up and away as Beauty stalked closer. Mom moved forward in an attempt to grab the horse, and Dita scrambled back from Sam's side.

Before Mom could reach Beauty and grab her reins, the horse lowered her big body down next to Sam's. And she . . . she gingerly nudged him with her nose. And again.

Sam didn't move.

Two stable hands rushed in, in front of a team of blue-uniformed medics. Mom gripped Beauty's reins, coaxing her to her feet. The noise Beauty made was an apology. A mourning cry.

Dad hovered near Mom's side like he was unsure what to do.

Thurston did his best to calm the crowd. "Everyone please stay seated and let us clear the ring."

Nan's polka-dot dress caught my eye as she lowered herself next to Sam, a medic on his other side pulling back his eyelids. Dita hadn't left, and she eased down by Nan.

Nan peered at Dita with confusion, then shock, as Dita said, "Sam, wake up. Wake up, Sam," over and over.

Remy and I went to them, separately. He pulled Dita up and into a hug and she shattered against him, sobbing. I went to Nan's side. Everything felt unreal.

Mom held Beauty's harness, offering quiet words of encouragement as the stable hands directed the horses out of the ring.

Remy said, "He's going to be okay." He met my eyes over Dita's head. "He'll be okay."

I didn't think so. Not without some miracle. I dropped down next to Nan, and I begged her. "You have to save him. Use your magic. Fix him. Please."

Nan shook her head, so sad. Sadder than I'd ever seen her.

"There's no magic that does that, Jules. Death cannot be undone. I'm sorry. I'm so sorry."

The rest unfolded like a terrible movie that wouldn't stop. The staff doctor gave CPR, even though Sam's face was more blue than flesh-toned by that point. It hurt to look at him. I kept flashing on his black, swollen eye the night we'd arrived, and in the days after. Maybe we should have left then . . . but even thinking it, I knew that wasn't the answer. There were no answers to this.

Paramedics came. One of them told us all about head and internal injuries. Sam had gone quickly, without much pain, he said. A terrible accident. These things happen.

They were lies.

That green scarf had caused this, and whoever put it there. Mom hadn't been wrong. Sam had been ready. He'd never have made a mistake if that scarf hadn't been on his costume. Never.

The person behind this had targeted me until tonight— until Sam had put himself in the spotlight. It couldn't be coincidence that this happened the day after everyone discovered he was seeing Dita Garcia.

I had been wrong about what the Tower card in my Three Fates reading had foretold. Falling for Remy wasn't the shattering of my illusions.

Sam's death was.

act two

twenty-five

All further Chicago shows were cancelled. Besides being in poor taste, no one would have agreed to go back into the tent and perform at the site of a fatal accident. Sometimes superstition and common sense are the same. There are things that stain the very air.

Sam's parents had arrived that morning. Surely they couldn't believe that they were about to bury their son. Neither could I.

There are few circus customs that go along with mourning. I suppose it makes a kind of sense, that people who live every day defying death would be the least comfortable around it, would want to leave it behind and move on as quickly as possible. There are exceptions, the legendary funerals of this person or that person, with a full complement of clowns or a circus band.

Nan told Sam and me a story about an equestrienne's funeral once, when we were just kids. She made it into a tragedy fit for a ghost story, emphasizing that it was passed down from her mother and hers before that, and we ate it up like sweet, macabre candy on that Halloween night. So it went, the sixteen-year-old May Jackson was in love with the bandleader on the Al G. Barnes Wild Animal Show. One night in 1915, while the show was traveling via train from one place to another, the two of them had a nasty argument. She left mad and drank some sort of poison, was discovered in the morning. Dead.

The whole circus mourned her. Nan had traced her hands through the air to describe the grieving performers without their costumes and makeup, the band playing a sad tune, which she hummed so we felt it in our bones, clutching our hands together, listening. Sam had been most transfixed by the part of the story where May's horse was brought out to lead the procession. They had put on the saddle and bridle, but left them empty, and tethered her boots into the stirrups pointing backward. The townspeople were riveted as the circus went down the little Main Street, where six more white horses waited, three on either side, and were told to kneel as her horse ambled past without its favorite rider. She was buried in a small cemetery, and then the circus got back on the train and sped away.

Sam, well, he only wanted to know what happened to the horse.

There was one way the circus still honored some of its dead. A handful of cemeteries known as Showmen's Rests existed, with plots set aside for those performers who wanted to be buried where the larger community could find them. Chicago had one of the largest such cemeteries in the country, a section of Woodlawn in Forest Park that was home to the victims of the famous Hagenbeck-Wallace Circus train crash and resulting fire in the summer of 1918. And many others besides.

I knew being buried there was what Sam would want, and so I insisted. Thurston could make anything happen, and when Sam's parents agreed, he took care of the arrangements.

Once I finished donning the only completely black dress I owned, I went out to the living room to meet my family and head out to Sam's funeral service. I was far from ready. But I could never have prepared for this.

Nan and Mom sat on the couch, both clad in dresses absent of color. They stood as I entered. Dad had on a dark suit, and paced like a tiger in a cage.

"Shall we?" he said.

The four of us walked to the big top. Everyone was meeting there an hour before the funeral was set to start at a nearby cathedral rumored to be an old and impressive local landmark: Old St. Pat's. I didn't know where the idea for the processional came from, but I approved. Sam deserved it, more than they could know.

Nan glided along like a Mafia widow, complete with a hat and veil, alongside me, Mom, and Dad. When we reached the tent, the tableau outside resembled a circus escaped from the underworld. Everyone wore black, no spangles or sparkles. No overdone makeup, no greasepaint, no stilts. Just black and gray and quiet. They wore sadness like a costume—put-on grief for a Maroni or maybe guilt at how they'd treated him, but my bones ached with it.

I felt someone watching me. Remy. He was a heartbreaking specimen of handsome in a tailored black suit, a dove-gray shirt beneath. He even wore a tie.

We needed to talk about what caused this. I needed his arms around me. But I couldn't have that. Not now, not until this was over.

Nan blocked my view of him, and I put my arm through hers. When I glanced back over in Remy's direction, his attention was on his sister. His arm curved around her, her black eye makeup already in tatters above a suit the twin of Remy's. Novio joined them, his hand gentle as he took Dita's chin and said something to her that earned a soft nod. He didn't look that well rested.

Maybe he wasn't a total jerk.

The horn section started up then, emerging from the tent in a cluster. Their usual bright tones had been transformed into a dirge, the register almost out of tune, underscoring the wrongness of the occasion. They were going to lead the procession.

The crowd parted to make way for them. I nearly moved to follow when they passed, but Dad's hand on my arm stopped me. Thurston left the tent flaps, holding them to let the two people behind him pass through.

Sam's parents, hunched over in black like crows. They hadn't blamed my mom and dad, but it was somehow fitting that they were slightly apart from the rest of us. An invisible force field of grief surrounded them. After the two of them had passed, with Thurston behind them, we fell in line, and then everyone else did.

When we reached the streets, the sidewalks were thronged with people.

"The papers," Dad said.

The front pages of the big daily newspapers had featured a story about Sam's death and the funeral. One had included his last class picture and a larger candid of him working with the horses, his grin spread wide over several columns. A cruel photo to use.

The people who'd come to watch didn't call out or move forward. No flashing cameras, and only a few phones held up for pictures. Children on their fathers' shoulders waved. Men took off their hats—Cubs caps, mainly—and held them to their chests. Some people were crying. The city was making a beautiful gesture to honor Sam. I told myself it mattered, even if he wasn't here to see it.

The half hour we took to get to the cathedral floated by like a bird in the air. It took forever. It took no time at all.

The Gothic structure was appropriately solemn, turrets thrusting into the air above. Several TV cameras and reporters jostled for position in the park opposite.

We made our way in, past a stone basin of holy water and up the center aisle. We fanned into the rows along either side, shoes scuffing on the floor.

Sam was in a coffin that seemed bigger than the entire building from where I stood, and we were expected to go and gawk at him in a gleaming wood box that would go in the ground. To pay our last respects. And so I did.

I went with Nan and Dad, each of them gripping one of my hands. I shuttered my eyes so they were nearly closed.

I might regret missing my last chance to see his face, but I wasn't able to look. I wasn't able to grasp that I would never see him again, never tease him again, never fight with him again. Too many nevers.

We went back to our pew.

I stared at stained glass without seeing it, listened to the gentle tones of the robed priest who presided over the service without paying attention to what he was saying. The whole time I wondered how I could ever manage to tell Sam good-bye, to apologize for not managing to protect him. The circus was supposed to be a family. And someone in that family—someone probably under this roof—had caused his death.

I wouldn't forget that, grand gestures or not.

A fleet of hired cars and vans drove the entire circus out to Forest Park for the burial. When we reached the cemetery, I climbed out and admired the pale stone elephant statues that guarded the Showmen's Rest section. Our party assembled at a tent erected over the freshly dug grave. The clowns acted as pallbearers, setting down the casket on the green cloth that covered the gaping hole Sam would soon be lowered into. The friendly cigar smoker was the one who had saved my mother. He'd accepted my thanks with a bent head and apology that he hadn't been able to help Sam too.

The priest began to speak again, which resulted in more muffled weeping. Mom and Sam's mother held on to each other and sobbed, while Nan stood straight and tall next to my dad and his brother. All around our family were the miserable faces of people who hadn't known Sam. Except for Dita, no one had known him but us. I couldn't take it. I didn't want a rose from the flower arrangement to remember Sam by. I didn't want to toss a handful of dirt into that hole.

Without making a scene, I backed away slowly, passing Kat, whose sympathetic expression nearly brought on tears. Once I was clear of the group, I ran across the grass to the other side of the nearest elephant statue.

I reached out and stroked the stone flank like Sam would have stroked Beauty's. There had been whispers about putting her down, but I had intervened. His last wishes were clear.

Beauty would never see the inside of a ring again. That much was inevitable. She was being sent to a rehab home for old horses. It would have broken Sam's heart.

Another never: even though I'd tried to tell him, he would never know that what happened hadn't been his fault. I sank down to the ground and leaned back against the base of the monument.

I would not cry. Not where whoever put the scarf on Sam's costume could see me.

Footsteps sounded through the grass behind me, and I expected Dad. But Remy eased around the side of the statue like he was approaching a skittish horse, and I reached up for him. He sat down beside me, putting his arm around me and pulling me in tight, so my head lay against his chest.

Anyone could notice that we'd disappeared, or round the monument to check on me and discover us. But right then, I didn't care. I slid my hand inside his coat and held on to the fabric of his shirt. It was the first time since Sam was pronounced dead that the world around me stopped shifting and heaving, too unfamiliar to get my bearings in.

"We shouldn't," I said.

"I don't care. Shh."

There were a million things I wanted to say, but all that came out was, "Sam. *Sam.*"

"I know," he said.

And that broke my grief open. I cried until the ocean inside me was dry.

It was Nan, her mascara streaked on one cheek behind her veil, who came, who discovered us. "Up," she said to me. And to Remy, "Wait here until we're clear." Then to both of us: "No one can see you together. Do you understand? You can't be seen. I will not lose Jules too."

This was not the time to argue. I went with her.

twenty-six

Mom and Dad weren't with us when we arrived back home. They'd gone with Sam's parents to their hotel. So it was just Nan and me alone for the first time in weeks. Since the night she'd given me that fateful tarot reading.

She asked me, quietly, "I gather Sam had been seeing the Garcia girl?"

There was no point to lying now. "Yes."

Her fingers worried at her lip, pinching it as she thought, the usual red lipstick long since worn away by the day.

"Tell me, how long had they been together? Or, rather, how long had others known?"

"For a while, but they only let everyone know the other night. The night before . . ." I didn't need to be more specific.

She took in the information, but I had more to tell her. Now that I was certain she'd been right all along. There was no way Sam would have screwed up without that scarf on him. "Nan, there was a green scarf on the back of Sam's costume. A bright square, like we'd tie around our necks . . . or maybe like someone would use in a magic trick or a clown would use in a gag. I only saw it when he was running out to perform . . . but I couldn't be sure it was anything to worry about, not until it was too late. When I ran to him, I saw it in the ring—it must have come off during the accident. But someone took it before I could pick it up."

"The scarf." Wrinkles cut deep lines in her face. Nan always tried not to frown, said it protected her face from telling all her secrets. "It caused him to fall. I see now . . . How did you know about it?"

"I've seen it before."

"Where?"

I hesitated.

She pressed. "It's like the elephant hair. Maybe worse. The scarf went with the trunk, they were used together. It's what I was looking for when I threw your things out onto the ground. I hoped that its absence meant it was lost. Where did you see it?"

There was nothing for it but to tell her. "Remy showed me a photo of it. But it was in black and white, and the trunk was in the photo too, so I didn't recognize it fast enough. I shouldn't have doubted you. I could've . . ." I stopped for a breath. No point attempting to change the night, no matter how much I wanted to. The past was done, fixed. That was why it cast such long shadows.

"Remy found a corkboard with old photos and news clippings. It was outside with his family's gear the day they transferred their things from their house in Sarasota out to winter quarters to join the Cirque. He doesn't think anyone else saw it. Whoever made that board must be the person who planted those objects on me, and on Sam."

"You should have told me. It's happening all over again. The objects, people dying who shouldn't. Someone is punishing us. Sam was punished because he got involved with a Garcia. I won't let this harm you the same way. We're going to pay the Garcias a visit."

"What?" I asked, confused. "No. Why would we?"

"Come with me, if you're coming."

I had little choice. Nan marched us through the darkened, tight-packed RV maze like she was head of a battalion.

I'd seen Nan focused and in command, but never like this. She must have been tired—*I* was bone-weary beneath the adrenaline, and I'd gotten used to nights with less sleep sneaking out—but she showed no sign of it.

When we reached our destination, she paused to take in the RV's elaborate mural. Remy's likeness grinned out, Dita flying above him, a beaming Novio holding her wrists. But Nan was looking at the patriarch, Roman Garcia, one arm thrust up as he stood on a platform, with a few other men rendered in less detail behind him.

Her expression gave away nothing. She finished the trip to the door and raised her hand to knock. I reached out to grab it. "You're not going to accuse Dita . . . or Remy . . . of anything, right? They didn't do anything."

Her eyes narrowed. "You couldn't stop me if I was, but no."

I let go, feeling foolish.

She knocked, and I expected it to take a minute or two for someone to rouse and come to the door. But it swung open almost immediately. Remy and Dita answered it together. They had changed, but they didn't look like they'd slept.

"Jules?" Remy said. His tone communicated both concern and relief to see me standing there. He peered past Nan, eyes only for me.

"Remy," I said.

"Invite us in," Nan said.

"Of course." Remy was looking a question at me. "Sure, please come in."

Dita clenched the rail by the steps like she'd collapse if she released it. Her short hair was in spikes. She was wearing a plain black T-shirt, dressed the most informally I'd ever seen.

The hush inside the RV wasn't like normal quiet, a simple absence of sound. It was the loud silence of things not yet said.

Dita released her grip and escorted Nan by the gleaming marble counters and into the many-cushioned living room. Remy grabbed my hand as I passed him, our touch concealed by the bar that divided the two areas.

I wanted to fold myself against him and let him hold me again and tell me we'd figure it out, to tell me everything would be okay.

But I didn't know if it could be, ever again.

The gentle pressure of fingers as he held mine, giving a light squeeze of support, helped ease the desperate pressure inside me.

"What's going on?" he asked.

"I'm not sure," I said, low. "Remy, I didn't get to tell them yet . . . about, you know. Us."

"I figured," he said. "But your grandmother knows. How are you?"

"I'm . . ." I searched for the word that would make him understand, and it came to me with the speed that only the truth can. "Furious. I'm furious."

An echo of my own anger flared in him.

"Me too," he said.

"Jules?" Nan called from the couch. "Join me."

Remy gave my hand one last squeeze, and followed me toward the living room. He stopped at the bar, leaning his hip against it. Dita emerged from the back with her mother, Maria, in a fuzzy belted robe. Remy's father and Novio were behind them. Novio hadn't even taken the time to put on a shirt. The two of them blinked in the opening of the hall.

Maria wasn't the least bit drowsy. Her sharp eyes settled on Nan. "What are you doing here?"

Nan didn't back down. "I figured you'd rather I accuse you to your face."

"What are you talking about?" Maria asked.

Nan smiled a smile as chilly as the Arctic tundra. I went over and joined her. Even though I wasn't sure where she was headed, I didn't want her to be alone. We were family.

Dita said, "I don't understand." Her confusion was plain.

Nan reached into the pocket of her coat and removed the tarot deck. "Shall I give you a reading, Maria? See what the Fates have to say. Or will you answer my questions?"

Maria Garcia stood for a long moment, unmoving, and I had to remind myself to keep breathing. Then she walked to the bar, pulled a chair out so it was facing us, and sat. "You're accusing me of . . . ?"

"This has to stop. Now," Nan said. "A boy is dead. I'm not the one being punished anymore."

"What do you think happened?" Remy asked, watching me despite the question being for Nan.

I was pulled between them, my loyalty to Nan and my knowledge that Remy wasn't the enemy. "Nan, I don't think they had anything to do with this."

Nan said, "You don't know."

"Wait," Maria said.

She reached into the pocket of her robe and removed a pack of cigarettes. She shook one out, the lighter *snick*ing as she lit it. She sucked in a long drag, blew the smoke out in a billowing screen. "I can't believe you have the nerve to come in here and point your finger at me. Everyone knows *you* were the witch. What you did—"

Maria broke off. Another long drag on the cigarette, another smoke cloud. "My father was never the same. He was convinced you'd stolen his luck. Even when he was dying, he kept saying it. 'Nancy Maroni stole my luck.' He and my mother . . . they might as well have been strangers after that summer. You were *never* the one punished."

"I lost everything," Nan said. "Roman kept his career. His life. So is it you, somehow, behind this? Because you're still angry that he cheated on your mother? I don't blame you, but you have to stop this. If you planted the thing on Sam that caused this . . ." She bowed her head for a moment, then looked up fiercer than before. "These children are innocent."

Remy's dad put his hand on Novio's chest to keep him in place. Novio's eyes were hollowed out by shadows. Maria ignored the rest of her family. She stood and stalked over to Nan. The tip of the cigarette glowed at the end of her fingers. She put one hand on her hip. The other waved the lit end of her smoke, as if for emphasis.

"Get out of my house. Or search it, if you want. Look high and look low. You'll find nothing here. I admit I had the cards, but I thought *you* left them here."

I blinked. "What—" Nan had claimed she'd given them the cards, as a peace offering. She reached over and put her hand on my wrist, and I swallowed the question. I could ask her later.

Maria went on. "I admit, I think about that time too much, still. I do blame you for my parents' unhappiness— that was when it reached the point of no return. Nothing was good enough for Dad after we ran you out of the show. Especially not Mom or us kids. He was a bitter man for the rest of his life. But I would never hurt a member of this circus, no matter what their family had done. Remember, Nancy, the Garcias aren't your only enemies. We weren't the only ones hurt by *you*. Take your accusations elsewhere."

Nan absorbed that. I waited, not sure what her next move was. For my part, I believed Maria Garcia was telling the truth. She sounded too affronted not to be.

Nan said, "You swear on your father's grave that you aren't behind this?"

The two of them stared like they could see inside each other.

Maria said, "I swear it on my father's *and* my mother's graves."

Nan rose, tucking the cards away. She reached for my arm and pulled me up. "We'll see ourselves out. My apologies."

She wasn't softer when she said it. She was—if it was possible—harder. Brittle. I worried she'd crack into a million pieces. Gone was the strength that had carried us here.

Remy was blocking our way. But when I gave him a slight shake of my head, he pressed against the sprawling marble counter, allowing us to pass. Slinking out together, it was like we'd committed a crime, rather than come to avenge one.

We didn't speak on the way home, and when we got inside, Nan pushed me down onto the couch as she went into the back. "Wait here."

I melted into the cushions, knowing if I closed my eyes I'd be out no matter how much I didn't want to sleep. I expected to have one of those terrible nightmares, and that it would be about Sam and Beauty. He had died because of something that had taken place decades before. Something everyone blamed Nan for. He died because of magic.

Magic. Yes, finally I was almost convinced it was real. Which was a *crazy* thought, but what made the most sense. Even Sam would probably have been forced to agree with me at this point. Except he couldn't anymore.

Nan returned, and I didn't miss that her right hand was closed in a loose fist. She was holding something. She settled down, facing me.

I sat up. "What do you have?"

"In a moment," she said, "I'll explain in a moment. I wish I knew this was the right thing." She tapped her empty hand against the back of the couch, watching me. "But there's no way to be sure. It's all I have."

She was clearly talking to herself, so I waited until she finished. I asked, "Your affair with Roman Garcia back then . . ."

Nan sighed. Every line in her face showed under the overhead light. She looked much older. "It's not important. Not right now."

"He had a family," I said. "So did you—didn't you?"

"My boys were still little. I don't know what your dad would remember. I think he only knows what people said when we left."

"You weren't married, but Roman was." She claimed it wasn't important, but it had to be.

"The woman is always at fault in an affair. At least, as far as everyone else cares. I was the one who got blamed. Roman . . . he was magnetic. He could get his wife to forgive anything, even that."

"It doesn't sound like it worked out that way," I pointed out. "The Garcias hate us."

"And we them. Or we should." She sighed again. "Are you just mad that it turns out I had a relationship with your boyfriend's grandfather?"

I stilled.

"So he is your boyfriend. I thought so, after that scene at the graveyard." And then she unfolded her fingers and held up her palm between us, as if that fact alone had decided her.

The light didn't reflect off the small, round object. It was metal, but dulled by the passage of time. Bronze, maybe? A coin of some kind.

There was something that pulled me. My hand rose before I could stop, reached out to touch the coin. The effect was the opposite of what I'd felt when I touched the elephant hair. I wanted to grab it.

I hesitated.

"Take it," Nan said. "It's the only way."

The coin warmed in my fingers, or at least I was almost sure it did. Having it in my hand made me feel different. I studied the small bronze coin. Roman numerals were engraved on it, and the rough shape of someone's head. "What is this?"

"It is from the Circus Maximus, the very first circus of any kind. An ancient Roman coin the Garcias passed down to their family patriarchs. I don't know who got it to begin with, or where, but it was their luck. The reason they said they never had bad accidents and always achieved great performances. Roman . . . treated it like a talisman. I took it from him when I left the circus."

I had to digest that. "You stole it?"

"He owed it to me."

Holding it in my hand, it was hard to imagine letting it go. Rationally I knew that was an insane thing to think. But when magic begins to make sense, rationality leaves the building. I weighed the coin's unusual warmth in my palm and started talking.

"The people who were hurt . . . killed . . . that summer. Those tragedies had to do with those other objects, didn't they? Were those things his too? What happened?"

I bathed again in the loud silence of things not yet said.

"You told me you gave the Garcias the cards, before, as a peace offering. Why did you lie?"

"Because I hoped it wouldn't matter," she said.

"That has to mean they stole them. You realize that?"

"It doesn't. I don't think she did. Whoever broke in that night . . . whoever's doing this . . . they know the whole story. They found the objects and planted them, and they left the cards in the Garcias' RV. It must have been to deflect attention. Send us in the wrong direction."

The idea that someone had thought this through enough to misdirect us made the whole thing even scarier. And more infuriating. "Glad *someone* knows the whole story."

When she finally responded, she said, "The coin is something more than good luck. It's powerful enough to protect you. After what happened to Sam . . . It needs to be on you when you perform. Promise me."

"How do you know? Have you used it before?"

"Never. I wanted to leave all this in the past, where it belonged. I swore I would never do anything more than lay the cards, read what they told me the future held. Tarot is a small magic, compared to what is in the coin."

Nan pursed her lips, then, "Jules, you can't tell anyone you have it. Especially not your boyfriend."

"You're not going to tell me to stop seeing him?" *I dare you to.*

"I'm not a fool. Not anymore. Just promise me you'll keep it quiet. Look what happened to Sam."

"Who besides the Garcias and you and Dad would care about Sam and Dita dating? It could just be a coincidence."

Nan narrowed her eyes, crow's feet deepening. She looked as old as the earth, as the stars. And yet fragile. "It isn't, and you know it. I don't know who's doing this, but I'm sure of that. And it would only worry your father. Just . . . be discreet. You have been so far. It shouldn't be any hardship."

I waited to see if she'd say anything else. When it became clear she wouldn't, I said, "I'm not going to stop looking for answers."

She smiled, and that sense of her being an ageless elder vanished. She was Nan. Herself, amused and sad. "Why do you think I'm giving you the luckiest charm there is?"

I closed my fingers around the coin. "Can I do magic?"

"I don't know. Probably not. Not many people can now. And even if you could, I wouldn't teach you how. I will never work that kind of magic again. It only leads to pain."

"Damn," I said.

Her eyebrows lifted.

"I was hoping for a bright spot in this sea of awful," I said.

If I had magic, I'd find a way to use it to fix things instead of breaking them. But at least I had the coin, maybe the one piece of magic in all this that could do good, if what she said was true. A piece of magic would have to be enough.

twenty-seven

I was up early the next morning to pack my gear and costume. The night before, I'd taken a tiny pair of scissors from Mom's sewing kit and slit the lining in my right walking slipper. The opening was the fraction I needed to tuck the coin safely inside. The slippers went in the oversized bag last, and I zipped it up and lugged it out to the kitchen.

Not believing Nan from the start had resulted in losing Sam. My grief was so raw that it felt like an open wound in my chest. So I was embracing a new strategy. I would believe Nan. I would proceed under the assumption that her magic worked.

Dad was drinking coffee at the table. He blinked at me over the edge of his cup like I might be a mirage. The dark circles under his eyes echoed the sloshing liquid in the mug. He took in the bag. "Where do you think you're going?"

"My walk's today. Why aren't you ready to go?"

He paused, cup in midair. "Julieta, is this really what you think is best?"

"I am walking the Board of Trade at noon. Everyone else doesn't think it's canceled, do they?" He made no answer. "Do they?"

I tossed the bag on the floor. "Get ready. I'm going to tell Thurston it's on."

He set the cup down. Mom called from the back, "Emil? What's going on?"

I could sense things about to go south. I had a plan. It was my *only* plan, and it involved doing this Fourth of July walk.

"Listen," I said. "We have to go on. Sam wouldn't want everything to stop. It's the *Batman* building. I have to do this, for him. People will think this family is done for unless we prove that we're not."

And I wanted to show whoever planted those objects that I wasn't done for either.

Nan entered the room in her red dressing gown. Dad sighed. "I'm not sure this is a good idea."

Since he was now looking at Nan, I did the same. I pleaded my case to her.

"I'll be perfectly safe. Every precaution will be taken. *Has* been taken." She'd know what I meant. "I need to do this. There's a reason they say the show must go on. It's not just for me, it's for *everyone*."

Nan narrowed her eyes. She said, "It's not your first time up there, and if you promise you'll take . . . care, then I don't see any reason to stop you."

"I promise," I said, quickly. "Dad, please."

I was prepared for him to keep arguing—and Mom too, once she emerged. Depression had kicked in hard over losing Sam, and Beauty being shipped off. She felt responsible.

Dad stood in one clean motion, like he was preparing for a walk or a fight, his muscles controlled. I waited, trying to settle on an argument to convince him, while he took the three steps to stand in front of me. He lifted a hand and laid it on my cheek.

"You're certain?" he asked. "You're up to this? It would be fine not to be. You and Sam are close."

"Were close." My throat was tight. "I need to do this."

His hand lowered to my shoulder. "We're leaving town later, going back to work at the next show anyway. I don't see what it can hurt. Go find Thurston. I'll take care of everything here."

Thurston must have stayed up late the night before, and had many drinks. When he answered the door of his trailer, he badly needed coffee, a shave, and a shower.

"Jules?" he said, dazed.

He struck me as genuinely crushed by the events of the last few days. Enough that I had serious doubts that he could be our culprit, though I still wanted to get my hands on the letter from Roman he'd held on to. If the guilty party wasn't him or the Garcias . . . then who?

"Has something happened?" he asked.

"Not yet," I said. "But we're not done, right? You do want the show to come back from this week."

"I do," he said, but slow with confusion. "Why?"

"I'm doing my walk. Today. The Fourth of July walk."

By the time I got through to him why I was there, that my parents were on board, he was picking up the phone to call his assistant. He told her to get the mayor for him. The guys had just started breaking down the tent so we could leave, and his next call was to order Remy's dad to get his crew and the rigging for the wire together instead.

The scouting had been done at the location. And by now getting the wire strung for the outdoor walks was old hat.

"So, we're on?" I said, standing in the door of his giant RV, nervous that someone would say no, that it was too late.

Thurston held his phone to his chest. "I'll take care of it. Give me a half hour and meet me back here."

I ran all the way to get Dad and my bag.

An hour later, Thurston, Dad, and I stood on the street below the forty-story art deco monster in question.

Because of the holiday, the sidewalks and streets around us were free of the busy traffic that would have usually clogged the area. No fast-talking men in suits lingered outside, phones glued to their ears, like I'd seen when I'd initially scouted the building. There were a few families scattered on the sidewalks and a couple of street vendors setting up, but it was early in the day. Thurston's press team and the city's July Fourth celebration organizers were just putting out the word that the walk was back on.

I slowly took in the view of the building from this low vantage, starting from the bottom and working my way up the impressive brown stone structure. There was a bank of revolving doors at the bottom, and, a story and a half above, an old-fashioned clock, its white hands and numerals stark against a black and gray background. It was the standout feature up to the twentieth floor, which featured a setback and broad open gap—which I'd be walking across. The rest of the building continued to thrust upward.

The silhouette narrowed until finally, at the very top, a silver statue of the robed goddess Ceres balanced, as if she'd climbed up the building for the view. She was a Roman deity who had something to do with fertility and crops. Financial types—I'd never understand them.

At the upper levels, the building was tall enough for the sun to hit the stone and turn it nearly golden. Fluffy white clouds lazed in the sky above. There was almost no wind, almost no humidity. The conditions were perfect.

I watched as our guys stretched the wire across the sixty-foot gap.

Dad strode over to me. I followed his gaze as he looked behind us. The building stood at a T-shaped juncture of streets. LaSalle Street unfurled into a canyon of buildings stretching back and back and back. After appreciating it, we turned to face the building again, looking up to where the men were working.

"That's a beautiful line," Dad said.

"It sure is." I left him standing there and approached the building. I put my hands on the stone and peered straight up, focusing on the wire. "Me and Batman," I whispered, with regret that Sam wouldn't see it. I called to Dad and Thurston. "Let's go on up."

I was meandering around the flat section of roof that led to the wire when I had a shock. Remy was here, supposedly on-site to help his father and the rest of the setup crew. But that wasn't the real reason, and I knew it. I was keenly aware of the coin hidden in my slipper and what I intended to do because of it, and of Nan's instructions not to tell him.

I made excuses and went to put on my costume and finish my makeup in a nondescript women's restroom on the twenty-first floor. The filmy grouted tile wasn't what I wanted my favorite pair of slippers touching, but no way I was going barefoot on it. I glossed on red lipstick. I added another coat of mascara. I straightened the lines of my red sequin costume in the smudged square of the mirror. I shook out my hands, and smoothed my hair back into its already tight knot. I bent and tucked my finger into my slipper and felt the solid shape, waiting there.

I was about to trust it. I was about to trust Nan. To trust that magic could be *real*. No reason to be nervous then, was there? But I was.

For all my reassurance to Dad, part of me wasn't sure I *was* ready for this. Whoever had been toying with my life all summer had killed my surrogate brother. My best friend. And they'd thought afterward to scoop up that emerald scarf and take it back. I had to prove to them that their plotting didn't matter. They weren't going to scare me off or get away with tormenting my family any longer. We were part of something important here at the Cirque—finally—and that wasn't going to be ruined over a grudge. I owed that much to Sam.

I checked my reflection one last time, marveling that the girl I saw there looked so familiar. Like she hadn't changed a bit.

When I opened the door, Remy leaned against the wall in the long, cheap-carpeted hallway. "I'm alone," he said, "though probably not for long."

He peeled off and came toward me, took my hands in his. The worry in his face was unmistakable. "Jules, what are you doing?"

"I'm . . ." *I'm believing in magic. Using a good luck coin my grandmother gave me, which she stole from your grandfather, to make sure I survive this walk, and memorialize Sam and strike back at our enemy, whoever he or she might be.*

I wanted to just tell him. Say the words. But, no, I'd vowed to trust Nan this time. And she said I couldn't. "I'm . . . doing a walk in memory of Sam. It'll be fine."

"But—"

"Someone will come along any second. Remy, we can't tell anyone about us. Not yet. Not until we know who planted the objects. Nan made me swear. She thinks it's why Sam was targeted, because of him and Dita."

His head tilted back a fraction, like I'd surprised him, but he nodded. "Whatever keeps you safe. But . . . Jules . . . do you believe the scarf hurt Sam?"

I have to. "We can't dismiss it. Not anymore."

"We'll consider everything. We will find out who was behind this."

I heard Dad's voice trying to soothe someone, and pulled back. Remy disappeared into an open office door beside us.

When Dad turned the corner, I saw who he was trying to calm.

"Mom," I said, putting on my best long-suffering voice, "the ideal view is from *below*."

"I'm worried. Upset is the worst way to perform. You know it." She crossed her arms over her chest.

"It's too late for me to back out now." I pulled on her crossed arms, dragging her forward until we reached a window. The streets below were packed with red, white, and blue. Or, rather, a lot of people wearing those colors.

"No, it isn't," she said.

Dad chimed in to agree. "Your mother is right. Say the word and we'll stop this."

But he only said that because he knew I was set on doing this. My no was a slice of my chin through the air. "I'm ready," I said, "to get started."

Mom said, "I trust you. Take care out there." She pecked my forehead lightly enough to leave my makeup undisturbed.

Dad led me to the unremarkable corner office we'd taken over and made into our staging ground. There were two old leather chairs and a desk hidden by stacks of papers. Dad handed me the small canister of gym chalk for my palms and feet.

"You should go down too," I said, opening the top of the tin. "You're just making me nervous."

He lingered uncertainly, but I shooed him. "I can't believe Nan didn't come up here to try and interrupt too." Except she knew I'd be safe . . . if the coin truly was magic. What if she only *believed* it was? What if none of the objects were? I might be wrong about everything. Still. "Go, be with her and Mom. I'm fine."

"I'm very proud of you. You're a strong girl, and you're right that this will help. It will lift spirits to see you being so strong."

"Go." I shooed again, waving my chalk-coated hands.

He gave me a small nod and left.

My balance pole was next to the open window, ready for me to climb out onto the roof. Remy's dad and his crewman were waiting, and so was Thurston. I'd cross the section of roof to get to my starting point on the wire.

This next part was going to be tricky.

I took off my slippers and chalked my palms and the soles of my feet. Then I fished in my duffel until I found what I was looking for: the large pale-pink parasol I sometimes used during my act, folded to the size of a big umbrella.

I stashed it behind the businessman's desk. "Thurston," I called. He poked his head in the window, and I motioned him inside. "Hold me steady for a sec."

I used his elbow to balance while I added a tiny bit more chalk to my foot and tugged the slipper snug, checking again for the small, solid shape. I plopped the chalk container in his hand. "Can you put this with my stuff?" I nodded at the bag. The moment he bent, I grabbed the parasol and went out through the window.

Remy's dad started to say something to me as I breezed across the roof, but I just said, "Thanks," and walked at as fast a clip as I could to the wire. But Remy was beside him, and I heard him shout, "Your pole!" at the exact moment I flicked open the parasol. Thurston said, "Wait, Jules!"

"Don't come closer," I said, loud and calm, so they'd all hear and understand. "Interfering will only make this dangerous."

I waved the parasol, getting a feel for how it would hold the barely there wind. Bird had balanced with one at a height close to this. I gazed out into the canyon of buildings in front of me. LaSalle Street was thronged with people, and I was going to give them—*and* the person who'd killed Sam—a show to remember.

Don't mess with a Maroni. Not when they have Garcia luck.

"Jules," Remy said, fear in his voice.

I'd have to do something about that.

I put a foot on the wire, and then another, leaving behind the safety of the building edge. This was madness, but not if I trusted Nan. And I did. I did.

I hadn't fallen since I was a child, until that rose wrapped in elephant hair turned up. I had stalled on the bridge because of the peacock feather. And Sam would never have toppled from the back of a horse if that green scarf hadn't been on his costume.

If Nan said the coin would protect me, I had to trust her.

I traipsed forward on the wire.

I took two steps, then three, letting my feet find the surest path, learning the feel of the wire and its slight sway. I didn't look down, but I looked out, at all those people, at the city beneath my feet. The parasol wagged gently at the end of its handle, a vibration against my palm's firm grip.

For a pounding heartbeat, my step faltered. A vision of myself falling to the street took my breath, it was so real.

But a phantom gust of wind tugged at my parasol, guiding me back where I belonged.

Wait.

I lifted my foot and dangled it to the side, letting the parasol dip. The wind pushed it up, my foot hitting its mark with as much grace as if I'd done it intentionally . . . which I hadn't.

For the first time in days, I could think. I no longer felt trapped, horrified by things I couldn't control.

I'd learned something from falling for Remy, and from burying Sam. Everything could end at any moment. The difference between life and death was one breath, one second, one act. And that meant that life was worth everything, every minute of every day.

I walked a simple walk, like an old-fashioned girl in the park holding a sun umbrella, until I got to the middle. Being here was so right, the wire so perfect . . . Maybe it was that small wind gust, or the feeling that no one could touch me up here. I didn't close my eyes or anything insane, but the rightness of this walk coursed through my limbs, bringing a certainty.

I wasn't going to fall. Not today. Not with that coin in my shoe. The coin was magic. It *worked.*

And so I did a single pirouette, using the parasol like I would have in my act. I danced forward out of it. And I did another one. The certainty flowed within me. I couldn't fall. Not with the magic. I laughed, and did another pirouette, letting the parasol help me find my balance at the end of each. The wind that had been absent before now buffeted strategically like it was a friend called in to do a favor.

The roaring cheers below reached me, but it wasn't them I thought about. It was how I wanted to stay up here forever, because there was nothing but the wire and the air and my moving through it.

It was the biggest middle finger I could give, and I did it with gusto. With glee.

When I reached the far end of the wire, I intended to turn and go back across. I didn't want the walk to end.

But Thurston was waiting there—he must have raced through the halls of the building—and he grabbed me as soon as I got close and pulled me onto the roof. There were Dad and Mom, hopping over the window ledge and jogging toward us. Nan came through behind them, slower, but no less pale. Their faces were washed of everything but worry. I didn't know why Nan would be worried.

Thurston had called me the Princess of the Air before, but now I was.

I imagined my own flushed cheeks, success coloring them. That had been a walk worthy of Bird.

There was a TV camera waiting behind Thurston. He'd told me the crew would be there for a postwalk interview. I waved the female reporter forward with a deep breath and a smile, using the same hand to tell my family to stay back. Her camera guy was open-mouthed in awe. Remy, behind them, was wide-eyed with a lingering panic.

"That was something," the reporter said, a woman with shiny brunette hair and lips as glossy as my own. I focused on her. "What were you thinking of while you were up there? Do you ever get scared?"

I looked straight into the camera, holding the parasol so it would frame me, and said, "I was thinking of my cousin Sam. That one was for you. It was good-bye, not just from me and the Maroni family, but from the entire circus."

I imagined the reaction of our foe on hearing that, and my smile bloomed wide as the building.

twenty-eight

Our next stop was Milwaukee, a short two-hour drive up the interstate.

We settled into a grassy field adjacent to the fairgrounds, mercifully roomy after the cramped quarters in Chicago. Being back on the road felt as right as being on the wire had—and as wrong as not having Sam with us, as wrong as keeping secrets from Remy. I didn't have an outdoor walk scheduled, and so I stayed close to Mom and Dad during the parade. People in the crowd kept calling out to me, and I dutifully smiled for their photos.

There were definitely more of those calls than usual. But I was too busy hoping the person I'd most wanted to had caught my big walk to pay much attention.

At the evening mess, after I went through the line, I hesitated, lost when I realized that I didn't have Sam to sit with. But I recovered and ended up claiming our usual spot. The acrobats and Kat were at the next table, and a sense of fragility clung to everyone, left over from the accident and its aftermath. But people had been nice to me all day. The irony wasn't lost that pity was what it took to make the circus embrace us.

"Excellent!" "Beautiful!" The eldest acrobat brothers stood and congratulated me in tandem for yesterday's walk with broad smiles, and then sat back down and resumed chattering away to one another in Mandarin.

According to Thurston, the Board of Trade performance had landed me—and the Cirque—on the front page of a half dozen of the country's major newspapers, and the twenty-four-hour news networks were playing it on repeat. Nan had been watching it earlier on CNN, in place of her usual TCM, and she'd shot me a warning look. "Such daring. You promised me care." But that was all she said, and I went on my way.

You couldn't just give someone a magic coin and expect them not to use it.

After a few bites of the roasted-vegetable dish on my plate, I decided to try catching Remy's eye. A few stolen moments here and there weren't enough, not anymore. He was across the room, surrounded by his family—including Dita, still radiating misery and clad in another ratty T-shirt. He must have been waiting, because our glances snagged immediately. I worried someone would notice, but ticked my head the slightest bit to the left anyway.

We both went back to our meals. I barely tasted the food, and soon enough, I was finished. I left, hoping he'd managed to read my cue. I didn't head toward our RV, but to the back of the tent. The least likely place to be spotted by someone randomly passing by was the far left corner. I leaned against the line tied to the stake, where we'd made out what felt like ages ago, back when even the most complicated things had been far simpler.

In moments, Remy came around the corner, and I said, "Great minds," and launched at him like a missile. He caught me, easily, and we stayed like that, holding each other. I'd missed everything about him. Including the way he smelled. I inhaled that mix of faint sweat from physical exertion and the scent of a men's shampoo I'd probably have turned my nose up at before experiencing it like this. Up close and so very personal.

Finally he pulled back, and I stared into his kind eyes. *What am I going to say? I want to tell him everything, and I can't.*

"Everything feels like a wreck," I said.

"Dita can't stop crying," he said.

I nodded. Her eyes had been red earlier. "So . . . how awkward on a scale of one to ten is it to talk about my grandmother accusing your mom of being behind everything the other night?"

"No one else in the world talks like you." He smiled. "I would say it's a nine."

My heart had skipped at the compliment. At least, I was pretty sure he meant it as one.

"Flatterer. Not a ten?"

"I hate to give anything the highest ranking. For all we know, something even more awkward is coming. We did already uncover our grandparents' affair." He transformed into what I recognized as serious-as-a-fall Remy. "I finally got a chance to ask around about whether any trunks were missing, and no one knew of any that were. But we know that scarf is still out there, and so we have to assume the person behind all this has it. Why would anyone else bother to pick it up?"

"Logical," I said.

"I looked through every picture I could find posted from the crowd that night, but I couldn't see anyone take it. There were too many people in the way."

My stomach tightened at the idea of such photos. I could envision Sam's battered body in the ring. All I had to do was close my eyes. "That was smart, to look at them. Those crime books have turned you into an excellent boy detective."

He stayed serious. "I didn't tell you, because I would never have asked you to look at them. And I know you'd have wanted to help. I also studied the pictures on the board again. It does make sense that Nan accused us. You know I looked for evidence of the same thing at first. I wasn't offended."

"But it really only makes sense if your granddad is doing all this from beyond the grave."

"That occurred to me," he said.

Really? "I was joking."

"But what my mom said seems most likely—that someone else is involved. The thing that bothers me is the picture of him and my grandmother."

"Why?"

"Because of whatever shiny thing he's got in his palm. It must still be out there too. Another object."

I didn't have the coin on me, but I felt like I did. A completely illogical need to protect it spiked through me.

The missing lucky coin obviously wasn't something the whole family knew about—wasn't a story Remy had ever been told. I'd figured that was the case, since he'd never brought it up, but part of me had wondered if he was keeping the facts about the coin from *me*. Unfair, since I was the one keeping it from him.

"I have something for you," he said, and reached into his pocket.

"Or are you just happy to see me?" The joke made my cheeks blaze.

"Close your eyes." He said it slowly, and so I complied.

His hand slid down my arm, turning my palm up, and then . . . placing a chunk of metal in it. I opened my eyes and peered down at a cell phone.

"My number's already programmed in. I want you to be able to reach me anytime. Call, text, whatever you like best."

"Cell phones are so inelegant, but thank you," I said, touched. "I'll try to think of texts like a telegram, but without the STOP at the end. I won't use those awful abbreviations like Sam used to."

Saying his name hurt.

"Well, then I'm number two in your directory, STOP," he said. "I refuse to take any more chances with your safety, and you should do the same. That walk . . . it was amazing, but I have never been so afraid that something was going to go wrong. I don't know what I'd do, Jules." He took my hands in his, phone still in mine, and cradled them against the gloriously solid muscles of his stomach. "You have to take care."

I was more careful with my answer than I had been danc-ing on the wire above LaSalle Street.

"I did. I will. I promise." I ditched the phone into my jeans pocket, then flattened my palms against his body, slid-ing them up to his chest, but keeping them on top of the thin T-shirt he wore. Neither of us looked away. "You know how sometimes you can just tell that a performance is golden, and you just follow it through, like the momentum is coming from a force beyond your body?"

"I do," he said, "but that was all you."

I didn't have to respond. Luckily. He leaned in and kissed me, and I put into my response everything I wasn't saying. Everything I couldn't tell him, yet.

But Remy wasn't finished. He cupped my chin, and said, "Now, the next thing we need is a plan to search Thurston's trailer. We need that letter."

I was already in my costume when Dad came into the RV and waved me to come with him before the evening show. "Jules, you have to see this."

My father's tone was so flat I wouldn't have been surprised by anything—not an elephant, or a spaceship, or the ghost of Roman Garcia. I followed him toward the tent. But he steered us not toward the backstage entrance, but the front. When I saw why, his face split into a wide grin.

There was a crowd of about twenty girls, a few guys mixed in, outside the tent. Three of them were holding oversized signs with blown-up photos of me with my parasol walking in front of the Batman building. Some of the others were dressed in cheap tutus dyed red and wearing bright red lipstick. Others had hearts painted onto their cheeks or clutched frilly parasols. One of them spotted us and pointed, and they started our way.

"You better go speak to your fans," Dad said. Then, "You'll need this." He handed me a pen.

"Fans?" I said. "It's only been a couple of days."

But the squealing and shouting as they approached made it clear they were real. I took a deep breath and went to meet them, checking over my shoulder to make sure Dad was staying, in case I needed, well, help.

The first to reach me was a girl with curly blonde hair, younger than me by a few years. She had a heart stenciled on her cheek and gripped one of the posters. "Oh my God, I can't believe I'm meeting you!"

I didn't know what to say.

"Would you like her to sign your poster?" Dad asked.

She nodded. The others swarmed in. I took it from her and drew a heart—since that was what she had on her cheek— and paused, not sure what to sign. After a second's hesitation, I went with my full name: Julieta Valentina Maroni. But I wasn't sure what to do next. I handed it back, and another poster was thrust at me.

"Do you know Remy Garcia?" one of the girls asked. Another beside her said, "He's *sooo* hot!"

"Um, yes. I know him." I didn't look at Dad. Was I supposed to answer questions like that? I had no idea how to act.

But they had so much energy, practically bouncing with it, that I was charmed.

"Do you ever get scared?" one of the older girls asked. She wore a red tutu, but no makeup.

"On the wire?" I asked, signing another poster. The girl nodded. "You can't get scared while you're doing it. You have to save your fear for before or after. While I'm walking, that's all I'm doing. If it's going well." I remembered being frozen above the bridge in Jacksonville, and lowering myself to try to find my composure. I'd lied to her—I had been scared on the wire. Just not often.

I heard the strains of the band start up inside. "You'd all better go get your seats. You don't want to miss any of the show."

"But we're here to see you," a lanky boy with a floppy haircut protested. The girl beside him must have been his sister, from the resemblance. She elbowed him and said, "He's in love with you."

The boy stared at the ground in horror.

"Thank you?" I offered. "But you really don't want to miss anything. The other performers are just as amazing as us Maronis."

A few of them started toward the tent, but several lingered. The girl closest to me had one of the hearts outlined on her cheek. I touched my own and asked her, "What are those for?"

She turned as embarrassed as the boy who thought he was in love with me. "We're Valentines. You know, like your middle name—it's what they're calling us."

I was confused. "Who?"

"The media."

I was going to have to start watching the news. Or not. Guilt gnawed at me, like it had when I was with Remy.

"Nice meeting all of you . . . Valentines," I said, waving.

I booked it to Dad's side. He was smirking, far too amused by the whole thing.

"They call themselves Valentines. Did you know that?" I asked him.

He burst out laughing. Disconcerted, I frowned at him, though it was rare to hear him laugh these days. "Yes, I'd heard," he said, attempting—without success—to stop cracking up. "You should just be glad they didn't go with your first name and call themselves Jew-els," he said, sounding it out, and laughing even harder. "Now *that* would be priceless."

I punched his arm. "Shut up."

"Sam would have been proud, you know," Dad said.

And he was right. I knew he was, and I took heart from that. I needed a shot of confidence. Because just when I'd assumed I couldn't get in any further over my head, I now had a fan base—and a boyfriend determined to break into the owner's office.

twenty-nine

Overnight success is a myth. I'd been working since I was too young to remember, dedicating myself to the wire. But *celebrity* can happen overnight. One minute very few people— considering the number of people on earth—know who you are, and then you go to bed and wake up and your name is *known*.

That was what happened after Chicago. The Milwaukee Valentines were just the beginning. We encountered crowds of them in Madison—where we also received a visit from the performers at the small one-ring at Circus World Museum in nearby Baraboo, the site of Ringling Brothers' original winter quarters—and in Eau Claire. Fan mail started coming in by the box load, and the show's main email account was so flooded with messages that they created a special one for me: CirquePrincess@CirqueAmerican.com. Ridiculous.

Minneapolis had delivered the biggest crowd awaiting our arrival yet. It was mid-July and *all* our shows were selling out in advance now. The rest of our summer was set as if the Fates themselves had woven a pattern of full audiences for every performance. My high profile must have stung the person I wanted it to, but it hadn't lured them out into the open yet.

I hadn't gotten used to signing autographs and taking pictures and the existence of the Valentines, and I wasn't sure I ever would. My newfound popularity also made it harder for me and Remy to hook up in secret with our former ease . . . as did my guilt at not telling him why my performances had become so much more thrilling.

The fear of getting caught with the coin seeped into my bones. I felt it all the time. Meaning that my answer to that girl among that very first group of fans—that I wasn't scared—had become an even bigger lie.

I missed Sam, who would have helped me figure out what to do.

None of us had forgotten what happened in Chicago. There were even some new safety restrictions, despite the fact that Thurston owned the company that insured us. He hadn't learned that disaster could also be courted by guarding against it too much.

No one protested my pirouetting high above the streets. It was too profitable. And I had to keep doing it, because to stop would be to give in. Surely all this would flush out the responsible party, one way or another. Eventually.

From my vantage point on the roof, the crowd on the street below the Hennepin County Government Center in downtown Minneapolis looked wider than the Mighty Mississippi flowing not far away. The building had two tall towers with a glassed-in atrium between them that stretched over a street, an opening at the top forming an architectural *H*. The throng below included a line of news cameras. We'd also negotiated with a local TV station about their helicopter, giving strict instructions about how close it could get.

The extra attention on this particular walk was undoubtedly due to the fact that Philippe Petit had reportedly walked this same site—though we'd tried and failed to find any footage of it. Still, he was a living legend who'd had his own circus ties when he started out. The Twin Towers walk and the movie made about it had turned him into a celebrity, the best-known wire walker in decades. I kept waiting for a reporter to ask him what he thought about me and for him to say something snarky in response, but so far he hadn't.

I wouldn't have been surprised if he knew who Dad was. Dad was the best on the planet, but Petit was a close second. They were both artists.

The wind blew stronger than was strictly safe for an outdoor walk, and the sky was filled with heavy gray clouds, which led to a frowning discussion between Dad, Thurston, and me on the roof just before it was time to start.

"It will be fine," I insisted.

"You should use the pole," Dad said.

Twirling my parasol, I said, sweetly, "Not a chance. The wind's not that bad."

A gust stopped the umbrella midmovement and sent it spinning the other way.

"My point," he said. He was about to pull the command card and order me not to proceed. I sensed it.

Thurston didn't like butting in when we were arguing, but he offered, "Maybe we should postpone? The weather's supposed to be better tomorrow."

"No," I said. "I'm ready. I can't disappoint them."

I bolted, realizing too late that the cameras on the roof had probably caught the whole disagreement.

Oh well.

"Julieta!" My dad was angry, but when I turned at the head of the wire, he only threw his hands up. "You throw caution to the wind, it may blow you away."

Thurston was also thunderously unhappy, I could tell.

"I'm sorry," I said. "But you don't need to worry."

When they started toward me, I moved smoothly forward and began. Like it had every time, the coin somehow sang to the wind, and my feet had no wrong place to land.

The crowd loved it. All the more for the reports of a "dispute beforehand." I had a new nickname to go with Princess of the Air. Daredevil Maroni.

Remy texted me after the performance: *Taking care?*

I'd gotten decent at reading between the abbreviated, inelegant lines. He hadn't been a fan of my walking in those conditions either. I stared at the phone, trying to figure out what to respond, but it buzzed again before I decided. *Meet me at Thurston's office @ midnight. Tonight's the night.*

That we were going to search for the letter, he meant. There was no way to protest without raising other questions I wouldn't know how to answer.

See you then, I sent back.

thirty

From the side curtain that night, I watched the Garcias' act. When the quad attempt came, the band did a drumroll, and Remy sliced through the air, gathering speed, then gathering more, putting every ounce of energy he had into it as he launched out into the spin, spin, spin, *spin*—

And just missed his brother's grasping hands coming out of it.

I watched his tight bow, the confident-but-chagrined performer's smile that said, "I'll get it next time." He would never forgive me if he found out about the coin. He'd be right not to.

As midnight rolled around, I discovered I didn't have the right clothes for a break-in. There was not enough black in my wardrobe, especially since I wasn't planning on wearing my funeral dress ever again. So I showed up outside Thurston's trailer in the closest thing I owned that I was willing to don: a deep-red dress that had a scoop back and grazed my knees.

A flashlight beam spotlighted me, before going dark, and Remy sighed. "Why not just wear a neon sign?" he whispered, but amused.

"Doesn't go with my complexion."

"I don't know how long we have, so we better get going."

I checked in front of the office trailer and confirmed that Thurston's actual rolling home appeared deserted. "Where is he?"

Remy waved me toward the door to the massive office, which he opened with a key.

"How?" I asked.

"After we're in," he said.

I hurried past him, and he shut the door behind us with a soft click. He flicked on the flashlight, and prowled toward the desk. "So . . ." I prompted.

"I had Novio invite him into the poker game he and Dad run once in a while." Remy was already rifling through the top left drawer of the desk. He held the flashlight between his neck and shoulder.

I walked over and took it, positioned it to illuminate the papers. "You didn't tell him what we were doing?"

"Don't worry about Novio," he said. "He's been nice lately—even to Dita, maybe especially—after what happened."

I didn't say anything.

He shut the drawer, moved down to the next. "No, I didn't tell him that I was meeting you or why I wanted Thurston in the game. It was just a suggestion I made that they might have fun fleecing him. He is rich, after all." He glanced around at the proof, surrounding us.

"Oh." But then, "The key?"

"That I might have lifted and had copied. Don't worry, he doesn't know."

The light dipped, and he waited for me to put it back on the papers he was paging through. Another drawer and nothing. "What am I thinking?" he murmured, to himself. "The middle. I should have started there."

I practically vibrated with foreboding, but I trained the light on the shallow tray when he slid it open. Nearly empty. A box of binder clips. A checkbook. And a white envelope I'd seen before.

"If Thurston finds out, he'll fire you, Remy. How can I not worry?"

He picked up the letter. "How can *I* worry about *that* when you're determined to risk your life up on the wire showing off? We have to do this now, get to the bottom of things, or you're going to get hurt."

But I'm not in any danger. The scarf can't hurt me. Nothing can.

"You don't understand."

"I'm beginning to think I do. We still don't know who's been sabotaging your family. But you don't seem to care about that anymore. Or about anything you used to."

The last line could have been about the mystery or about us. Or both. I stepped in closer, grabbing his shirt in my fist. "Remy, no. It's not like that. I'm doing all of this for that reason."

"I know you," he said. "And that 'Remy, no' is different from 'Remy, you're wrong.'"

Remy, you're wrong. I wanted to say the words. But what he was wrong about was me. And it stung that he was right about a few things. For example, the past week or so, I'd stopped trying so hard to find the culprit who was planting the objects. I'd been too busy using the good luck coin to put on magical shows, and signing autographs. And too busy lying to him.

"You don't need to worry about me."

"It doesn't work that way, Jules. Now, come here. Let's read this." He took the letter from the envelope, slid the drawer closed, then sat in Thurston's desk chair.

It was almost like forgiveness when he tugged me into his lap and put his arms around me to hold the letter in front of us. I shone the flashlight down so we could read it at the same time. My heart was pounding so hard I was sure he'd hear it.

Roman had typed his reply on family stationery, a miniature of the mural on the side of their RV gracing the letterhead at the top.

Dear Mr. Meyer,

I read your letter with great interest. You must truly be a devoted fan, to have uncovered what it seems you have. I can confirm that the rumors that circulated then are true, and I can also tell you that if you can bring Nancy Maroni's family back into your circus, you will have access to what I believe you are seeking.

You must not trust her. I did, and it is my single greatest regret. You see, the old magic

she has is not solely her own. She stole my luck,
in the form of a coin that had been passed down
within my family for generations. She still has
it. Of that I'm quite certain.

I am old, sick, and it is of no use to me.
But I would have it back for my family. My legacy
must continue. I will ensure that they sign on to
your effort, and we should discuss this further in
person. However, my one condition is that if what
she took from me can be recovered, you return it
to my family. They will stay in your circus, and
so you will benefit. They will do as I say.

Yours,

Roman

We were both quiet for a moment. Remy, no doubt taking
in the content of the letter. Me, waiting for the ax to drop.

"That must be what's in the photo of him and my grandmother," Remy said. "This coin. Don't you think?"

I swallowed, throat dry. "Yes."

"Jules, what's wrong?" He nudged me, shifting me to face
him. He gave me a long, searching look. And then he shook
his head. "You have it, don't you? How long?"

I could lie. I *should* lie. I'd promised Nan.

"For how long?" he asked again.

If I could have reached over and touched my fingers to his
pulse, it would be racing. The energy in him, always barely
contained, was greater than ever.

"She gave it to me right before my walk in Chicago. After Sam's accident."

"After she accused my mother of being behind it all."

"She told me after we left your place. She took it from your grandfather that summer, before she fled the circus. Look, it's complicated. I didn't want to lie. She told me I had to."

"You, who always do exactly what you're told. You had *no* choice but to lie to me. That's what you want me to believe?" The force of his arguments unleashed all that energy, and focused it on me. "You want me to believe that your grandmother stole a *magic coin* from my grandfather. That the magic is real? Jules, you are risking your life."

"Remy . . ."

"I can't do this. It doesn't matter how I feel about you. I can't be with someone who lies to me. I won't. I won't let you turn us into them. I won't be your fool. You are not invulnerable, no matter what your grandmother has convinced you."

I felt a tear slip down my cheek, and I swiped it away. I had to fix this. There had to be some way to apologize. "I screwed up, I know that I—"

Remy made a scoffing noise, an angry one, and so I almost missed the sound of the door opening. We both froze as feet sounded on the stairs, their owner humming as he climbed them. Thurston.

Jamming the letter back into the drawer, Remy dropped the flashlight between us. We needed a cover for being here . . . and this might be my last chance to kiss him. Before he could say anything, I clutched his shirt and pulled him toward me, winding one hand into his short hair. I kissed him hard, and he kissed me back. I moaned against his lips without meaning to. His hand glided along my bare spine, tracing the low dip along the back of my dress. His other hand tangled in my skirt. I wanted to pretend that we were alone, that everything was all right between us.

The light flipped on.

"What's going on here?" Thurston demanded.

I would have gone on kissing Remy, if it would've made a difference, changed his mind. But he stopped. I squinted at the bright overhead glare.

"Oh," Remy said. "Uh, hi, boss."

"Jules, is that you?" Thurston said. "With *Remy*?"

The shock of seeing us together seemed to have him nearing a heart attack. Remy gave me a little push, and I got to my feet.

"Sorry, Thurston," Remy said, with a shrug. "We needed a place, and I knew you were at poker night. It was just a hookup. Nothing serious."

That hurt like a punch.

"How did you get in?" Thurston asked, blinking.

"Picked the lock," Remy said. "You really should get a better one."

Thurston looked around, and apparently seeing nothing disturbed, decided to let us go. "Fine. But your parents would not be thrilled about this, I'm guessing."

"All part of the appeal," Remy said, wearing a smile that was not like any I'd ever seen on him. Like he was that cocky jerk he'd promised he could never be. Thurston clearly bought it, though, and I had to admit, Remy was convincing. He went on, "Forbidden fruit is the sweetest. And I do like a bad apple."

I winced, and started for the door. I turned to Thurston. "Please don't tell my dad."

"Don't worry," Thurston said. "But, Jules, you should associate with boys who value you. And, Remy, you owe her an apology. I expected more from you."

"Sorry," Remy said, acid.

I walked slower than slow once I got outside, creeping along the quiet grounds, giving him every opportunity to catch up to me. To finish our conversation and see if I could undo the damage. But he didn't come after me. I wasn't even surprised.

Remy Garcia had broken up with me, and he knew all my secrets.

thirty-one

The next morning I lay in bed—still in my dress, still in the midst of a personal pity party—and listened to Mom leave to check on her horses and Dad head out for a walk. I heard Nan making coffee in the kitchen. No one bothered to force me up.

The weather was gray, rainy, and we were leaving for a long, eleven-hour haul to Cleveland that afternoon. We had been lucky all summer—only two or so rain dates. The thunderstorm matched my mood. That letter had implied that Thurston knew lots about the Garcia and Maroni feud from the Garcia perspective, but it didn't mean he'd acted on anything except hiring us. Still, I would have to be more careful around him until I was sure. At least the way he'd walked in on Remy and me, I had a good excuse for avoiding him.

I burrowed my face in the pillow, reaching between the mattress and box spring to feel the note from Remy there.

I ruined what we had. Me. He was right to be mad, right to break my heart.

Out in the cabin, familiar music swelled for the opening credits of *Midnight*. It wasn't as famous as some of Nan and my standby favorite old movies. The movie's star, Claudette Colbert, reportedly went a little nuts when *she* got famous. According to Hollywood legend, she decided that the left side of her face was the good one, and refused to be photographed from the other side. The difference was imaginary.

I dragged myself to my feet and emerged from my room with my blanket wrapped around me. Nan's eyebrows lifted as she took in my disheveled state and . . . whatever else was noticeable about my bleak situation. She made no comment.

We watched together as Colbert—playing a beautiful lounge singer—arrived in Paris after losing everything in Monte Carlo. I couldn't help but observe that she didn't seem as bad off as me. At least she still had a gorgeous evening gown. Colbert bantered with a cute taxi driver, and the chemistry crackled, and yet she left him anyway, landing herself a gig impersonating a baroness for a rich fairy godfather.

Nan passed me a handful of peanut M&M's as the scene changed to a fancy party at a giant mansion. Colbert shimmied magnificently in the middle of a conga line. She didn't even stop dancing when the fairy godfather checked in to see how the scam was going, just crossed her fingers that things were going well. I didn't bother crossing mine.

Nan stiffened beside me, and when I thought through the scene I realized why. I gave the line myself in tandem with the fairy godfather's response to Colbert: "'Superstitious?'"

Nan shot me a sideways look and said Colbert's line back: "'Don't forget, every Cinderella has her midnight.'"

Suddenly we were talking about me. About us. About our situation. *I* was Colbert as a sequined Cinderella. Dressed up as someone I wasn't, using magic to pretend I was more than I was. Queasiness hit me in a wave. It was true, wasn't it? Just like everything Remy had said.

Nan looked at me like she saw every thought pass through my brain.

"I can't stay to the end," I said, rising, shedding the blanket.

The irony wasn't lost on me. But it wasn't anywhere close to midnight. To *my* midnight. As far as I knew.

"Why not?" she asked.

"I need to go somewhere." I didn't specify where, because I had no idea.

"The coin," she said. "Roman was obsessed with it. You can't just expect to use it with no consequences."

I didn't breathe. "Do you want it back?"

"Nothing is free," she said. "The problem with success is it can become a form of blindness. You can't see what you really want anymore."

"I have what I really want." *Except for Remy. Except for Sam back.* "I want our family where we belong. And we are. Higher than we've ever been."

Out the window beside us, the rain had stopped, but the day was grayer.

"I gave you the coin to protect you, but it only protects you from the harm of those objects. It won't protect you from what you can do to yourself. I understand." She softened.

"More than you know. But someone out there does still want to hurt you. And if they can't? They might try the ones close to you next."

I chilled. "I'll give the coin to Dad, to Mom—"

"There's no way to protect everyone." She didn't have to mention Sam. "And your parents would want it to be in your possession. They would accept nothing less."

"I could hide it in their costumes."

"But which one?" she asked. "You are the one who's a target. The only one who has been except for Sammy. We need to keep it that way."

"Why won't you help me find the person doing this?"

"I tried, and I failed. I'm the reason all this is happening." She lowered her gaze. "The more I'm involved, the more I fear it will escalate. The worse it will be. I shouldn't have come here."

Her refusal to come clean almost made sense to me, seeing how guilty she looked. What had really happened all those years ago? "You're never going to tell me the details of that summer, are you?"

"Not if I don't have to." She turned back to the movie.

"That's what I thought."

I didn't feel any satisfaction at getting the last word. Outside, I wandered aimlessly around the grounds, where people were packing up. Distracted. I was half hoping to find Remy, half hoping I wouldn't—especially given that I probably looked like death.

But the Garcia I bumped into was Dita. She was wearing a man's black shirt, collar unbuttoned. No makeup. She'd been wearing black ever since Chicago, whenever she was out of her costume, in mourning.

"How are you?" I asked.

We didn't really know each other, no matter what I wished. When I looked at her now, I couldn't help remembering how she'd sobbed at Sam's side in the ring, clinging to his unconscious body.

She bit her lip, shook her head.

I said, "That good?"

"You seem . . . not yourself," she said. "Remy told me."

My breath caught.

"That you broke up," she finished.

"He dumped me." I was curious what else he'd told her.

"He wasn't happy this morning either."

Knowing that helped, but it wouldn't change anything. He'd been so certain. And he'd been right.

That was the real problem.

"About that night when we . . ." I started. She'd been there for Nan's accusations, but I wasn't sure what to say that would help without revealing everything.

"Remy showed me the photos on the corkboard."

"Good," I said, though I was thrown. The photos had been our shared secret. I didn't *mind* her knowing. Not exactly. But it made the distance I'd put between Remy and me gape even wider. "It doesn't make any kind of sense. I wish Sam could have known about them. He was so practical . . . Maybe he could have fit it all together for us."

She dragged a hand through her short hair. "Sometimes I think nothing will ever make sense again."

It was almost like he was still alive, the way the two of us were talking about him. "This is going to be an awkward question," I said.

We started moving again, away from the trailers by unspoken agreement. We stopped when we reached a tree at the edge of the field where our RVs were parked. There was only one guy over here, sitting on a damp bench reading a worn paperback mystery like the ones on Remy's nightstand.

"What happened to your grandmother?" I asked. "Everyone talks about Roman, but not much about her."

Dita stared into the branches of the tree. "She hurt her back and had to stop flying. Then about ten years ago, she took a lot of pills. I was just a kid, but before that . . . I don't remember her ever laughing. Mom still misses her. Granddad, I don't know. He mourned her, but I don't know if he missed her."

"That's rough."

Dita tilted her face down to me. Tears glossed her eyes. I put a hand on her shoulder. "I'm sorry I asked."

"No." She brushed her cheek with unusually clumsy fingers. "I feel like an idiot, but in some ways I feel like I had something they didn't have, that my parents still don't. Just for a little while, I had it."

"What do you mean?" I applied a little pressure to her shoulder, in case she needed steadying.

"Sam, you know . . . when he first came up to me, I thought he would be a jerk. Not just because he was a Maroni. Because most guys are. They think because of how I dress I'm just a weirdo or a poser, or assume I'm gay. But he . . . he wasn't like that. He taught me how to ride. And he thought I was fascinating. He told me that, and he didn't mean because I was weird. He said it was the way my mind worked. But he didn't expect me to be able to answer every question. I don't know all the answers yet, okay? Whether I just like dressing this way . . . whether I'm into girls and boys, or just into certain people. But I didn't have to worry about all that. I just knew how I felt about him. I liked Sam right away. That was where it started between us."

I couldn't pretend Sam had confided everything to me. But I was sure enough of the main thing to say it. "He cared about you."

The breeze ruffled her hair as she nodded. "I know he did. We were in love. It happened so fast, but it was real."

I could see how much it cost her to say the words out loud and admit what she'd lost. Again, I felt a stupid pinch of jealousy at their good fortune. I hadn't ever been that sure of how Remy felt about me, and I was afraid to ask her opinion on the subject.

The truth hit me in that moment, though: *I* loved Remy. And *I* had lost him.

"I'm glad you found each other," I managed to say, and it was the truth.

That two people from our twisted, screwed-up, warring families had been able to be happy together was something—even if tragedy had ruined it. Too bad only I could be blamed for what had destroyed the chance of love between Remy and me.

thirty-two

Two weeks later, I trudged through the August heat to the costumer's for dry cleaning day. A big event. We had turned over our costumes the day before, after our last show in Nashville, so they could be sent out for one last cleaning under the supervision of the head costumer. She'd checked over everything, reaffixing sequins or spangles where needed, and posted a notice in the mess about pickup time.

With each city we passed through—from Cleveland to Pittsburgh to Louisville to Nashville—the season crept closer to its end. We'd just arrived in Birmingham, and from here we moved on to our final dates in Atlanta. I'd been unable to break out of my dull, heartbroken fugue, except during my performances. I was alive only on the wire these days, or at the side curtain watching Remy perform. When I saw him elsewhere, he ignored me.

As I neared the costume trailer, I spotted his familiar dark head. For a second, I questioned whether he could be waiting for me. But that wasn't likely. He was hanging out with a group of guys, crew members who wouldn't have costumes to retrieve. It was undoubtedly a coincidence, and so I tried to stamp down the surge of hope.

But when he spotted me and broke off from the group, hope soared anyway. I reminded myself of the risk in hoping. He was probably just being polite, even though he swung closer so we could go to the trailer together.

"How've you been?" he asked.

Or maybe he *was* here to see me. "The bee's knees. Whatever that means."

"Uh-huh."

He wasn't buying it. I'd have to do a better job of keeping up appearances.

"You going to tonight's party?" he asked.

Thurston liked to celebrate, even more so during the second half of the season. I suspected he wanted to distract people, give everyone an excuse to make merry and not dwell on the tragedy we'd experienced in Chicago. Tonight's was a "season's almost over" party.

"Thurston figured I'd skip it, so he told me I'm the guest of honor."

"I heard. Has he done anything to make you . . . suspect he's involved?"

I stopped. "No."

That he cared to ask was something. Wasn't it? Or did this mean he wanted the coin back? I'd played out that possibility again and again. I didn't know what I'd do if he did.

He said nothing else, but opened the costume trailer's door and held it for me to go in first. Politeness was better than being ignored—even if the cause was unclear.

The hair hanger exited past us, a blue dry cleaner bag across her arm. I ended up pressed against Remy. *So close, but miles apart.* I wanted to rest my cheek against his, to whisper how sorry I was in his ear. I wanted to grab hold of him, to never let go again.

I stepped away.

Inside, the costumer was visibly frazzled—this was a much busier day than normal—and peered at us over her cat's-eye glasses, nodding. "You both have two," she muttered, whirling to the rack behind her, thumbing through bags.

"Remy," she said, plucking one zipper bag down and extended it to him without turning. He took it with an eye roll of good humor. "And Julieta." She pulled mine down, turned and handed it to me. She *blink-blink-blink*ed at me and snapped her fingers. "Wait, I have something for you. Someone left this here. I found it this morning. An admirer?" Her eyebrows lifted over her glasses' frames as she handed me a small white box. There was no card, but someone had lettered in blocky handwriting: JULES MARONI.

My stupid heart assumed for a second that it was from Remy, but he crossed his arms, the costume bag hanging over them. "Open it," he said. "I'm curious."

"Me too," the costumer said.

I handed the dry cleaning bags back to her so I could open the lid. When I did, I promptly dropped the box on the floor. I bent to retrieve it.

"I thought it must be a dead rat for a second, the way you reacted," the costumer said. "Although I can see your point. That's not your style."

"What is it?" Remy asked.

The scarf in the box was made of thin red, white, and blue material. While not identical to the green one, the point was clear enough. And if it hadn't been, there was a note. Short and typed on a sheet of paper:

Best of luck until the end of the season.

No signature.

Remy's expression went darker than night.

"It *is* hideous," I said, pretending that the gift was nothing. "But a present's a present."

"Whoever left that is *not* for you," the costumer added. She thrust my bag at me, went back to the hanging rack, and rifled for the costumes of the next people coming in.

I carried out my bag and the box with Remy next to me.

"I knew it wasn't over," he said.

"Me too." I had to ask, but I hated to. "Did you . . . tell anyone?"

"No."

"I didn't mean . . . I wouldn't blame you. And so it's not over. What can I do? Nothing."

"Jules," he said.

I hesitated, trying to determine if there was concern in his voice, whether he might still feel something.

"You're not invulnerable. You can *always* do something. You can act like you know that."

"I'm—"

"Sorry, but still ignoring everything you say," he finished for me. "Got it. Trust me."

I dressed up for that night's party, more than I had been lately, when I was offstage anyhow. The dress was short and striped, a simple cut, high in the front and dipping low in the back. Nan's fashion advice stuck: better to leave a few things to the imagination.

It was harder to slip out of a mess-tent party early these days. People were nice to me now. I danced with three acrobats in a row, followed by one of the lighting guys. I was getting ready to snag a glass of champagne and leave to mope over my encounter with Remy and mull over the creepy gift when fingers tapped my shoulder as a salsa started.

There it was again. My stupid heart, hoping. But it wasn't Remy. Of all people, it was Novio standing there, with his hand out saying, "May I?"

I was downright shocked.

"No hard feelings," he said, starting to turn away, but I jarred into action.

"I'd"—he wouldn't buy *love to*, and I couldn't sell it—"be happy to dance with you."

"Really?" he asked.

"Of course," I said. "Water, bridge, things under it."

Maybe I could pry a few details about Remy's current emotional state out of him. Discover whether I should turn my hope into hopelessness.

The best thing about this type of salsa was that it required little touching. He barely had my hands. Our fingertips pressed together. Impossible not to wish he was Remy, that Remy and I were dancing together again. I couldn't help comparing his every step to Remy's, the way I had his looks the first time I'd seen him, before I saw Remy with his mask off.

Novio was sharper edged than Remy, though they were obviously brothers. They had the same brow, similar shoulders. But while Novio's eyes might be brown, they weren't warm like Remy's.

"Do I have something on my face?" he asked.

"Um, no, of course not," I said. Then, as our arms brought us closer in rhythm with the song, "Why'd you ask me to dance?"

"You're the star. Why wouldn't I want to dance with you?"

I didn't bother to answer that. Swallowing, I said, "How's Dita?"

"Heartbroken. You?"

The same.

He raised his arm, twirled me beneath.

"You're an excellent dancer," I said, deflecting the question.

He nodded agreement. I considered faking an ankle twist. I scanned the room for a savior, and he smirked at me.

"I don't bite, Julieta Maroni," he said. "You seem to like the rest of us well enough, especially my baby brother. Why can't *we* get along?"

"We do . . . we can." What did he mean?

"Is your grandmother here?"

"She doesn't like parties," I lied.

"Probably for the best. The older generation has the biggest difficulty moving on." I almost wept in relief to see Dita approaching. Maybe she intended to cut in and dance with me, but I whirled so Novio faced her.

"Looks like Dita needs a partner," I said, and waved as I backed away.

Dita closed her hand around her brother's saying, "This will be . . . new," and I cut through the crowd. Heading outside while trying to keep an un-freaked-out smile in place.

I pulled the phone out of my bra. Another handy tip from Nan. It was a good place to stash things. I started a text to Remy. I did it all the time—some were serious, some chatty. But I always hit Save, never Send. This time, I typed out: *Novio just danced with me. You're missing everything unnatural by refusing to talk to me.*

Lowering my hands, I inhaled the night air. The familiar masculine scent hit me as Remy leaned over my shoulder to look at my phone.

"*Novio* danced with you?" Remy asked, incredulous. "Who were you . . . This is to me. Were you going to send it?"

"Give me that. I must have hit your number by accident." I swiped the phone back from him.

"Stop," he said.

"What?"

He grinned. "Remember when you told me you wanted to add the word *stop* at the end of all your texts? To make them more like an old telegram?"

I smiled, momentarily warmed by the inside joke. *Our* inside joke. Then a chill slid over me.

When I'd imagined Remy talking to me again, I hadn't realized it would hurt to be so close in proximity—now that we didn't share any other kind of closeness. I changed the subject. "Why would Novio do that?"

"Novio," he said, not a question. "Who knows? Maybe he has a crush on you."

The way he said it made me pause, and then so did the words. "What does that mean?"

"You danced with my brother who you can't stand, so anything could happen. And how can you act so normal? You were *threatened* today."

"I told you already I'm the one person you don't need to worry about."

"I wish I could . . . stop," he said. "And I wish you would start. If you don't owe it to me, then don't you owe it to your cousin, Sam?"

Before I could say a word, he disappeared into the tent.

Nan sat at the table in her wrap when I got home, drinking a glass of wine. I went to my room and retrieved the white box with my name across the top, then plunked it in front of her.

"Jules," she said, "what is that?"

I took the chair beside her and pushed the box closer. "Look inside."

Someone who knew her less well than me would have missed her intake of breath when she saw it.

"Creepy, isn't it?" I asked.

She closed the lid, examined the block lettering. She traced one perfect red nail across it. "I don't suppose you know where it came from."

"Someone left it at dry cleaning day pickup."

She lifted the tacky red, white, and blue scarf from the box, and it took strength I wasn't sure I had not to cringe as she held it up at my neck. Like she was testing how it would go there. Then she cupped both of her hands and held the scarf draped within them, closing her eyes and murmuring unintelligibly.

"Nan?"

Her eyes flicked open and she dropped the fabric back into the box, shut the lid, and slid it toward me. "Throw that away. It wasn't a gift, but it has no power to hurt you." She paused. "But, remember, that doesn't mean nothing can."

She hardly needed to say it. I was hurting enough already.

I crawled into bed and tapped out a text to Remy: *That new scarf scared me. You're right. I do owe Sam. I owe you.* Then I plunked the phone onto my nightstand without sending it or even bothering to save it.

thirty-three

Finally, the next day, I did send a text to Remy. Not any of the ones in the saved drafts folder, but a new one, asking for help.

And then I nervously spent a half hour in my room sorting through outfits. I wanted to look my best, but without obviously attempting to look my best. It was an insanity-breeding state of affairs, especially since I couldn't consult with Nan, given what I was up to. I settled on a black top with a V-neck that segued into a gathered front seam with tiny red roses along it, paired with my favorite pair of worn jeans and sequined slippers.

I had no idea whether Remy would meet me or not. But I let myself hope as I made my way to Thurston's office. A place I hadn't returned to since our breakup.

When I arrived, there he was. Waiting. His eyes raked me from head to toe.

"Hi," I said, muffled when the wind blew my hair into my face. I had to fight to push it back. A few strands stuck to my lipstick, and then got caught on my costume jewelry ring. Nice and awkward.

He was *almost* smiling at my ridiculous flailing.

I extricated my hand from my hair. That part was graceful enough. "Thanks for coming."

Remy pushed away from the side of the trailer and went a few steps toward the door. "You know I have your back on this."

Well, that was noncommittal about *us*. But he was here at my side to confront Thurston. I wanted to map the territory, know if the distance I needed to travel to get back to him was impossible.

"What should we say if someone sees us together?" I asked, though we hardly planned to stay out here long.

"That we're just friends."

I kicked the grass. That had been our first cover story. "Are we?"

I didn't want to say anything more, and I didn't have to. He was so good at anticipating where my thoughts would go. I'd missed that about him too.

"Just friends, you mean?" he asked, quietly. He took a step closer.

"Friends," I clarified. "Are we friends?"

He gave me an odd look. "As far as I'm concerned, we are."

It was a starting place I could work from. After all the mystery was behind us, maybe it could be like the bad part of our past never happened. I wasn't ready to give up on the possibility, no matter how slim and delusional.

"Okay, then," I said, "friend. We'd better do this."

"You brought the new scarf?" he asked.

I nodded. "Nan said it's not magic."

He shook his head at that, but stepped forward and knocked on Thurston's door. "Remy," I blurted before I could stop myself. He half turned. "I've missed you. I watch your act, every time."

No visible reaction. But he said, "I watch yours too."

"I . . ." I wasn't sure what to say, but there had to be something else. Or I could reach out and touch him. Try to make things right between us that way.

The door swung open, Thurston checking his watch. "Right on time. Come in." But then he did a double take. "I was only expecting Jules. I hope you don't think I'm leaving you two alone in here."

"We have something to discuss with you," I said.

"Maroni-Garcia business," Remy added.

A spark of intrigue flared in Thurston. He swept a hand out, indicating we should come in. I could see him watching for any tiny clue about whether we were *together* together.

"I'd appreciate it if you didn't mention this to my family," I said, sending him a message that this wasn't for gossip. "For the time being."

He shut the door behind us, made the "lips sealed" motion with his fingers. "As long as they don't ask, I will continue not to tell."

The valise with the posters was out on the coffee table. I settled on the couch and Remy eased down next to me. Not so close we were touching, alas.

Rather than start with the creepy gift scarf and a direct confrontation, I decided to go fishing first. Giving Remy a look, I opened the valise and flipped to the poster of our grandparents' joint act. Nan was as radiant as I remembered, and Roman was the picture of strength.

Thurston sat down in a chair to the side of the table. "I'm aware you have a family rivalry," he said, "but I didn't think there was anything major between you now. Is there?"

Remy ignored the question. "What do you know about that act?"

Thurston studied the poster. "It wasn't long-running. That's why the poster is so rare. I believe they only did it for three months. By the end of the summer, your grandmother had retired from that show. She didn't perform again until the following year, and by then she'd moved to a small circus out in the Midwest."

Remy touched the plastic beside his grandfather's face. "What about Granddad?"

"You knew him," Thurston said, carefully. "I don't see how I can add anything more. I just know the stories. That he had a reputation for high standards. That he wanted everyone to excel, and that he expected it of them—demanded they try to be as good as him. That was probably impossible for most people. Your mom is said to have some of his hard-driving qualities."

"You know more about that summer, don't you?" I asked. "We want to hear it."

Thurston hesitated, then cleared his throat. "You must mean the way your grandmother left it. You've never heard the stories?"

"Never," I said.

"Well," Thurston said, his eyes fixed on the painted versions of Nan and Roman, "it wasn't pretty. The accounts I've read come from journals, a few personal interviews. It was . . . operatic. Your grandmother was confronted by the entire circus community. They showed up at the door to her small caravan, where she lived with your father and Sam's, both just boys then. Roman, I'm sad to say, was leading the charge. When she opened it, they stood there, a sea of angry people, convinced she was a witch and that she'd caused harm to the circus. I know the circus is a family, but families can be cruel. They told her she was no longer welcome. One person remembered people shouting that they would not suffer a witch to live among them. She had no choice but to leave. She had to protect her children."

Somehow, despite everyone saying Nan had been run off, I hadn't taken it so literally. Hearing this, it made sense that she'd had no second thoughts about taking Roman's coin. "That's terrible," I said.

Remy reached out, and took my hand. It helped. More than he could know.

"That's not all you know, boss," Remy said. "We read the letter my grandfather sent you. We know he told you about the old magic everyone believed in back then. Do you believe in it? We want to know if you've been trying to scare Jules, to get the coin back."

Thurston's head went back like he'd been struck. And then he leaned forward. "I never believed the coin he mentioned had any power. I believe in illusion, not magic. I believe in feats of daring that are real. I chose to court the Maronis with a more generous paycheck. Now, what has happened to Jules? What do you mean about scaring her?"

I nodded, convinced. I'd never felt like Thurston had any desire to cause me harm. But Remy said, "Show him."

So I removed the scarf I'd received from my jeans pocket. Being balled up on the trip here had caused creases in the thin fabric, but he'd recognize it if he'd seen it before. I lay it on the poster of our grandparents.

"What is that?" he asked, genuinely bewildered.

"Nothing," I said. "A practical joke."

"It's the furthest thing from a joke," Remy said. Tension stretched out in the air between the three of us. I said, "It's not him."

Remy said, "I think you're right. Did my grandfather tell you anything else we should know?"

Thurston shook his head. "I assumed it was all a fantasy of his. He was bitter when I met him. Like he had a poisoned soul." He blinked as he realized what he'd said. "I'm sorry."

Remy swept the scarf off to one side and closed the book. "You're right. He was."

There was a long silence, and then Thurston spoke again. "You know, when I decided to start the Cirque, it was just something I could afford to throw money at. It didn't really matter if it crashed and burned. If it did, I could have gone back to HQ and rededicated myself to my original mission. And if it succeeded, then I'd have another win on my hands. This summer has helped me understand that I'll never be born-and-bred circus the way you and your families are, never understand it like you do. But the safety of my performers is of the utmost importance to me. I'd never put them at unnecessary risk."

"Give it a generation or two," I said. "Or at least a few years. After a while, no one will ever know you weren't circus to start with."

He nodded, thoughtful. "How did *you* do it, Jules? Push yourself from good to great? *Should* I put stock in the notion of magic coins?"

Remy stilled. It was impossible not to notice when he went motionless, because he was usually so filled with energy. He was rarely truly still. Some part of him was always swinging through the air at high speed, even when he was sitting next to me.

I worried that Thurston would notice. The last thing we needed was to have him start believing in magic now.

"You should know my secret better than anyone," I said. "Aren't you the king of the overnight breakthrough?"

He rolled his eyes at himself. "You're right. We don't know. It just happens, after a million hours of work. And then we forget about the million hours."

A little truth wanted to show itself, to offer an apology that we'd come here to accuse him. "I do think something spurred me on, during that walk in Chicago. It was anger. I was angry about Sam."

Thurston's relaxation vanished. I was almost sorry I'd said it.

"Oh," he said. "But that was an accident. Terrible. But an accident. One I will never forget as long as I live."

I wanted to say, *No, no, it wasn't.* Instead I said, "That you kept going after that tragedy, despite the pain, is what will make you circus. Just give it a while."

Those of us who were born into the circus grew up with the sad stories. The fires, the train crashes, the overtired brother who brought down a pyramid stunt. They were the worst-case scenarios, not something any of us would ever court. All the superstitions were designed to protect us from them. But whoever had planted those objects was flouting that tradition. The red, white, and blue scarf was a reminder that someone else's clock was ticking. The note had said "until the end of the season," a handful of shows away now. The coin prevented me from being harmed directly, but the fact was plain: whoever had started this twisted game was playing with our lives.

That girl above Jacksonville had been desperately certain that all she needed was what I now had. Our family's spot on top reclaimed, our name remade. But she'd been wrong.

Remy stood. "Sorry about this, Thurston." He looked at me. "We'd better be going. Shall we?"

I was surprised to see Remy offering me his elbow. I picked up the scarf and put it back in my pocket, then linked my arm through his. Every nerve in my skin gathered in the crook of my elbow as we touched. Thurston saw us out, and we kept walking.

Finally Remy stopped and gently removed his arm from mine. I wished I could protest.

"You're going to have to talk to her," he said. "Your Nan. Demand to know the truth. Jules, do you think . . . She wouldn't hurt you?"

I pictured the coin, and the scene Thurston had told us she'd endured all those years ago. I didn't have many answers, but I had this one. "She would never."

"Just making sure."

"I'll talk to her," I said, and left him there, even though I wanted to stay.

I finally had to look, unblinking, at the possibility I'd denied since the beginning of the season. What if Nan had been guilty all along? Not of coming after me, but of something bad enough that the circus performers had justification in casting her out as a witch. Terrible, destructive behavior that was still haunting her, and that had put a target on my back, and on Sam's.

thirty-four

Nan was alone in the living room when I returned. I pulled over a chair from the kitchen and sat down in it in front of her, blocking the TV and whatever movie was on TCM. It was in color, and something I didn't recognize. Which meant she hadn't really been watching it.

"Yes?" she asked.

"You did it, didn't you? Those accidents that happened back then, you did it out of jealousy—over Roman Garcia."

She didn't respond right away. Her lips pressed thinner. "It's not what you think. Not exactly."

"What is it? Because I'm not leaving this chair without knowing. Not this time. This time you have to tell me the truth."

Our eyes met.

I said, "We have to figure out who's behind this, and there's not much time left. It has to end. For Sam, for me. For you. It needs to end with this season. Our lives can't go on this way forever, wondering when that green scarf will turn up and where. The coin may keep me safe, but no one else is." I realized with a sense of panic that it was true. I had been fooling myself. No more. "Someday whoever this is will get tired of failing. Or they'll realize I have Roman's good luck coin and move on to someone who doesn't. Then what? What if they target Dad?"

Nan wrung her hands like she held a cloth and was squeezing water out of it. It was a painful motion to watch.

"The truth. Part of me has been waiting for you to demand it all along. I don't know if it will solve anything, but okay." Her fingers twisted around each other, over and over, while I waited. She began to speak.

"My mother could always do magic, but she mostly confined herself to small tricks. Her talent was that she could make things more than they were. Whatever essence was in them, she knew ways to draw it out. It was a skill passed down in whispers. For her, it was about helping someone with a good luck charm, or maybe getting rid of someone who was in the way of a romance. Bringing out the essence of a mixture of herbs to heal a bad cough, to make an illness fade. Nothing so big. Nothing so dangerous. She also had a gift with the cards—the set she made was different. Special. I know how to read them because of her. But she truly just wanted to help people. She was circus, but my mother, above all, she was content with her place. Happy to be where she was, who she was. You would have loved her, Julieta. She was a light. She never hurt a soul."

My breathing felt thin. Souls had been hurt, just not by Great Grandnan. That was the implication. I gripped the edges of the chair beneath me on either side.

"But I was more ambitious, I guess. I was never satisfied. I had the idea to move past simple, honest remedies. I got my start by picking the most superstitious objects I could think of and empowering them . . . and, in the process, I discovered new ways that the old magic could be used."

I shot her a questioning look, and then she took a deep breath and continued.

"I'm getting ahead of myself. I told Roman about what I could do, how I'd learned to one-up her magic. How I'd found ways to call *more* out of certain objects, to make them actively powerful. I suppose I was . . . no, I know, now, that I was bragging. I wanted him to love me, to be fixated on me the way I was on him. To see how unique and different I was from his other women. I was young, Jules. I was all alone except for my sons. I was lonely, I wanted so much more."

"You don't need to apologize to me. Just explain."

"It was Roman's idea. He gathered the things and brought them to me. The peacock feather. The trunk and the green scarf. The elephant hair. He picked those things because they were part of circus lore. Our beloved superstitions. He could charm anyone into giving him anything. He could charm anyone into doing what he asked. He had me . . . make *them* more. He wanted to harness the power of good luck, of bad luck—and it was bad luck for those objects. *Hexes.* That's the word my mother would have used. I went through the steps, but I wasn't sure they'd work. And I didn't ask him what he planned to do with them. I regret that now, but I was blindly infatuated. I wanted to trust him. He gave the peacock feather and the rose wrapped in elephant hair to other girls he kept on the side, like romantic presents. Told them there was nothing to the old superstitions. He dared the clowns to use the trunk after he moved it, gave them the green scarf for good measure, and told them it was silly to believe in bad luck. There were three terrible accidents in just a few weeks. I couldn't tell anyone."

Nan squared her shoulders. "What I'd done was wrong, but I did it for him. And, God help me, when he came back, empowered by the knowledge of what I could do, he demanded that I work the coin. And I did it. The luck it naturally possessed become *more*, as if it held all the goodness in his soul. But I gave it to him at a price. I made him swear those first objects would be destroyed. The coin was already something powerful. I could feel it during the working. But once I put it into his palm, he wouldn't have anything to do with me. He started rumors, and they caught on. People who knew about my mother helped spread the idea that the accidents were my fault. What could I do? I told you already, the woman always takes the blame for an affair, for anything that goes wrong because of it. He didn't deserve to keep that luck. Not after what he'd done. So I took it and I left."

We were both quiet for the longest time.

Then, she said, "Now you know why I never used it. I couldn't bring myself to touch it. Not until I had no choice.

But those objects? He should have destroyed them. He told me he would. I never dreamed he would keep them."

"Clearly he was very trustworthy."

That earned a wry smile.

"And you really don't have any idea who might have gotten their hands on the objects after Roman's death? Could they have been lost and then found? Could he have given them away?"

She shook her head. "He wasn't a good man. But he saw firsthand what the objects were capable of. I don't think he would knowingly give them to anyone."

The corkboard Remy had found floated back to my mind's eye. Thurston was in the clear now. Remy wasn't a suspect, and his mother had convinced me—and Nan—that she wasn't behind it either. Novio had been busy fighting Sam that first night when the rose was laid at my feet and our place was broken into, which scratched him out. Dita wasn't on any list. If her dad wanted to hurt me, he could have screwed up my wire at any point. It didn't seem possible that the culprit was a Garcia. Though whoever was behind it must have known about the Garcia-Maroni connection, or Nan's cards wouldn't have ended up at their place.

Which basically meant that, even after her confession, we didn't have an answer.

"You let him run you out of your own life." What she'd done was wrong, and I wasn't making excuses for it. But the thing that hit me hardest was that she hadn't stood up. She'd run away. No wonder she was so threatened by returning.

She'd given it all up. To come back must have made her see how much the family had lost because of her decision.

"I've been hiding," she said. "All these years, hiding, pretending it was my choice to leave and never return. But it was the coward's way out. I didn't have the backbone to try to make things right. I watch these old movies because of the heroines . . . I wish I was more like them. Strong, singular, able to best any man. That's the woman I wanted to be. If I'd been like that, I would have had the strength to say no to him."

"Why didn't you tell me? When this started . . . why not just tell me?"

"I'd lived with the secret for so long. Your father never asked me, you know, why we had to work on our own, why we hated the Garcias so much. I think he suspected he might not want the full story. Sometimes the truth doesn't set you free, Jules. Sometimes it cages you."

I couldn't imagine my father shrinking from anything. "I was caged, we all were," I said, not that I meant to say it out loud. "We almost lost our place in the world."

Her face was full not of sorrow, but regret. "I never wanted you to look at me like you're looking at me now. You thought I hung the stars, you thought I was one of them. I'm not. I'm just a woman in the shadows, holding on to secrets so tightly I don't know if there'll be anything left, now that I've let them go."

Nan's confident persona had convinced me completely. The ways she'd changed in the time it took for us to have this conversation were unfathomable. I measured the woman I thought I knew versus who she said she was, and what the truth meant for both.

For her. For me. For *us*.

Finally I said, "I don't love you any less, knowing the truth. You're still here, no matter what mistakes you made. And so am I."

"So we are," she said. "So we are. What will you do now?"

thirty-five

Thurston had set up lots of press for me in Birmingham, wanting to ensure the upcoming last dates were sellouts. Between interviews and performances, I tried to decide what to do about Remy, about everything. On our last morning in Alabama, I entered the mess tent and spotted Remy eating a bowl of cereal. I decided to text him here, so I could gauge his reaction. The message told him I needed to see him after our first show in Atlanta. Talking in person was the only solution.

I watched him glance down at the screen of his phone beside him as the alert popped up. I held my breath while he read it, but he *did* read it. That was a good sign, maybe? He looked up, and I met his eyes. He didn't nod *yes*, but he didn't shake his head *no* either. I grabbed a pastry and took off.

The whole Cirque caravan was hitting the road to head to Georgia after lunch, and I had a big outdoor walk scheduled for the next day. I was fine with postponing my and Remy's inevitable conversation until after our first performance there. Never one to rush in front of a firing squad, I still needed a little more time to figure out exactly what I was going to say to him when I gave him the coin. Because that was what I had to do.

Hours and hours later, as we got off the interstate and drove into Atlanta, I was sitting at the kitchen table with my cheek against the cool glass of the window. We passed a bus shelter with a large poster hanging inside, well lit, that had the Cirque's name and—

I sat up. Beneath the name was a painting of me, gleaming smile and glimmering red costume, balancing on a wire over skyscrapers. It advertised the Princess of the Air's final outdoor walk of the year.

That walk would also be my last one with the aid of magic. Would this be the last poster I ever graced too?

I wasn't going to say anything about the poster, but Mom was across from me. She had a short glass filled with clear liquor in front of her, but even mellowed by a drink she must have noticed my change in posture. We passed another bus shelter, and she spotted an identical poster.

"Look at that," Mom said. "You're more famous than all of us now."

"No," I said.

I'd never wanted that.

Our exchange drew Nan over from the couch, yawning as she joined us. The advance team sure hadn't taken any chances. We passed yet another poster, this one smaller and pasted to a light pole.

"You're a headliner now," Nan said. "All eyes are on you, and what you'll do next."

"I can't wait to find out either," I said, and waved as I went to my room. I stayed there until we stopped for good at the edge of a giant parking lot.

If all eyes were on me, I had to try not to disappoint anyone. Including myself.

That well-advertised final walk arrived before I felt anything like ready for it. Already, looking down from my high vantage, I never wanted to give up this view. From so far above, I wouldn't see anyone's expressions of disappointment even if they were aimed right at me.

Sprawled below me was Atlanta, city of sultry summer days and our closing weekend, a mix of glittering towers and people having a lazy afternoon. It was fitting that a city famous for once having been set on fire was going to host my own personal conflagration. But if I was going down, better to be in flames, casting a bright glow.

I watched as the circus paraded up Peachtree far below, crawling along the broad street.

I was at the top of the fifty-story Peachtree Tower. The building had two crowns, which was what caused me to select it immediately from several photos of potential sites for this walk. I was the Princess of the Air, after all. I'd be too high for the people below to see the details of my performance. But there was a network TV crew positioned on the roof to get footage. The sidewalks below were clogged with red tutus and T-shirts worn by the Valentines, my fan base that had somehow just continued to grow.

This was one of the highest walks I'd done, but deceptively so. I was only walking a sixty-foot gap between the two points at the top of the golden-brown-toned building, the flat portion of roof below not nearly so far off as usual. It was still far enough to shatter every bone in my body, but not so distant compared to some of my previous stunts. There was a slight breeze, but it wouldn't be a problem. Not with the coin safely in the side of my slipper.

I bent and rubbed it, tracing the rough circle through the thin fabric.

"It's time," one of the rigging crew said. He was new, his first time doing support for a building walk. "Now or never."

I flicked open my parasol, tested it against the breeze.

"I've seen the footage, but you really just use that? Up here?" he asked, and waved to indicate the sky around us.

"Magic," I said.

I went slowly to the side of the wire, took a breath, and climbed on. This was too high to expect the sound of cheers to reach me, or to risk looking down. There was something majestic and, in fact, regal about the building.

I stepped out, twirling the parasol. I danced forward on the wire, then back. I waited until the middle before executing the trio of pirouettes, feeling the wind catch in my parasol and root me in place. I high-stepped back to the side, and when the rigging crewman stepped forward to help me off, I turned and went across again.

There would be cheering down there now, but the people on the street might as well have been a dream. It was only me up here. The city and me and the air. I wanted to stay right where I was.

I pirouetted again, and knew I should be smiling, but my face refused to move. I tried to hold on to the seductive sense of certainty, the knowledge that I couldn't fall.

You don't have to give it up. Ever. No one will make you.

The wind sang against my ear, twisted my hair into itself, and I never faltered. I twirled the parasol into it. And I forced my feet forward. One step, then another. And another.

Easy, faultless steps that were the hardest I'd ever taken.

I climbed off, folded down the parasol, and took a bow, sinking low to the buildings, to the sky, to the world. The wind sang to me: *Don't give this up.*

I suddenly understood the myth about the sirens. I was a sailor on a ship passing by the most beautiful place on earth, and the wind, the sirens' voices, beckoned me. I could stay here forever. Protected. I'd run no risk of disillusioning anyone.

But I'd learned that was a false promise. There are some things none of us can control, some consequences that must be faced. By finally understanding that, I discovered what I was going to say to Remy.

We met at the time I'd set, after the first show here had ended. Remy stayed backstage until everyone else was gone, and so did I.

We drifted into the main tent, and sat on the second row of the stands. The lights were off, the center ring completely empty.

"This is weird, being here when it's like this," I said.

Remy didn't dispute it, so he must have understood. It felt more deserted than it had for his midnight practices. Back then, the night had folded around us, and we'd been hidden in the tent like it was a pocket and we were safe inside. Now, it felt cold. It was no longer a place I wanted to linger. This conversation was a bandage that needed to be ripped off. I should just do it.

"What do you have to tell me? Is it what you found out from Nan?" he asked.

"I need to give you something."

"What?" His eyes were nearly black in the shadowed tent. The angles of his face were familiar, but we might as well have been strangers. I couldn't reach out and touch him. I could barely believe I'd ever been able to.

I slid my finger into my slipper and wiggled the coin free of the lining. It warmed against my skin. "Open your hand."

His palm unfolded before me.

I placed the coin in the center of it, and he bent forward to examine its ancient contours.

"Jules, why?"

I didn't answer. My fingers itched to grab it back, but I forced my hands onto the bench seat on either side. His palm did close then. He held the coin in a loose fist. "Explain."

"When the accidents happened and people died all those years ago, our grandparents were . . . together. You already know that. And my grandmother *can* do things. She can make objects powerful. Make them stronger. When your grandfather found out, they worked together. It was both of them. They caused those tragedies."

"On purpose. You're saying it was on purpose, that they weren't accidents?"

"I know it sounds crazy. Maybe neither of them really believed the objects would work. Who would? It makes no sense. But they tried anyway." *Your grandfather talked people into taking the hexed objects. They were gifts.* But I didn't say it. What he knew already was bad enough.

"Why are you giving this to me then? I know you believe it works." He raised the fist with the coin.

"Your grandfather wasn't lying in the letter, when he said she stole his luck. You should have the coin back. It belongs to you."

He was quiet for too long.

"I didn't mean to lie to you forever. I don't think I realized what I was doing at first. I was just so angry about Sam's death, and about getting nowhere when we tried to find answers," I said. "Then the shows were selling out. And everyone here was nice to me. Like they never were. They accepted me."

Remy's expression turned to disbelief. "When your family showed up at the Cirque, the only thing anyone here knew about the Maronis was the old stories about your grandmother. But we saw how you were. Your dad acted like he was better than everyone else. You did too. But then, when Sam died, you all lost something. And despite that, you went on. *That* made you one of us. Part of this circus. That's why people are nice to you. But you betrayed them using this."

"I'm telling you I screwed up. I know that."

"Everything that happened, I was right there with you for so long. But then you shut me out. You knew I wouldn't go along with you trusting in this coin, so you didn't tell me."

I banged a palm on the bleacher between us. "Nan said it was too dangerous for you to know. I wanted to tell you."

"Jules, you don't follow orders. Nan's instructions are not why you kept it a secret."

"I know it was wrong. I was heartsick over Sam. It got out of control."

"Jules, do you know how many quads I've made in the last month?"

"Four," I said, not needing to stop and think.

"And you're telling me I could make every one from here on out. That it wouldn't ever be a problem again, because of this? That I could use this?"

"Yes."

I wanted to reel the word back in as he reached out and grabbed my hand. He forced the coin into it and let go, like touching me had burned him.

He said, "I don't want this. I won't take it. You keep it. Your secret's safe with me."

"Remy, no! I don't want it anymore."

"The green scarf's out there somewhere, and the end of the season is here. Keep it for now. If you're right, it'll keep you safe."

My pulse quickened, but I didn't dare hope. "How can you care about that?"

One corner of his mouth tilted up. "You think I want you falling on my conscience? Knowing I sent you out there— never mind. But, know, like I thought you already would, that I would *never* use that *thing*. Do you even know what you're really capable of?"

"I'm capable of using this." I hefted my hand. "Says it all, doesn't it? Do you think I don't know what a fraud I am? Do you think I ever wanted you to know? I know you wouldn't use it. I never thought you would. But I don't want it anymore."

He stared at me with an expression I didn't have the decoder ring for. And I drank in the sight of him, ridiculous as that sounds. The darker separations in his irises, the way his black hair was longer than usual and messy from raking his hand through it. That little scar over his eyebrow. We might never be this close again. We probably never would be.

"Remy . . ." I started, though I had no further defense to make for myself. What I'd realized on the wire above Atlanta was that I didn't want this magic, even if giving it up made me vulnerable. Telling the truth was one step. But playing this game, using the coin—whoever was behind the sabotage was winning as long as I kept on participating.

I wasn't about to let that happen.

But it was too late to explain. Remy was already gone. Leaving me alone in the enormous dark of the tent, holding the "good luck" charm I'd sworn to give back.

thirty-six

I put the coin back inside my slipper and used it for the next two shows, the night show and the following day's, and during them I was more aware of its presence than ever. There was heaviness in my feet, but that didn't translate into any klutzy mistakes or problems. My performance was as perfect as ever. The Valentines in the stands roared after my act, both times. And every second that passed, I was thinking.

After breakfast the next day at the mess hall, I plodded back to my room and stretched out on top of my covers fully clothed. In my gut, in my bones, was the knowledge that this needed to be resolved by the end of the season. I just didn't know how I could keep that resolution from being awful.

But I had to do something.

I considered Bird for a few moments, until my eyes drifted away—as they always did these days. She hadn't had the benefit of an ancient good luck charm keeping her buoyant above the city. She'd been strong enough to do it alone. Who had I become?

When Dad poked his head into my room, I bolted upright. "Jules? You busy?"

He sounded skeptical, with a slight undertone of concern.

"Nope, just killing time." I should have known that would earn a frown. I wasn't much of a time-killer.

But he didn't ask why I was moping in my room. Instead, he said, "Thurston asked for you and me to come see him." I nodded, barely curious, sure it was nothing to pull me out of this dilemma, and got up.

On our way out, Dad paused at the kitchen table and took in the state of Nan. I did likewise. She hadn't been up when I went to the mess earlier.

She had not a fraction of makeup on, but she was dressed. Her hair was not bound up by a colorful scarf. She looked plainer than I'd ever seen her. And still beautiful.

"Are you feeling okay?" Dad asked her. He gave me the eye again, as if her appearance and my mopey staring were related. They were, of course.

"I'm feeling like myself," Nan said. "More than I have in a long time. Where are you off to?"

"To see the boss," I said.

"Thurston, she means," Dad clarified, his frown lingering.

Mom was the boss as far as he was concerned. Thurston was our employer.

"Right, that's what I meant," I said. "We're off to see Thurston."

"Have a nice time," Nan said.

Dad cast one last worried glance at her before we continued out. Light rain pecked at our arms.

"Did something happen that I missed?" Dad asked.

Yes. "Not really."

"You know I'm proud of you, Jules. You've worked hard for all this."

The only time in my life I don't want to hear that. "Thanks, Dad."

"I know it's been tough on you with Sam gone. You've been isolated, but dealing with all this"—he raised his hands and framed an invisible marquee—"Julieta and her Valentines. I haven't checked in with you like I should have."

Because with Sam gone, Mom had needed to be with the horses more—especially with their equine leader, Beauty, also missing in action—and Dad had supported her. "I understand. Being there for Mom is more important right now. I'm fine."

Nothing can touch me up there, and it's down here I have to deal with now.

"You're a good girl."

I was spared from having to respond by our arrival at Thurston's trailer. Dad knocked, and a Thurston making a poor attempt to hide a grin admitted us. "Maronis, it's so great to see you both. Jules, you know I've been thrilled with how your season has gone."

Thurston was fighting that grin hard. I didn't like it.

"Let's all sit down," he said.

I shrugged. Dad and I took the smaller sofa beside the long one. Thurston stayed standing, despite his having asked us to be seated. *Oh well.* He could be a space cadet when he was distracted.

"I had a call from Hollywood about you, Jules. The network team here called someone important and raved about you."

"What?"

"They'd like to feature you in a special of your own. Like Nik Wallenda, but younger and hipper. Your stunt walks caught their attention. They want you to do something even bolder than the ones you've done already. This will cement your stardom, make you a household name . . . which you're already well on your way to being. Say yes? You'll say yes too, won't you, Emil?"

Dad said, "Whatever Julieta wants to do, her mother and I are behind her."

Thurston had stopped battling the smile. I nearly cringed. Since when was I a cringer? I should be more thrilled by this than anyone. I should be beaming. Dad and Thurston noticed my reaction at the same time, and both frowned.

I covered as fast as I could, pasting on my best fake smile. It was a good one. They relaxed when it showed up. "I'm thrilled."

Thurston said, "I've got another surprise too. In order to celebrate, I think for the last show, you should do the finale, Jules. We'll make the announcement about this right after it's over. You wouldn't mind, would you, Emil? Turning over the spotlight for that last big moment?"

"Wait—" I started, but Dad shushed me with a look.

What he said was awful, unimaginable. "Of course. She deserves the finale."

I kept pretend-smiling, ignoring the sting in my eyes. Ignoring that terrible tightness in my father's face and body. Couldn't Thurston see it? He'd refused to wear a mask since we got here, and now it was plastered on him. I'd put it on him, as surely as I'd gotten a TV special I didn't deserve. That coin never did anything for me except raise me up so high I'd never survive the fall.

I held up a hand and rose. "I'm just going to go tell Mom. Dad, you stay here. Have some champagne."

Thurston paused at the fridge, as I made my way to the door. "Congratulations, Jules. Who needs magic with you around?"

One last fake blast of blinding white smile and I was out of there.

I felt like I'd hit my head. Like I was tumbling through the air, already falling even though my feet were on the ground. My father's quiet nod replayed itself over and over. His "Of course. She deserves the finale." The emotion that showed in his face was pride, but that wasn't all it was. He was injured, and doing his best to hide it.

I didn't *want* to take the finale, *or* his career. Dad wasn't anywhere close to retirement. He didn't need to, he didn't want to. He lived up there. He was made for the wire. The earth was an inconvenience. He wasn't showy about it, had no need to brag, because it was just the truth. What he did up there was something true.

He would never have used the coin.

What I did next would determine whether I ended up with years of regret like Nan. I didn't want that. I could still make things right, couldn't I? I had to.

A series of ideas lined up in my mind like dominos. Just like that, I had a plan.

thirty-seven

All that was left was the finale. As the minutes ticked by, I
felt more like myself than I had in weeks. Jules Maroni didn't
wait for a shoe to drop on her. She didn't shrink away from
trouble like a violet. She made a plan, and she carried it out.

And that was what I was going to do.

Standing in my room before the evening show, I removed
the coin. I held it in my hand. Bird was Zen cool above the
Chicago skyline on the wall in front of me. "Do you even
know what you're really capable of?" Remy had asked me.

"It's time I found out," I told Bird.

Half-past time, I imagined her saying back.

I could face my hero again. I'd earned that back. The coin
went into a small velvet drawstring purse.

My phone lay on the windowsill. I picked it up, thumbed
through the screens to the saved drafts folder. I edited the
latest version of the message that had been waiting there for
Remy, adding two words of punctuation.

I'm sorry STOP Forgive me for being an idiot STOP

I didn't hesitate before I hit Send. Maybe the telegram style would clue him in about the magnitude of *how* sorry I was. With that, phase one of my plan to set things right was complete.

Now for phase two. I was already wearing my costume, and I tied the creepy red, white, and blue scarf around my neck, knotting it at a jaunty angle. It wasn't the best look I'd ever rocked, but it definitely made the statement I wanted. I painted my lips a red that matched, and went out to the living room. I brought the velvet bag with the coin inside along.

Nan sat on one end of the couch. She wore a slight gloss of lipstick, but otherwise was as subdued in appearance as she had been all week. She wore a plain black dress, belted. She could have been a widow waiting to go to a funeral instead of a grandmother preparing to attend the final show of the season and announcement of her granddaughter's big score.

My father sat on the couch too, on the opposite end from her. He wore a suit.

"Ready to head over?" he asked.

I settled between them, my tutu rustling. I shifted toward him. "I have a condition."

Dad said, "We don't have enough ti—"

I put up my hand. "I'll go, but only if you perform with me."

He stopped cold, taking it in. "That's sweet, my heart, but you don't need to do that for me. I will be fine. I'm your father, still."

I didn't budge. "My father is the best wire walker in the world. It would be my honor to perform alongside him. It would be no honor at all to prevent that crowd from seeing him up on the wire tonight."

We'd performed together plenty of times in our one-ring. The truth was, much as I liked having my own wire, I missed that. I'd brought us here to be *us*, to be amazing. Not to lose what we had.

He was quiet, but then, "You're set on this?"

"Remember when I ran away to bring us here?"

His face slipped into a frown. "Like I could ever forget."

"Well, I'm three times as determined as I was then. Maybe three thousand times. Three thousand million even. So get dressed."

He gave his head a shake, but he rose and made his way into the back. Nan turned wide eyes on me. She touched her neck. "Explain. Why are you wearing that?"

"The time for explaining is done." I smoothed a stray hair back into place. "It's half-past time for action."

Her head tilted. "Well said."

"What is it?" I asked, because there was a note of disbelief in her voice.

"For a minute there, I thought you must be quoting one of our movies, but . . ."

"Nope. Tonight's all me."

She took in what I was saying. There'd be no magic protection tonight. She stood, and I could see her fear. Feel it. "No, you're provoking . . . whoever it is. Jules, it's not safe."

"I'll be as careful as I can live with," I said. "I haven't always been, but I will be tonight. Promise. But this can't go on forever. It just can't."

Dad rushed out of the back, clad in his simple black walking outfit. "Our costumes aren't that well coordinated," he said.

"Maybe if you lost that scarf?" Nan suggested to me.

"Maronis always look good together," I countered. "It stays."

Backstage was the kind of frenetic chaos that only comes for the first and last shows of a season. From Thurston's patter, I judged that the Garcias were getting ready to begin their act. I'd hoped to catch Remy before, but we were too late for that. Nan being with us had made it uncouth to suggest running to get here faster.

We barely made it before the panic about my whereabouts—and the night's new finale—set in. Or maybe it already had, because when I found Thurston's assistant she vibrated at an extra-high pixie frequency. "Jules, *thank God*, you made it."

She stopped and absorbed the fact that my father and I were both in costume.

"We'll be performing as a duo tonight," I told her. "Can you find Nan a seat?"

"Isn't it just supposed to be, well . . ." she started.

"Both Maroni wire walkers will be participating in the finale," I said. "It's clear enough. Nan needs a view."

She didn't argue, perhaps assuming that Thurston had known this tidbit and forgotten to share it with her. "We're sold out, but"—she must have read my expression—"I'll find her a spot." She took Nan's elbow. As an afterthought, she asked, "The control-booth guys know about the finale?"

That was a minor problem I hadn't foreseen. Good thing they only needed a little warning, because that was all they were going to get.

"Better tell them too," I said.

She hesitated, then hurried away. Wearing the scarf might well provoke our saboteur, by sending the message I wasn't afraid. But that didn't mean I wanted to court disaster.

Mom strode across backstage toward us in her equestrienne getup. Everyone had been given dispensation to wear their costumes to the after-party, if they wanted. She extended a hand and rubbed my bare shoulder. "I'm so proud of you," she said. She included Dad. "Both. I'm proud of you both."

The music for the lead-in to the quad attempt started. "Be right back." I didn't wait to see if this earned a frown from Dad. I scurried through the crowd to the side curtain.

Remy was swinging high and fast, gathering speed. He let go and soared, curling into a tight spin—once, twice, three times, and the fourth—

And then Novio caught him beautifully.

The two of them dropping into the net meant Dad and I were up. I darted back over to the main entrance to the ring. Dad was waiting on the far side.

"Coming!" I dug for the coin and pulled it out, tossing the bag aside. Instead of joining Dad, I lingered opposite him.

The blonde flyers drifted out, giggling as they passed. Dita came next, and Novio loped out behind her. He did a slight double take when he saw me, and said, "So, you really are doing the finale? Taking it from the old man. Wow."

I ignored him, since that wasn't happening. He moved on.

Dad waved for me to come to him. "Julieta!"

"Just one more sec!" I held my breath, and *finally* Remy came through. Grabbing his arm, I pressed the coin firmly into his hand and a kiss onto his sweat-damp cheek. I stayed where I was long enough for him to take me in, and then went across to Dad before he could push the coin back to me. Or push me away.

Phase three, complete. I couldn't control anyone else, but I *could* control what I did.

Dad asked, "Back together?"

I gaped at him. He had that knowing father expression on. "You knew?"

He gave a sharp nod. "We're not imbeciles."

"No," I said. "Not back together."

"Oh well." He tried not to look pleased. Which was easier when he frowned. "Wait. Where's your parasol?"

Oh no. He walked without any aid, but I needed my frilly umbrella for balance. More than ever, since I was doing this act without the coin.

I dodged through bodies to our dressing tables, hearing the sweeping build of our cue music, and then it building over again. The parasol lay on its side and I bounded over a chair to snag it. I raced back to Dad's side. He caught my arm when I would have gone on through the curtain and said, "Breathe."

I sucked in a breath. We each slipped into performance mode like a second skin.

"Now we go," he said.

We jogged out into center ring together, Dad waving to the crowd while I twirled my parasol. A second ladder came down on the opposite side from the one already lowered. I headed toward that one.

Thurston had a momentary hiccup as he realized there were two of us coming out, but he covered it in the flowing patter he'd become so good at. "As I told you, tonight we have a very special treat for you. You may have noticed that you were deprived of a performance by Julieta Maroni earlier . . ." He paused to let the Valentines in attendance shriek their approval. "But that's because you're going to be getting *both* of our Amazing Maronis on the wire together. The first performance of its kind!"

Well, the first one with the Cirque, but it's not like we could stop and correct him.

Dad and I had reached our ladders and—with a synchronization that would have convinced anyone we'd rehearsed for days—leapt on and flourished with restrained dignity while the ladders retracted, flying us up to either end of the high wire.

The crowd was already applauding in wild approval of the surprise. Dad and I had discussed how we'd do the act on the way over. He was going to walk across to me first. I insisted he play lead to my second. I'd follow him back, adding some pirouettes if the wire felt good. We would stop at the center and do a couple of tricks—lying back in tandem, similar to what I'd done on the wire above the bridge—and then we would switch positions in a move that looked more dangerous than it was, ending up on the opposite platforms from where we'd begun.

There was no sign of our saboteur's work so far, and it occurred to me that the gift of the scarf might have been a bluff. Why else wait so long, all the way to the end of the season?

I waited patiently on my platform, holding the parasol over my shoulder, as Dad stepped onto the wire. Watching him walk from this vantage was a pleasure. And in the tent below, the Valentines were appreciative too. Some of them had their hands clasped in front of their hearts, gripped by the spectacle.

The tent was as full as I'd ever seen it. There were people crammed in between the sections—standing room only, except there wasn't room for another body to squeeze in. I imagined all the other performers crowded up to the side curtain watching too, and wondered if Remy was among them.

Dad reached my end of the wire, and the band launched into a drumroll. I smiled at him, and twirled my parasol. He extended his hand, whirling into a turn and stepping forward so that it would look from below like he'd led me onto the wire. I stepped onto it. Cautiously.

So far, my plan had gone well. But the plan was only to right the things I'd messed up, to make up for my own trespasses and mistakes. And to try to convince our foe to blunder out into the open, revealed at last.

I wasn't as sure of my footing as usual. I tilted the parasol this way and that to make up for the subdued quality of my performance. Hopefully Dad's inability to be anything but jaw-droppingly wonderful would distract from any perceived lackluster on my part.

We made it to the middle of the wire where we'd agreed to the do the lie-downs. That was when I glanced up at my parasol in preparation for lowering it. I intended to hook the handle over the wire behind me, to dangle there during the trick.

The green scarf was attached to the inner net of metal ribs. Tied there, the loose ends pointed down in either direction, like some crazy grin directed at me.

This, too, was my fault. I should have checked the parasol, but I'd been in such a hurry. I'd left the perfect opening for someone else's plan to overtake mine. Here I was, trapped on the wire with Dad.

Breathe. You have to get through this.

My hand trembled around the grip of the parasol. I placed my other hand over it, and tried to stay calm as the trembling spread to my limbs.

My whole body began to quiver like a leaf. There was so much noise. The band, the hum of conversation, Thurston's patter.

My father smiled as he held position, waiting for me to hit my mark so we could lower ourselves in tandem as we'd agreed.

I closed my eyes, opened them. Sucked in a deep breath. Looked up again at the scarf. So bold and green. Such bad luck.

"Julieta." It wasn't a whisper, not with all that other noise. He spoke it with flat calm. "What is it?"

If I hadn't given the coin to Remy, I'd be safe as ever. I'd smile at Dad and pirouette and show the world that no one could touch me.

My hands tightened around the base of the parasol. No. *No*. I didn't need the coin. This was the moment it all became clear: What was I capable of? Who was I now, after everything that had happened? What was I willing to give up?

"Jules," Dad said again, more insistent now.

A rivulet of sweat trailed down my temple and slithered across my cheek. Another ran oh-so-slowly down the center of my spine.

Thurston's patter had turned nervous in tenor, but none of the words penetrated.

"Dad," I said, my voice even, "I need to take a rain check. I'm going to turn and go back to my platform. You finish this."

He considered what I'd said, his worry plain.

"Always trust a performer when they tell you they need an exit," I said.

He'd taught me that. I stayed as still as I could manage, my fingers shaky around the parasol grip. I would have let it go, but I didn't trust my stability without the aid.

Dad nodded to me. He lowered his body to a crouch, hooking one leg over the top of the wire and eased back, like he was going to take a nap. There was applause, but not wild applause. Because there I was, still standing.

I had to get off the wire.

I turned with more care than I ever had, and took one step and another. My platform wasn't that far. If I could just make it there, I could let go of the parasol and be safe. Only a few more steps.

I didn't make the mistake of looking down. This time, I made the mistake of looking up, and seeing that flash of green. Flickering in its place, I saw the old photograph on the murder board, the clowns around the trunk, one of them brandishing the scarf. And then I wasn't on the wire at all. I was running toward the ring the night of Sam's accident, Beauty rearing and screaming. Sam bleeding in the sawdust, the scarf discarded beside him . . .

I dropped the parasol, tracking it as it sailed through the air and jounced into the ring with enough force to cave in on one side.

Raising my arms straight out to my sides, I tried to find that line, that invisible tether of spine that led to balance. But I lifted them too quickly and—

I was falling too. I grabbed for the wire, caught and held on to it with both hands. I held on to it for dear life. Mine.

The thick cable hurt my palms, but I couldn't let go. I was no longer a girl on a wire, but a fish on a hook. The parasol would have been hanging just like this, if I'd completed the earlier trick.

My father was sitting up, out of the lie-down that had protected him when I'd lost my balance. If he'd been standing, my fall would have been enough to knock him off.

GIRL ON A WIRE

"No," I said, pleading for him to stay where he was. "No."

"Julieta," he said. "I'm coming."

"No, don't." I struggled to get the words out.

There was a commotion below us in the ring—shouting, familiar voices—but I couldn't look down. Not and hold on.

"Yes," Dad called down to whoever it was. "Yes, bring it out! Now!"

My muscles screamed at being asked to hold this position, the wire cutting into the tender skin of my palm. I needed to lift myself higher if I was going to have a chance.

What was I capable of?

I was capable of fighting with everything left in me.

Using every last bit of strength I had, I inched upward until one forearm was level with the wire and I could hook an elbow over it. I didn't have the power to get the other one up. But it was enough to stabilize me, so I could see what Dad was telling whoever was below us to bring.

Remy was in the ring, and he was directing the crew to position a net beneath our wire, maybe the same one they'd just used for the trapeze act.

My father was telling them to bring me a net. My father, who had never believed in them.

Nets might be for amateurs, but there were worse things to be. Like dead. "Dad," I said. "Finish the act. Get an ovation."

Remy backed up, the net strung wide, ready and waiting. If I had the courage to fall, it would catch me.

If Nan was right, her magic was about amplifying what already existed inside something. So all I had to do now was amplify my own courage. That was what I tried to do. Finally I would be strong enough to let go. Strong enough to get back to the honest performer and person I knew I could be. Steadying myself as much as I could with one arm to hold me up, I took a breath.

And I let go.

I

let

go.

As I fell, I pictured Remy doing it. I'd watched him jack-knife into the net so many times. He fell with intention.

I pulled my body into that approximate V shape—falling, falling—and bounced in at an angle. As soon as I landed, the net threw me up again, not wanting to keep me.

A moment later, Remy's hands were on my waist, and then they found mine. He pulled me onto my feet. "Pretend you've got a limp," he said, putting an arm around my shoulders.

He wanted it to look as if he were supporting me, like I'd had to come down off the wire because of an injury.

"No." I pressed him back. "Thank you, but no."

I lifted my arms above my head and bowed low. Valentines applauded, even though all I'd done was . . . fall. But it *had* been one of my most important acts ever, hadn't it? I raised myself even taller and bowed lower.

When I finished, Thurston was frowning at me, which transformed into gawking as he glanced up at the wire. Where my father was *prancing*, putting on the show of his life. He *never* showboated.

"Did you see the green scarf?" I asked Remy. I knew no one would be watching us when Dad was doing that. Which, I was positive, was why he was doing it.

"No," he said, "just that you were in trouble. Jules, I could barely breathe."

"Thanks for the save. But we need my parasol. It has the scarf in it."

Remy took my hand—earning a few wolf whistles, I was guessing from fans so devoted they were missing the walk of a lifetime to keep an eye on us—and steered me toward the parasol. Letting go of his hand, even though I didn't want to, I plucked it off the sawdust. Dirt smudged the half-caved-in canopy. When I flipped it upside down, the green square of fabric that had caused so much trouble was still there.

We reached the curtain just as my father finished. Thurston had recovered and was saying into the mic, "Please show this man your appreciation. Now that was the sight of a lifetime!"

I looked up to see Dad bow to the crowd from the middle of the wire. They were on their feet.

"We always get our standing ovation," I said.

Remy touched the parasol. "Do you have any idea how it got there?"

"None," I said. "I left it where I always do."

Nan and Mom were on top of us as soon as we exited the ring into backstage. Mom patted me from head to toe to make sure I was okay. "I'm fine. A little net rash tomorrow probably, but fine," I reassured her, pressing her back with my free hand.

Then I dropped the parasol to the ground and bent to remove the scarf. *Such a small thing to have caused so much pain.* I handed it to my grandmother.

"Give it to *her*, that's a great idea," Novio said, appearing with a sneer. Behind him, Dita tried to pull him away, but it was clear that she'd have no effect. She backed off. It was too late to stop him.

"Now's not the time, Novio," Remy said. "Jules could have been killed."

"Yes, she could have," Nan said, closing her hand around the scarf. "This is what killed Sam."

"What do you mean?" my mother asked, aghast.

Maria Garcia had apparently been summoned by the presence of Nan and controversy. She echoed her son. "The girl's careless on the wire. That's all."

"Was it you who set Jules up?" Remy asked her.

"No," she said, dismissive. "How could you think I would harm her? You're my son."

"You'll give us the coin back now, won't you?" The words were low, and they came from Novio. I almost thought I'd misheard. But he repeated it. "You'll give it back? Now you see that I know everything. It's time to make this stop. Just give back what belongs to us."

Remy stepped between Novio and me, or maybe he was putting me behind him. "Novio?"

We were all quiet, and Novio began to talk. "I was his heir. The oldest Garcia son. It should have been mine. He told me everything. What had happened. How it was stolen.

That Thurston would bring you here, and that I could get it back."

Maria scrubbed her cheek. "Dad put you up to this before he died?"

"He told me about the ancient coin that should have been my birthright. How it's powerful enough to make you the best you can be. Nancy Maroni stole it from him. I just wanted what belongs to us. I put all the pieces together. Granddad had the clippings and the photographs in his study, up in the attic. The objects were in the trunk. All these years."

"The murder board," I said. "It was *yours*."

Everything clicked into a sad, sick kind of sense. My mother couldn't have understood half of what was going on, but she said, "If Nan says you endangered my daughter, you have no life on this show."

Novio ignored her, nodding at me. "I wanted Remy to know, to see it when we got here. I knew Thurston was trying to hire the Maronis, because Granddad told me. I thought Remy would come to me, and I'd tell him the whole story. That he could help me. But you tricked him. He stopped caring you were a Maroni. But I can never forget. The coin belongs with me."

I moved in closer, standing beside Remy. "That's why you picked a fight with Sam. So we would think there was no way the break-in could be you. And the rose was you too?"

"I meant to give it to her"—he jerked his head at Nan—"but she wasn't there, and I didn't find the coin in your RV. When the lights went out in the big top, I gave it to you on impulse. I had the rose in my jacket." He shook his head.

"The coin was my birthright. You were here to steal the spotlight, just like she took it."

And I understood. He was in the same shadow that had consumed his grandfather. Something darker drove him than his siblings, the same hunger for recognition and power that had driven Roman. Remy was all about work and achievement. Dita was fighting to be herself. But Novio, he was a creature of family. I understood him. I might not have gone about it in the same way, but I recognized the need to secure the place he believed belonged to him.

My plan had worked, even though drawing out the culprit had been the longest shot part of it. We knew who was responsible. But what would we do, now that we knew?

Dad and Thurston exited the ring. "Explain," Thurston barked.

I could see Dad had plenty of questions of his own, but he took in Nan and the Garcias, Mom and me. He faced Thurston and said, "This is family business. We will talk with you later."

Thurston's assistant emerged from the curtain, with a phone in her hand, and she gave Thurston one sharp shake of her head. "Producer who was here for the announcement says no," she said, regretfully, to both of us. "No special. Not this year."

Easy come, easy go. Thurston stood where he was for a long moment, and I expected him to challenge Dad. But he said, "Come with me," and went off with his assistant.

Which left us with the very messy family business to conclude.

"Give me the coin," Novio said.

"Novio, I understand why you think you want it—" I started.

Remy took two steps closer to him. He looked from me to Novio and back. He laid his hand on his brother's shoulder. "Jules gave it to me before. And it's gone. I got rid of it."

My mother's arms were crossed. "The boy must be punished. He can't stay here. Nancy says he caused Sam's death, tried to hurt Jules."

Maria apologized in her smoker's voice, face lined with years of unhappiness. "I had no idea. You're right. He won't be back. He is no longer part of this family."

"Wait," I said.

The line of balance that had eluded me on the wire, sent me tumbling when I tried to locate it . . . there it was. I stood straighter, like gravity didn't apply. "Just wait. I'm not sure that's what we should do. Think about it. We can't send him to jail. He hasn't committed any crimes, exactly. What are we going to say? This jerk kid took objects he believed were *magic* that had belonged to his grandfather and used them to cause an accident that led to Sam's death?"

I stopped to drag in a breath. When no one jumped in to argue, I went on. "While kicking him out *would* feel good, it wouldn't make anything better. Not really. Your father had Nan cast out, and it solved nothing. I don't even think it's what Sam would want. He loved Dita, and he understood the importance of family. He wouldn't want her to lose a brother too."

"I'm not a kid," Novio said.

But it was Nan who shushed him. She wasn't born to the wire, but she carried herself like she was. "I think all the goodness that Roman possessed went into the coin, all those years ago. He was so closely linked to it." She touched Novio's shoulder, and he flinched. "I might be able to figure out how to take the poison from this one, put it somewhere we can destroy it. So the good in this boy can come back into the light." She held up her hand to Maria. "I won't make any promises, but I wrote myself off, all those years ago, for making terrible mistakes. I didn't think I could earn my way back, and I refused to use my gift any longer. But he's just a boy still, no matter what he says. Roman's gone, but no one knows better than me how hard it can be to shake his influence. The boy, he might come through this yet."

"What are you talking about?" Novio said, fear shining out from him. "I won't do it."

Maria and Nan stared at each other, like they had that predawn morning in the Garcias' RV, seeing past the surface of each other. This time, Maria nodded and turned to her son. "Yes, you will. For Sam Maroni, Novio. You will do whatever she tells you."

He shifted toward Dita. "I didn't mean for that to happen. It was all just supposed to scare them into giving us the coin."

"If they're right, you killed *my* Sam. *You* broke my heart," his sister told him. "You do this for me."

"I knew she had the coin," Novio said, a weak protest. "I was right."

Nan held up her index finger and said, "Lesson one. Sometimes being right doesn't matter."

Novio didn't volley back an insult. He lowered his chin in a grudging but unmistakable nod.

People were filtering out of the backstage area, giving us a wide berth. No doubt they were heading to the mess tent. Drama between the Garcias and the Maronis was juicy, but it couldn't compare to free booze and an after-party.

The Cirque had made it through the season. Everyone wanted to celebrate that. And I agreed. That our families in particular had made it through—even if we weren't intact, and would never be the same again—was worthy of recognition.

"So, it's over?" I asked. "It's all really over?"

No one disputed it, but Dad looked like he wanted a fuller accounting later.

Remy returned to my side, and reached an arm around my waist. "Yes, STOP. It's over, STOP."

I faced him, grinning like a fool. If that wasn't an apology accepted, nothing was. When our lips met, it wasn't like going back in time, and it wasn't like forgiveness. It felt as new as the first time.

Our kiss was a beginning.

thirty-eight

After the crew broke down the tent in Atlanta the next day, the caravan returned to Florida. But most of us wouldn't be here long. There was going to be one final, epic party to mark our last night in Sarasota. With a few exceptions, the performers and crew wouldn't spend the entire winter here. Everyone would head back to their homes—the nonmoving ones—and then early next year either we'd come back here to start training again or head off to other shows. The verdict on the Cirque's future remained out, especially after I'd flubbed my chance at the TV thing. But I had faith in Thurston. What he'd created was too special to give up.

Just before it was time to leave for the party, I went out into the living room. Mom gave me a sparkling smile from the couch. She and Dad sat beside Nan. "What is it you say, Nancy?" she asked.

"*Bellissima*," my dad and Nan answered in stereo.

Nan wasn't quite as glam as she would have been before the truth came out, but she wasn't entirely plain either. A polka-dot scarf was knotted at her neck, and she wore a little lipstick. Her new look suited her.

A knock sounded at the door. Dita came in first, in a white tux, smiling sweetly. We'd invited her to join us, rather than go on her own. But my breath caught when I saw Remy in his suit—and how *he* looked at *me*. I was wearing a vavoom-y ensemble I'd picked up in Atlanta. Red like my costume, but with a slinky shape.

"You look amazing," Remy said.

"Of course she does," my father said, clearing his throat. "She's a Maroni."

Remy dropped into a gallant bow in front of my parents. "I'm sorry. I just—"

"Stop before I rethink this whole date-night thing," my father said. My mom swatted his arm affectionately.

And then the third Garcia entered. Novio wore a polo shirt and jeans. He was banned from the party, and this was going to be the night when Nan set the ground rules for her plan to try to save him from his own darkness. His inherited darkness, the poison Roman had given him. He ducked his head. "Hello," he said, and slung himself into the first open chair—a kitchen one, facing the living room.

Nan was examining him like she couldn't wait to get started. I noticed her tarot deck lay on the table, and suspected he was about to get a reading. I almost felt sorry for him. Almost.

I still missed Sam too much to forgive him. Maybe someday.

"Home by eleven," Dad said, as we made our way toward the door.

"Ish," I said, and shut it firmly behind me before he could object.

The party had already started when we reached the big top. I had a momentary déjà vu, thinking back to that first night and our masks. Remy must have sensed it. My arm was tucked into his, and he said, "Nervous, First of May? Don't be. I hear you're a good dancer."

Things were good between us. It turned out that almost plummeting to my doom off a forty-foot wire and being rescued clarified a lot of feelings. If Novio deserved another chance, so did we.

Thurston was in the middle of an announcement when we made our way into the crowd. People smiled at us indulgently and a little cynically, the way older people do when young people pair off.

Think what you want. This is going to last—or if it doesn't, it won't be for the reason you think.

"I've decided I'm going to give us five years to turn a profit," Thurston said, and, over the cheers, "I'm having too much fun not to." He punctuated the news by opening a bottle of champagne. He added, "Plus, *someone* keeps telling me that one day everything will make sense. After enough years, I'll wake up and it'll be like I've always been circus."

The finale had bewildered Thurston, but Dad had assured him it was a momentary problem on my part and wouldn't happen again. Thurston wasn't as bothered as I expected by the TV thing falling through. "Always a long shot," he'd said. "But I'm beginning to rethink my stance on the idea of magic being illusion only." I hadn't responded, and he didn't force the issue. Thurston was full of surprises.

I wasn't disappointed about it either. I had more than I'd ever realized I wanted. My family had found our place. And now that I knew for certain we'd be coming back next year, it was all the sweeter. I only wished Sam could be here to see it all.

"He meant me when he said *someone*," I said, gloating. "I keep telling him that."

Remy said, "Not surprised."

We had this one night here left, before we went our separate familial ways for a few months. That stupid cell phone was going to come in handy. I'd have to keep it.

"Dance?" Remy asked.

"Or we could go make out."

The music started, and, in answer, Remy spun me into his arms and around the ring.

"Do you still have the coin?" I asked, leaning close to his ear.

"I don't know any safe way to get rid of it." Remy had finally become a reluctant believer in the power of the coin. What happened during our finale night in Atlanta had convinced him.

"We could ask Nan, I suppose. Explain that you were lying when you told Novio you'd gotten rid of it." I smiled. "But I've been thinking. And I have an even better idea."

"Oh no," he said, but there was no sting in the comment. "What's this idea?"

"You'll see. It involves sneaking out later."

He grinned. "Just like old times."

I checked over my shoulder to see where Dita had gotten to. She was dancing near the edge of the ring, smiling shyly at a girl in a plaid dress. I approved.

We all carried our grief about the night we lost Sam, but we had to move forward. Our losses, our wins, they were what bound us together. The circus *was* a family.

And *that* was what had given me the idea.

Remy hissed. "Hey, pretty lady, you by yourself?"

I nodded cartoonishly. It was quiet, the middle of the night, the party cleared out at last. He emerged from the side of the big top where he'd been waiting. We both wore practice clothes.

"You ready?"

He gave me an *I was born ready* face.

"Fine, but do you know how to get us into the rigging?" I clarified.

"Yes."

"And you have it?"

"Yes." He put a hand in his pocket, and I rushed to say, "No, you keep it. I have the needle and thread in mine."

The tent was dark inside, and Remy had turned on the lights only right in the center spire. He lowered a ladder, and we had to climb and climb and climb. I wasn't used to it, but he was from all those nights practicing. "Tired?" he asked.

"You?" I countered.

"Not with this view."

"Nice," I said, looking down to where he was, below me on the ladder. But we finally made it up above the rigging, to the beams and railings and poles that supported it. We climbed like monkeys, and when we got to the last section, I rose to my feet on a flat beam several inches across. I extended my arms out for balance.

Remy had gone a little ahead of me, so he could pull me up into the last section at the top of the tent. Over his shoulder, he said, "Are you sure?"

I nodded. I needed this. The last time I'd walked, I fell.

So I let the beam beneath my feet feel like a wire. I kept my spine straight and I called on every ounce of my talent. There was no packed house to applaud, only Remy watching in the dark, but I'd remember this performance for the rest of my life.

"I can still do this," I said, when I made it to him.

He lifted a hand and brushed it along my cheek. "Of course you can. Coin or no coin, it was you doing it all along." There we sat, high above the ring, and just below the stripes of the big top. Together. What a difference a few days made.

"We'd better do this." I got to my feet using one of the bars, and he joined me. I climbed one more step until the very top of the tent was inches away. I took out my sewing kit.

He didn't ask how I knew how to sew. Everyone who is circus knows how to mend small tears and rips in costumes.

I sewed the piece of fabric I'd brought into the lining of the tent, and said, "You do the honors."

"You're *sure* this is a good idea?" he asked.

"The coin is good luck, but it shouldn't belong to one person. This way, it'll belong to all of us. Or it'll do nothing. Either way, it will do no more harm. Besides, this feels right, doesn't it?"

"It does," he said.

He placed the coin inside the pocket in the lining, and I sewed it closed. We pulled the tent fabric back over it. Concealed as if nothing was there.

He put his hand at the back of my neck and I took a step toward him, getting so close there was only space around us, and none left between us. His lips met mine and we kissed in the empty air. That felt right too.

When we separated, he clambered down to the next level and waited for me to join him. I paused for just a moment, reaching up to put my hand over the fabric where the coin was hidden and to admire the grand sprawl below my feet. In not that many months, we'd fill this tent again.

I couldn't wait for next season.

acknowledgments

My eternal gratitude is due to everyone at the inaugural Bat Cave Retreat in 2012 for reading parts of this book in first draft—shout-outs to Alan Gratz (organizer extraordinaire), Megan Miranda, Carrie Ryan, Megan Shepherd, Tiffany Trent, Kristin Tubb; to Wendi Gratz for providing sustenance and cheesecake; and most especially to the divine Beth Revis and Laurel Snyder for reading the whole messy thing and helping me figure out how to make it better. A tip of the top hat to writer friends who let me bend their ears along the way: Kelly, Karen, Gavin, Holly, Cassie, Josh, Delia, Sarah, Kim, and Chuck. And to Clint Hadden for serving as my man on the ground in Chicago, and finding me the perfect location for a special walk there. I'm sure I'm forgetting someone, but I'll make it up to you: promise. I also owe many thanks to Tim Ditlow for his excitement about the manuscript, and to the magnificent team at Skyscape for their support in making this book a reality, particularly Amy Hosford and my genius editors Courtney Miller and Kate Chynoweth. Many thanks to fabulous copyeditor Kyra Freestar too. Thanks are due, as always, to Jenn Laughran, my fabulous agent, whose enthusiasm when I showed her the first chunk of this kept me moving (and who *is* circus folk), and to my wonderful husband, Christopher Rowe, who is always there to hold a net for me.

As you might guess, I have long been obsessed with circuses and wire walkers. Some resources that turned out to be helpful when I discovered I was going to write a circus of my own were Bruce Feiler's *Under the Big Top*; Taschen's gorgeous, glorious *The Circus: 1870s–1950s*; the great Philippe Petit's *On the High Wire*; and the PBS documentary series *Circus*. Like Thurston, I was not born circus, and so any errors or flights of fancy here are entirely my own.

And, last but never least, my biggest thanks go to you for reading.